Family Assets

Samara Black

ISBN 979-8-9898465-4-2 (eBook)

ISBN 979-8-9898465-5-9 (paperback)

Printed in the United States of America

Book Cover Design by Cheshire Gato Media

Front and back photos by Samara Black

First edition 2025

For Evafaye, aka "Sis"
The OG badass of the family who always had it handled, got it done,
or made it happen and made it look so easy while doing it.
I miss you everyday. I know you're damn proud of me, and would've
totally read my books while giggling at the spicy bits.
I love you, Gramma. Happy 100th.

Contents

Author's Note

THIS IS THE THIRD and final book in a series. It's highly recommended you read the first two books (The Asset, Seized Assets) before continuing.

The following story includes the following content that may be inappropriate for readers under the age of 18:

- Cursing, profanity, dirty words

- Consensual sexual content – open door

- Violence, sometimes graphic in nature. See below for specifics

This story also contains the following content that might be sensitive or triggering for some people:

- Rape or threat of rape (RP took place in the past off-page and is briefly mentioned; threat is briefly described)

- Graphic violence, including against women (multiple, described)

- Torture (multiple occurring off-page but mentioned; one

described)

- PTSD (described)

- Threat of forced breeding (briefly described)

Chapter 1

Back to the Beginning

Felton

October 7, twenty-three years ago
Alexandria, VA

"All right, let's go over it one last time," Syd bellowed, pointing to the diagram on the chalkboard.

I rolled my eyes and took a long drag from my cigarette. It wasn't like we were robbing a bank. Then again, our target was one slippery son of a bitch. I half shrugged to myself and decided to pay attention. Technically, it was my hit.

Tonight was finally the night I would take what was mine. A part of me hated it had come to this, but they'd been warned. I knew she wouldn't listen. She hated me too much. He had no goddamned excuse. We were both from the streets and knew how it worked. Had either of them been willing to work with me, it would've been different, but now...fuck that. Now was the time to end this shit once and for all.

"Syd, I really don't think we need to go over this again," Gio announced as he entered the room. "It's pretty simple. Wait until they head to bed, knock them out, snatch the kid and torch the house."

"Yes, boss," he replied.

Gio walked to the front of the room. "With that said, I'll still advise everyone to be cautious. Seamus Donovan is not one to be crossed. If you give him the chance, he'll break your neck and then piss on your corpse. Make sure you neutralize him first."

"Think he'll mind if we have a little fun with his wife?" someone asked from the other side of the room.

My head whipped around to get a better look at the man and was shocked to discover he was a young kid who couldn't have been much older than fifteen. There was something unsettling in his silver eyes, something almost inhuman. The hunger in his smile only made me more uneasy.

"Patience, Marco," Gio chuckled. "Let's see where the evening takes us, shall we?"

The kid nodded and turned to the guy next to him with a smirk and it was then that I knew I wanted him nowhere near that house. Unfortunately, it wasn't my choice. It was my hit, but the manpower belonged to the Sardis. Hopefully, he was one of Massimo's men and would be headed back to Italy after this was over.

A hand on my shoulder caused me to jump as Gio sat next to me. "Is there a problem, Soren? Don't tell me you're having second thoughts about tonight?"

I'd had second thoughts when I first told him the Donovan family needed to be wiped out. Seamus refused to listen when I approached him about coming to an agreement so he could do the right thing. I knew I'd screwed up, but I deserved to make amends. Instead, he threw my misdeeds back in my face and shut me out. That was when my second guessing stopped.

"Hardly. This has needed to happen for a while now. It was bad enough he was ratting on the family, but now he's gone too far. He knows my true identity. That puts too much at risk, especially now that he's figured out the kid is mine."

He watched me closely. "Never took you for one to want kids. Didn't you say they were too much of a pain in the ass?"

"This kid isn't like the usual snot-nosed brats. I went to Seamus's house once and, even though he tried to keep me from seeing inside, she walked up to the door and started asking me a million and a half questions. Smart and fearless. I thought Sera was going to blow her top when she heard us."

"What about the wife? It's not like you're bringing a puppy home tonight."

I groaned inwardly. Karina wanted no part of the subject. We'd fought at least a dozen times, usually with her screaming that she refused to take care of someone's spoiled little heathen. I knew the real reason was because she hated Serafina with a passion, even though she had no reason to. Despite the fact I left that woman to be with her, the venom she spewed at the very mention of her name was astounding. Bringing my daughter home would piss her off, but she could either deal with it or leave. I'd already missed the first six years of my kid's life. No more.

"She's not, but I told her that's too bad. The kid's mine and she's going to live with us."

He chuckled. "That's why I never got married. They get all kinds of ideas and think they can call the shots once you make it legal."

"Only if you let them."

"Let's head out!" Syd yelled from the garage.

There was no traffic, which made the trip quick and easy. I parked outside the house while the other cars and vans lined the street. A light turned off in one of the upstairs windows. Out of the corner of my eye, I saw brake lights near the end of the block.

"He's not here," Syd whispered when I joined him near the van.

"That looked like his car at the end of the street when we pulled up. He most likely went to the store around the corner."

"*Follow him and make sure nobody sees,*" Gio instructed from the passenger seat. "*We'll take care of the house. Meet us back at the warehouse when you're done.*"

"*What about my daughter? You better make damn sure you don't leave without her.*"

"*Fine. We'll make sure we grab the rug rat before we leave,*" Syd drawled in a bored voice.

I wanted to be the one to grab her, but my thirst for vengeance won out. He thought he was so fucking clever by hiding her right under my nose, but it was about to catch up to him and the fact it would be by my hand made it even sweeter. As I stopped just before the end of the street, I watched the men cross the street toward the house and prayed they'd make good on their end of the bargain.

His silver BMW was parked at the small store around the corner. I parked next to him and cut the engine. Through the window, I saw the top of his head as he wandered the aisles. He was probably looking for those disgusting vinegar chips he liked so much that smelled like piss. I curbed my impatience and stood between our cars. When he finally got to the register, I checked the area for witnesses. The door chimed and broke the eerie silence in the air, and I rested my hand over the gun on my waistband as his footsteps drew closer. He rounded the corner and stopped when he saw me, narrowing his eyes before reaching into the front pocket of his jacket and grabbing a pack of cigarettes.

"*Evening, Seamus.*"

"*Wish I could say it was a pleasant evenin', but it would be a lie.*"

He leaned against the hood of his car and beat the top of the pack of cigarettes against his hand. It was an annoying habit of his, but according to him Americans didn't know how to pack the tobacco tight enough. After a long moment, he smirked. "*What brings you out here tonight?*"

"I wanted to have a word about our current situation."

He laughed. "Did you now? I think we said all that needed to be said the other day when I told you to stay the fuck away from my family."

"You're in no position to order me around," I snapped.

"Oh, really? All I have to do is tell my guy at the CIA what I know about you, and it's all over. Then where will you and your Italian friends be, huh? Who's going to filter information to the Genovese then?"

"Like you're any better, you fucking rat. You've been informing for how long? Five years?"

"Aye, but at least my deal was done for the greater good. It kept my family safe. You know, the woman you abandoned when she needed you most?"

"And my daughter that you've been passing off as yours all these years?"

"You didn't seem to give two shits about either of them when you were off banging that Russian waitress," he scoffed. "When Sera told me she was pregnant, she begged me not to tell anyone. She knows what a slimy monster you are and didn't want you anywhere near either of them. So, out of the love and respect I have for my wife, I agreed to keep her secret."

"Well, now I know, and you can bet that I'll be a part of my daughter's life. You won't keep her from me. Period."

He flipped the lid closed on the pack and laughed. "Damn, that's probably the funniest thing I've heard tonight, Felton. Or is it Soren? Which name do you really prefer? More to the point, what name should I tell my daughter to call you? Assuming you ever get to see her again."

"You bastard," I snarled. "You're completely crazy if you think you're going to stand in my way."

"I'm leaving this up to Sera. The decision whether you get to see Lissi is entirely up to her."

"You can't keep her from me."

"No, but her mother can. Like I said, I'm leaving it up to her."

"Did you really think...," I yelled but stopped.

"I don't think," the son of a bitch roared. "I know. And that's not how this is going to work. There will be rules and conditions that you're going to have to follow if you want to even think about coming anywhere near her."

I fought the urge to pummel the hell out of his traitorous face. Sera was a bitch for not telling me, but I knew that was my fault. When she caught me cheating, I'd been a coldhearted prick and accused her of fucking Seamus to get info on the Irish. He'd always been a lady's man, even when we were kids back in Ireland, so it wouldn't have surprised me if the rumors were true. Her facial expression made me regret my words the second I said them, but it was too late. She ran away and married the bastard two months later. When word got out that she was pregnant, I felt justified.

What was Seamus's damn excuse for not telling me I had a daughter? He'd spent summers with my family and met my grandmother, who treated him like he was one of her own. The man was like a brother to me at one point. Now he was the piece of shit who stole my woman and kept my child from me.

"Not if I just take what's mine," I hissed.

He smiled, a smug, arrogant fucking smirk, and stuck a cigarette between his lips. His laughter continued as he felt around in his pocket for his damn lighter. "Over my dead body."

"That's the idea."

I grabbed my gun and fired before he had a chance to react. As if in slow motion, he fell backwards against the hood of the car and then gracefully slid to the ground. The cigarette fell from his mouth and rolled away. I stared at his body briefly, shocked that the infamous Seamus Donovan had been felled by a single bullet to the head.

"Tú a fheiceáil in ifreann (See you in hell)," I whispered, feeling no regrets.

Reality set in a few seconds later and I knew I had to go before someone came to investigate. I got in the car and took off toward the warehouse, praying things went according to plan and my little girl would be waiting for me when I got there. Now that he was out of the way, she was the only thing that mattered.

One excruciatingly painful hour later, the garage door banged open and the cars all parked inside. The men were hooting and yelling in triumph, giving each other high fives and racing back into the meeting room. Marco emerged from the van with an evil glint in his eye. The blood on his shirt, as well as on his cheek, made my own run cold. His eyes met mine and he smiled. I fought the bile rising in my throat at the realization he was most likely Sera's killer.

"Where is she?" I demanded as Gio climbed out of the van.

Syd pursed his lips and scampered away, avoiding my eyes. I turned back to Gio, who sighed. "Soren, I'm sorry. We searched the house and we couldn't find her."

"What about Sera?"

"She came at Syd with a butcher knife, and well, there wasn't much talking after that. We took care of her, checked the house and when we couldn't find the kid, we torched it and left."

Blinding pain shot through me as my legs threatened to buckle, and my heart shattered. I took a deep, steadying breath and when I saw the indifference on his face, my sorrow boiled over into rage. I grabbed his shirt and threw him against the van. "You son of a bitch! You left a six-year-old little girl in that house to die!"

Several sets of hands grabbed my arms and yelled as I was pulled away. Someone punched me in the stomach, but the only pain I felt was the loss of the child I'd only recently discovered who was now gone forever.

"Stop!" Gio ordered, and everyone stilled. "Mr. Luccetti is clearly distraught. He needs to go home and rest. In the morning, he'll see there were no other options."

Nodding, I walked to my car. Feeling eyes on me, I turned and found Marco and Gio watching me as they spoke. Without another word, I sped away from the warehouse before I got myself killed.

My house was dark when I parked in the driveway. I knew I wouldn't be falling asleep anytime soon, so I headed to the backyard. Despite the frigid air, I leaned against the oak tree near the fence and lit a cigarette. Finally alone, I turned my face skyward and let the tears fall.

No matter how much anger I had over the situation, Sera's death hurt. She was my first love and a part of me would always love her. My heart broke all over again when images of our beautiful daughter appeared in my mind. She had her mother's face, but her wavy dark brown hair and pale blue eyes were mine.

"I'm sorry, Larissa," I whispered.

My cigarette had long since been stamped out, but I couldn't bring myself to go inside. I looked around the backyard, and saw the slight movement of a tarp covering the firewood next to the house that caught my attention. Thinking it was probably a raccoon, I walked over and yanked the cover back. What I found stole every last bit of air from my lungs.

Her face was covered in what looked like motor oil and grime. The tears falling from her eyes cut through the dirt and left two narrow trails down her cheeks. Blood soaked the back of her sweater, which had a large tear across her shoulder. Her little arms were wrapped around herself as she shivered violently.

"Uncle Felton?" Her voice was soft and uncertain.

I blinked, convinced I was hallucinating. My mind warred with itself, questioning how it was even possible. Several weeks earlier, before we stopped speaking, Seamus came to the house to drop off some papers as a favor to a mutual friend. She'd stayed in the car the entire time, but had somehow remembered how to get to my house in the dark. I stared at her in shock as her fearful eyes watched me cautiously.

"Larissa?" I croaked, trying to swallow the lump in my throat. "Sweetheart, what happened?"

"Some people came to our house and Mommy told me to run," she cried, her breath hitching between sobs. "I found my daddy at the store, but somebody shot him."

"Why are you bleeding?"

"I hurt myself when I was under Daddy's car," she hiccupped. "A man was yelling at him and then I heard a bang. He had blood on his head."

My stomach threatened to erupt, and I composed myself. If she had seen me, she would've reacted, I told myself. I picked her up and she clung to me. She buried her face in my shoulder as she continued to cry so hard her entire body shook. My heart filled with joy as I held her in my arms, determined to never let her go.

She could never know I was her father. The truth would either get me a life sentence or a bullet between the eyes. Even worse, if the wrong people learned she was my daughter, she'd become an extremely valuable bargaining chip and hunted for the rest of her life. I inhaled deeply to quell the hatred that I'd have to pretend that Irish rat was her father, but I quickly pushed it away. It no longer *mattered. No matter what lies I had to tell, I still won. She was mine now.*

"Let's get you inside, sweetheart," I whispered. "We'll clean you up and then I'll call the police and see what we can find out about your mom and dad."

* * * * * * * * * *

Present Day
Unknown Location

John shifted in the ugly blue metal chair. "What's your endgame here, Felton? I would think if you were going to kill me, you would've done it by now."

"A simple exchange with your uncle. You for her. Both of you will be safe and sound and allowed to live your lives in peace."

"You know he'll never go for that. All you're doing is making her death that much worse when he finds her."

"The family will need you to replace him someday. There's no way in hell he'd ever let Lucas take over as boss."

"She killed his brother. Nothing else matters. Once he realizes you're behind this shit, the only choice he'll give you is whether you want Marco or the twins to kill her."

Arguing with him was useless. We never got along when we worked together and now that my daughter was involved, we hated each other even more. I had my own sins to atone for, and I knew that would happen soon. In the meantime, I'd take some comfort in John's continued punishment for his sins against her.

I leaned forward in my seat. "When did you figure it out?"

"When she stumbled into the hallway while we were arguing." He chuckled softly and winced. "The way you and Lucas both tried to hide how worried you were about her was practically identical. My turn to ask a question."

"I guess I can indulge you. What?"

"How did it feel to see both your children together? Did it thaw that fucking glacier in your chest at all?"

"Surprising, to be honest. I never thought their paths would cross."

His eyebrows shot up. "That's it? You're going to sit there and tell me that's all you felt after seeing your son for the first time since he was barely walking?"

"How am I supposed to feel? I knew Lucas would be well cared for by his mother."

"And what about Liss? She'd be well cared for if you'd let me go so I can protect her."

"I can't let you go. You know too much."

"Then you've signed her execution order," he retorted, his voice cracking. "I don't care about your secrets. I don't even care why you let Gio lure her out in the open. You say you love her and yet you have some of the most fucked up ways of showing it."

"Don't you ever question how much I love my daughter," I spat. "Like you even know how to love someone as special as her."

"You have no fucking idea what she and I have. Whether you like it or not, she's going to be my wife someday. Now let me go so I can try to fix this before he rips her apart like a fucking rag doll!" he screamed.

Franz rushed into the room and belted him in the mouth. I calmly strode from the room and allowed him to continue his work, pummeling John as he continued to yell about being the only key to her survival. The moment the door shut, I slumped against the wall and tried to control my racing heart. After several minutes my body was calm, but my brain continued to scream at me. After trying to convince myself otherwise, I had to admit the truth.

I was in way too deep, so much so that my only hope was a desperate move that even I knew wouldn't work. All the impulsive mistakes I made haunted me. What was worse, my foolishness put Larissa in a position where she'd pay dearly for my sins if she were ever captured.

Over the years, I never worried about Lucas. Even when he was a baby, he was unbelievably smart and levelheaded. I knew Elena would raise him well. It didn't surprise me to hear John put his skills to work as a tactician and even though I had no right to feel it; I was proud of him and what he had accomplished.

Larissa, on the other hand, worried me from the time I found her in my backyard that fateful night. She was smart like her brother, but unlike him she didn't abhor violence. A cold and calculating rage was born inside her the night her parents died. One of her drill instructors saw it and warned me how easily she'd lose her humanity if it wasn't harnessed. I saw glimpses of it a few times, but it wasn't until I found her sitting on my desk with a gun in her lap that I realized she'd have no problem unleashing that rage on me. Thanks to my evil wife and her lies, I betrayed her and put her in harm's way. Karina paid with her life, and I thanked whatever force in the universe spared Lissa. However, I knew if she ever learned the truth, my death was certain.

After the mess in Cuba and hearing about the bounty on her, I was desperate to save her life. I hadn't expected to come face to face with Lucas, nor did I expect a bargaining chip to cross my path. John was barely a toddler when I left Italy, so he had no way of knowing the double agent who recruited him to join the CIA and helped him pass information to the family was his long-lost uncle.

Unfortunately, I saw the realization on his face in Tampa when he saw the three of us together, and I knew I had to act.

I realized then that kidnapping the one person who could have probably helped her was impulsive and foolish, but it was too late to reverse course. I was committed to the plan, and I had to see it through. If it didn't work, I wouldn't rest until I found another way to keep her from further harm.

Franz had knocked the chair over and was kicking John repeatedly in the ribs when I barged back into the room. To his credit, John merely laid on the ground and accepted each blow with little response. He'd been desensitized to the brutality weeks ago, enduring everything with little more than a blank stare. Lissa was the only subject that got any kind of emotional response, making me thankful there was no way of using her as leverage.

"Enough!" I yelled. The kicking stopped and Franz pulled the chair upright at my nod.

John winced and coughed. "I am begging you. Please let me go. I'll get her somewhere safe and he'll never find her."

"I want to believe you, but he found her the last time you tried that. I'm sorry, son. This is the only way."

I dialed my phone and steadied my nerves. It had to work. It just had to. I'd never been an overly emotional man, but I was willing to cry and beg if it meant she could live her life free from constant threats. I would sacrifice my own life if I had to. Just as long as it meant my little girl could finally be at peace.

"Si," a deep, heavily accented voice answered.

"Massimo. It's Soren. We need to talk. I have something here that you've been looking for."

"And what might that be? Another bastard child to betray? Or have you decided to cash in on the bounty?"

"I have your nephew."

"I see," he drawled after a pause. "Since you're calling me, I'm going to assume that you're referring to Gianni and not that useless son of yours."

"I am. I'd like to talk about an exchange. Your nephew for my daughter."

Silence and then the sound of boisterous laughter echoed through the speaker. I opened my mouth to speak and the line went dead. I stared at my phone.

"You stupid, stubborn son of a bitch," he rasped. "You've just killed her."

Chapter 2

Arianne

Larissa

I SCANNED THE FILE on my phone a second time, flicking through the pages of the encrypted digital reader. The app was in the testing phase before I went on my "leave", as was the shiny silver phone issued to me by the Bureau. Between that phone and the red phone Lucas gave me, I held links to vital information but none of it was the type I needed to find John.

Barton's description of the job that ensured my freedom was an interesting one. Arianne Shaw Reynolds, Ari to her close friends and family, was a twenty-four-year-old IT consultant who started her own firm with Georgia's son and a couple of their mutual friends. Their first contract was for a gaming company in Toronto. What nobody knew was Ari had a stalker who harassed her almost as soon as she arrived. When she started dating another man, things escalated from threatening messages to her ultimately being kidnapped, raped, and almost strangled to death. She and her boyfriend went into hiding once she was released from the hospital.

Once they felt safe enough they returned to Seattle, and the case took a strange turn. Because of Ari's background and criminal record as a computer hacker, she was on a special FBI watch list that alerted the agency if her identity was accessed. Someone performed a background check and tried to access her travel history.

The case went much deeper, but my job was to find the person who accessed her information. Marcus Vargas, an old hacker in the Miami area, was the master of travel records. The Bureau had tried to bring him in for years because he worked as a freelancer for anyone willing to pay. He would be offered a deal too tempting to pass up, and he'd give them what they wanted. For Georgia, she wanted him to corroborate that Ari's attacker, James Erickson, was one of his clients. James was still at large and had most likely fled the country. I not only had to locate Marcus, but Barton and Georgia also tasked me with finding James and bringing him home.

"Five minutes to landing," the pilot announced over the intercom.

The lush vegetation surrounding Joint Base Lewis-McChord came into view. Located about forty miles south of Seattle, the base housed both the Army's Fort Lewis and McChord Air Force Base and was my best way into Seattle without being detected. We landed and after I checked in with the base commander, I called Ari's husband from my Bureau phone. Since I was dealing with a computer expert who'd been arrested at thirteen for hacking the Department of Defense, I used one of my lesser known and therefore "cleaner" aliases. If, or when, she dug into my info, she'd learn that Special Agent Sarah Stone was a highly decorated senior field agent who paid all her parking tickets and liked to post multiple pictures of her cat on social media.

As I drove into Seattle, the pictures of her injuries played over and over in my mind. Not only did he break four of her ribs, but she'd also had to undergo surgery to repair her carotid artery from the damage inflicted by the strangulation. The fact she was brutalized so severely that she had to be put into a medically induced coma made my blood boil. Nobody deserved that, not when their only "offense" was not wanting to be in a relationship with her stalker.

I parked a couple of blocks from the Reynolds's home. The meeting wasn't for a couple hours, so I checked out the house and the surrounding area. Georgia told me a small fortune was paid to have everything checked by one of the best security consultants in the region. Satisfied with what I saw, I made my way to the restaurant.

Sitting near the back so I could easily see the front door, I read through my latest text messages with Lucas. It was frustrating that I couldn't tell him I'd been forced to take a job and couldn't call him, but I couldn't do anything from jail. He reported some of his contacts close to Massimo had intel he'd share as soon as he knew it. Shutting down my anxiety at the sound of the bell at the front door, I looked up. Now was the time to focus on the job I was sent to do.

Patrick Reynolds, Ari's former boyfriend and now husband, was a very tall, imposing looking man with a large frame and a muscular build. According to the file, he played football in college until a horrific knee injury derailed any hope of playing professionally. His dark blue eyes scanned the room as he led his wife to a table, their hands tightly clasped together. They sat next to each other, where he wrapped his arm around her shoulder as she looked through the menu.

Ari Reynolds was the physical opposite of her husband. She was at least a foot shorter, barely standing at the middle of his chest and I would've been surprised if she weighed more than a hundred pounds. Her long, curly red hair, which she pulled at as she glanced around the room, went past her shoulders. He said something to her, and her green eyes lit up as she smiled and brushed a lock of his light brown hair from his forehead. She'd been through a lot, but he had clearly been there with her almost every step of the way. My eyes met his and I nodded, which he returned. I watched him whisper in her ear as I strolled to the booth.

"Ms. Shaw, thank you for agreeing to meet me so late in the afternoon and in such a casual place. I was really excited to hear about the job opportunity," I said, extending my hand to her.

"It's my pleasure, Ms. Stone." She shook my hand with a warm smile. "Our pizzas should be done in a few minutes and then we can take them back to the office, where I'll show you the software."

"Sounds great! I really can't wait to get started."

We walked up the front steps to their home with two pizzas a short time later. The gray and white house had a modern design with a lot of windows facing the park and the beach across the street, offering a stunning view of the Puget Sound. The interior of the house had the same modern look: metal and glass banisters and a sleek kitchen with black cabinets and stainless-steel appliances, but the décor had a very warm and homey feel, complete with bright colors and a ton of pictures of family and friends on the mantle in the living room. As we ate, we chatted about Seattle and how they had only recently moved into the house. Afterward, the two of them leaned against the counter and looked at me expectantly.

"Well, let's start with someone explaining the situation to me," I said.

Her brows creased. "Nobody told you?"

"All I was told was you needed help to find the man responsible for your attack."

She motioned for me to come with her into the living room. "Let's all get comfy and start at the beginning."

They sat on the larger couch while I sat on the loveseat. She explained her past as a hacker, including her arrest and the deal she made with the government that kept her out of jail but shunned her from the community. She met James in college, but they were never more than acquaintances. Their paths crossed at a conference the summer before she and Patrick started dating, which resulted in a drunken one-night stand. James wanted a more serious relationship and aggressively pursued her. After a violent confrontation when he visited her in California, he left to avoid prosecution and agreed to cease all contact. A few weeks later, she started receiving harassing text messages, but could never prove the identity of the sender. The messages stopped briefly but started again almost right after she arrived in Toronto.

"Any ideas where James might be?"

"I tracked him to Amsterdam a couple months ago," she admitted quietly.

Patrick closed his eyes and drew a deep breath. "Why would you do that? He could track you."

"I masked the outgoing IP address so he can't track anything. The cops weren't having any luck finding him, so I embedded a virus into an email. Once he opened it, the virus did the rest. And I only checked it the one time."

He shook his head. "Have I mentioned lately that you're bloody brilliant and you're going to be the death of me?"

"Do you remember the name of the bar?" Thanks to her virus, half my job may have already been done.

"No, but I saved a screenshot."

I leaned forward and stared at the image, showing that the phone was tracked to the Geheim Bar in downtown Amsterdam. The name sounded familiar, but I hadn't been to the city in a while.

Explaining she'd just track him again, she typed quickly, muttered under her breath, and typed a few more commands.

"Shit, I think he may have disposed of the phone. It hasn't moved since the last time I tracked it."

I studied the address on the screen, racking my brain to remember where I'd seen it before. "Holy shit, I remember now! Ari, we just got extremely lucky. That bar belongs to a man named Yanislov Petrocova. He's a boss for the Russian mob out of—"

"St. Petersburg," she answered.

Patrick bumped his shoulder against hers. "And how do you know that?"

"My hacker group did the occasional favor for him. We erased the evidence the police had on one of his soldiers. I also helped find his daughter when she was kidnapped."

"Impressive."

She shrugged. "All part of my former life. What the hell was James doing in a bar in Amsterdam owned by a Russian mob boss?"

"He'd better pray Yani didn't find out what he did to you," I answered. "He's loyal as hell, and that could be very bad for James."

"So, how do we find out what happened to him?"

"Simple. I'll call and ask." I grabbed my phone.

Patrick looked at the clock in the kitchen. "Isn't it like one in the morning in Amsterdam?"

"He's usually in St. Petersburg, so it'll be three. But that's actually the perfect time since the bar will be closed and he's more likely to be in the office."

"Da?" a deep voice answered.

"Yani, it's Bianca Monroe. It's been a while. How are you?" I walked downstairs to the garage for privacy.

Yani was the boss of one of the larger bratvas in Russia. He also had a powerful network of associates around the world, including

Rome, Toronto, Paris and Amsterdam. I'd met him four years ear-lier when the son of a White House aide was kidnapped from a nightclub in Rome. Yani helped me get access to an auction house outside St. Petersburg when we discovered the young man was sold into an underground human trafficking ring. Unfortunately, we'd been too late and the nineteen-year-old's body was found a few weeks later in Moscow. The last time we spoke was eighteen months ago when I visited the Geheim in search of a Sardi family arms supplier.

He chuckled. "Hello, Miss Monroe. It has indeed been a long time. What can I do for you?"

"I have a bit of a mystery I'm trying to figure out. Does the name James Erickson mean anything to you?"

"What do you want with that scum?" The tone of his voice dropped several degrees in seconds.

"Justice for Prodigy."

"You are helping her?"

"Unofficially. So I need my involvement kept extremely quiet."

"Is she okay?" he asked in a rush. "My sister worked for the hospital she was admitted to."

"Physically, she's doing better. She's the reason I'm calling."

"What do you mean?"

"Apparently, she tracked James to your bar in Amsterdam at the end of June."

"She was always a smart girl. If she did that, it means she's going to be okay," he sighed. "James is in my dungeon. A mutual friend of ours hired him to do a job. After he found out what James did to her, I volunteered to hold him until he could decide what he wanted to do with him."

"That mutual friend isn't part of my case, so I won't ask."

"I appreciate that. What exactly does she need with him?"

"She needs James back here in the States so he can answer for what he did."

"When can you get to St. Petersburg?"

"Give me seventy-two hours."

"I will see you then," he said. "Bianca? Please tell her she's in mine and Ilya's thoughts."

"I will. See you soon."

Too excited to contain my squeal of victory, I raced upstairs and found Ari in Patrick's lap. He cupped her face while softly pleading with her to be more careful. After she nodded slowly, he shut his eyes and hugged her small body to his. I cleared my throat to announce my presence. She remained in his lap while they both gestured for me to sit.

"I'm headed to Russia," I announced. "James has been sitting in a cell in Yani's dungeon since the end of June."

Patrick's eyes widened. "What?"

"Yani knows about the attack. I won't go into detail about that because it's not pertinent to my assignment and he didn't tell me everything, but he agreed to let me take James off his hands so he can get what's coming to him."

"Oh, my god," she whispered. "How can it be so easy?"

"Getting him back here is the easy part," I replied. "The hard part is how to get him into a situation where he can be arrested once he's back."

Patrick shook his head. "Why would he ever come back here?"

"I have an idea," Ari blurted out.

We listened to her plan and then spent a great deal of time convincing Patrick it was the quickest and easiest way to get James into custody. It was only after I called Georgia and she assured him that we'd both do everything in our power to keep her safe that he grumbled his agreement.

I went downstairs to make my travel arrangements. When I returned to the living room, Ari was talking to someone on her phone while Patrick read on his tablet. Shortly after, she announced she was heading to bed. He whispered something in her ear, causing her to nod before kissing her neck. She said good night and headed upstairs. Sensing he had something to say, I turned to him the moment the bedroom door closed.

"What's up?"

"Two questions," he began. "One, do you really think this will work?"

"Honestly? Yes. Ari did most of the work already by finding him."

"Yes, and that's the problem. Which leads me to my second question. Can you keep her safe? Even if it's from herself?"

"Absolutely," I answered. "I know you don't like this plan, but Georgia will make sure we have the full support of the Seattle field office and anyone else she can wrestle into helping. Nothing will happen to her if any of us have anything to say about it."

The tension in his shoulders eased, and he nodded. "Thank you. I almost lost her once, and I don't want her to do anything else crazy to bring him down. It's bad enough she tracked him."

"How long have you two been together?" My guess was it had been several years, based on the way his eyes lit up whenever she was close and all the stories they shared during dinner.

"Believe it or not, we'd only been dating for six months before we got married yesterday," he answered. "We've been friends for eight years, but she's had me wrapped around her little finger since the day I met her. I just took forever to work up the courage to make a move."

"It's clear to me that you two have meant a lot to each other for a very long time."

"And that's why I'm willing to agree to this insane plan. I can't lose her again."

I nodded. "We'll both make sure you don't. Deal?"

"Deal."

He offered to show me to a guest room, but I told him I was still waiting for a call and had no problem sleeping on the couch. After he went upstairs, I leaned my head back and went through the pictures on my phone. John had been missing for two months and I knew the chances of finding him alive grew smaller with each passing day. The idea of losing him made my heart ache. I squeezed my eyes shut to stop the tears from flowing again. When that proved impossible, I quietly opened the glass door just off the living room and slipped outside to the patio.

The summer air had cooled under the night sky. I gripped the railing and stared out at the blackness of the Puget Sound. Turning my face skyward, I said a prayer, pleading that John was okay and would come back to me safe and alive. I wasn't sure how long I'd been standing when I felt someone behind me.

"Sarah, are you okay?"

"I should ask you the same thing," I answered, sitting down on the dark blue patio chair. "Couldn't sleep?"

She shrugged and sat in the chair next to mine. "One perk of my PTSD is insomnia. I don't want to toss and turn and wake up Patrick. He's lost enough sleep because of me. But what about you? Why are you crying?"

I blinked, feeling the tears I hadn't realized were still flowing, and gave her a small smile. "I'm okay. Just some things on my mind. Nothing important."

"Maybe not important to me, but certainly important to you," she observed, and then grimaced. "Sorry. Sometimes I have a habit of prying when I shouldn't."

"No need to apologize. That was a pretty crappy lie, wasn't it?"

"Well, if you ever want to talk about it I'm here. I know Georgia said not to ask you anything personal, but I'm willing to listen if it will help you feel better."

I was touched by her sincerity. Over the course of my career, I'd met dozens of civilians, but I'd felt nothing close to the bond I felt with Ari. Maybe it was our common backgrounds of losing our parents, a simple need for human interaction, or maybe even the humanity that Connor swore by. I didn't know, but I just knew she was someone I could confide in.

"Someone very important to me is missing," I murmured. "He's been gone for a while now, and I was just thinking of him."

"What happened? If you feel comfortable telling me."

"The security camera shows him walking into a café in Lisbon, and then nothing. He just vanished without a trace."

"But?" she prodded.

"Things aren't adding up. The guy he was supposed to meet didn't even know he was coming to see him. And whomever he did meet made sure not to show his face to the camera."

"Is there any chance the security footage is fake?"

"I'm told it's not. My brother had a few people look it over and they said it was real."

"That must be hard, especially since I'm sure you'd rather be looking for him instead of babysitting me."

"Not at all. I actually volunteered." It wasn't completely true, but knowing how important this woman was to Georgia made it easier for me to accept being voluntold.

"You did?"

"Georgia's a good friend of mine, and when she told me your story, I wanted to help. So, no thinking that I'm babysitting you or

I'd rather be somewhere else. I'm right where I need and want to be."

"Thank you," she whispered, staring out across the water.

We sat in silence, apart from the occasional squawk of a seagull from the beach below. I turned back to the card game on my phone and played quietly. Ari seemed to have a lot on her mind as she continued to stare at the sky, so I left her to her thoughts.

"I want to help," she suddenly announced.

"What do you mean?"

"I want to help you find him."

"Ari, that's very sweet and I appreciate it. But I don't know how you could. Plus, these are dangerous people involved."

"I know people. And I'm not saying I'm going to storm the café or anything like that. But I know people who can find the impossible."

"Hackers?"

"Maybe."

"Ari," I started, but fell silent when she held up her hand.

"Sarah, I know some of the most elite hackers in the world. They know how to not get caught. Hell, I know Marcus Vargas was the one James hired to track me. He had no idea the person who hired him was a dangerous sociopath, so I don't hold it against him. My point is, I can help you. All I need is his name and the name of the café. I could even have someone look at the video."

"I don't want you to get in trouble."

"No one will get in trouble. I promise," she replied. "But I know how frustrating it is to follow the rules to get what you need and get nothing in return. Sometimes the rules need to be bent a little."

I paused and stared at the wallpaper on my phone, one of my favorite pictures of John and me. We'd fallen asleep snuggled on the double chaise lounge by the pool, and Lucas stole my phone and took the picture before throwing water on us like the asshat he was. I smiled at the memory.

"All right," I sighed, scrolling through my phone and gathering the information for her. "Just promise me nobody gets caught. I honestly don't know who's connected to this, and the last thing I want is someone getting hurt."

We stayed on the patio until she yawned and headed back to bed. Not long after I laid on the couch, I received my flight information. I tossed a dark gray blanket over me and tried to get some rest. Sleep never came, but plenty of nightmares did. After a couple of hours, I gave up and returned to the patio. I exchanged text messages with Lucas for a while, leaving out the fact I was headed to Russia. Once the sun rose over the horizon, I wandered inside for a cup of coffee and opened the fridge to see what I could cook for breakfast.

We ate on the patio and toasted mimosas to the victory of locating James. I was unsure what lie ahead of me, but Ari's relaxed demeanor chased away all my uncertainty. The couple insisted on cleaning up while I showered. Coming downstairs, I watched them talk and laugh as they worked in the kitchen. The love they had for each other was plain on both their faces. I swallowed the lump in my throat and headed back upstairs to finish packing, determined I wouldn't fail the next part of this mission. I didn't know if mine and John's story would have a happy ending, but I was determined to ensure one for Patrick and Ari.

Chapter 3

The Side Quest

Larissa

"What in the actual fuck, Larissa Aednat Donovan?" Lucas bellowed into the phone.

"Settle down! You're gonna wake up Nonna and I can't deal with both of you right now!"

"You're willingly going to a Russian dungeon and you want me to settle down?" he growled. "Are you serious right now?"

I decided not to tell him about my plan to infiltrate Yani's dungeon until after I arrived in St. Petersburg. In truth, I didn't want to tell him at all, but I knew he'd freak out even worse if he couldn't reach me. Yani was a trusted friend who'd pass on any urgent messages.

"It's my friend's private prison, if that helps."

"No, it doesn't help!" he spluttered. "How would that possibly help?"

"It means I'm not in any danger, Lucas. Relax."

"You don't understand! Massimo is pinning John's abduction on you."

"Fuck."

"That's why I'm freaking out," he ranted. "He has a ton of associates in Russia who would be only too happy to cash in."

"Okay, Lucas. Deep breath. I have to do this to stay out of jail, so I can't leave. I'll be careful and as soon as I'm done, I'll get the hell out of here."

"How will I get a message to you if something comes up?"

"Get a hold of Yani Petrocova. I'll text you his number."

"Lissa, how are you friends with a Russian mob boss who has a personal prison?"

"I can't tell you right now. And it's not like you guys didn't have cells in Verona," I answered. "Anyway, I know Yani and most of his crew, so I'll be safe. They won't hurt me. I promise."

"Fine," he huffed. "But be careful."

"I will. Love you, favorite big brother."

"I'm your only big brother, you pain in the ass. And I love you too."

I hung up and placed the red phone on the arm of the couch where I'd sat for the past hour. The bar downstairs was busy as hell, which meant Yani was doubly so. I stood before the mirror near the door to check my appearance, deciding to look as close to Ari as possible. The door burst open, and Yani stormed in, cursing under his breath in Russian. He stomped to his desk, paused for a moment, and nodded at me before sitting down.

"Ms. Monroe, welcome to St. Petersburg. I trust you had a safe trip."

"I'm here in one piece, if that's what you're asking."

He rubbed his bald head. "Prodigy is still doing well?"

"She is. I was staying with her and her fiancé when I called you."

Patrick and Ari were married, but in secret. One reason was to shield his parents from some details of the case. The other reason was so we could leak news of their engagement to the media in order to lure James back to the States.

He smiled. "She always was a smart girl. It was nothing short of a miracle when she found my Ilya. Fiancé, huh? He better treat her well. I already have one man who mistreated her in my cells. I won't hesitate to add another one."

"That won't be necessary. They look very much in love and he treats her like a queen."

"I'm very glad to hear it," he replied, grinning slightly before his face turned serious. "The only reason I'm even agreeing to this plan of yours is because of her. She saved my little girl, and I would love nothing more than to tear the beast who attacked her to pieces."

"I know, and she's very grateful for your help. We all are."

"I hope this works. We should move you into the cell soon. The red hair and the green eyes are a nice touch. It will definitely make him more receptive to you. What story are we using?"

"I figured the closer I looked to her, the easier it might be. And I thought I'd be the dumb American tourist who accidentally witnessed a murder. Is Anatoly still the head of your guards?"

He shook his head. "Fucking Moscow bitches. Killed him almost a year ago."

"I'm so sorry. He was a good man."

Without a word, he reached into his bottom desk drawer and produced a large glass horse. He uncorked the lid and poured the brown liquid into two small silver cups. It wasn't often he shared his favorite Armenian brandy with anyone, so when he slid one to the edge of the desk, I grabbed it without delay. Raising our cups, we toasted and drank.

"Petyr is my new head of the guards. He's not Anatoly, but still a good man. Escaped all the bullshit in Moscow, so he's smart."

He opened his office door and yelled down the hall. A young blond woman ran into the room not long after. He took the large paper shopping bag from her hands and shooed her out with a flick of his hand.

"Here are some clothes for you to change into." He placed the bag next to me. "Petyr will take you to the bathroom to change before he takes you downstairs."

I headed to the hall, freezing when my gaze met Petyr's. His dark green eyes widened for the smallest fraction before narrowing to slits. I squared my shoulders, clutched the bag to my chest, and stepped forward.

"Are you Petyr? I'm Bianca Monroe. Yani said you'd be showing me downstairs?"

Clenching his jaw, he grabbed my elbow. I started to protest, but the look he gave me was a clear enough warning to keep my mouth shut. His boots were loud as they stomped down the hall and I did my best to follow him. After passing several hallways, he turned left and shoved me into a dark room. The lights came on just before the door slammed.

"What in the fuck are you doing here, *Bianca*?" he snarled.

Jesus Christ. Of all the prisons in all the world, I had to find the one where a fellow CIA officer and my former friend with benefits were working undercover. The last time I saw Jackson Michaels was when I ended our arrangement almost three years earlier. I wrenched my arm out of his grasp and stepped back.

"I could ask the same thing, Officer."

"If you were coming in on a job, I would've been told. So I'm going to ask again. What in the fuck are you doing in Russia?"

"It's not a job," I answered. "Your turn."

"So if it's not a job, it's...," he broke off and his eyes widened. "Why are you on a black bag, Officer?"

"A black bag would be if I were here on CIA business. And I'm not. This is personal, unofficial, and nobody, and I mean nobody, can know. Now, it's your turn. What happened in Moscow?"

He sighed, and his gaze went to the floor. "Anton is growing more and more unstable. He's still married, but he disappears every few months and spends days afterward drunk and coked out of his goddamned mind. His wife is a sadist who's a psychopath on even her best days. When she started imprisoning and enslaving lower level men, I knew I needed to get the hell out of there."

"Jesus."

"You shouldn't be here, Lissa. It's not safe for you."

"I can't. Someone very important to me is in danger, and this job will ensure I can keep looking for him."

His eyes narrowed. "And who is this man you've decided is worth dying for? I heard rumors you'd taken up with some rogue agent. Is it the man from MI6?"

"No, John killed him for attacking me," I blurted, and then cursed my loose lips.

"*John?*" he scoffed. "The only rogue agent I know named John is John fucking Martinetti. Don't tell me you fell for that piece of shit's lies."

"Hey." I shoved his shoulder, forcing him to step back. "You can be angry and disagree with my life choices all you want, but I was honest with you when I ended things. Were you so judgmental about your fiancée's drug charges, or were those forgiven when she got out of rehab? If not, maybe after the second or third time?"

His cheeks flared and he sighed. "Lissa."

"I'm here to do a job. You can either have my back like you've always had in the past, or I'll take care of it by myself. All I will ask of you is to not blow my cover and stay the fuck out of my way."

"I'm sorry. That was way out of line. I will always have your back. That's a promise."

"Then let's get this show on the road so I can take the obsessed rapist off your boss's hands."

He led me to a bathroom and I emerged minutes later in a pair of dirty light blue jeans, a black t-shirt with a few holes in it, and a pair of plain white canvas shoes. The temperature dropped about ten degrees as we climbed down the stairs leading to the dungeon. Once he led me through the thick metal door at the end of the narrow hall, the only sources of light were a few old bare bulbs hanging from fixtures in the ceiling. Further down the corridor, I heard the screams of several prisoners. He elbowed me in the ribs and I smiled. Showtime.

"Help!" I shrieked at the top of my lungs. "I swear I didn't see anything! Please!"

"You think I care what you say you didn't see?" he yelled. "One minute you say you see nothing and the next little bitches like you run to police and tell them you saw everything!"

I struggled hard against his grasp as he dragged me down the corridor. My sobs echoed off the walls. "Mister! Please! My family will be worried sick about me. I swear I didn't see anything!"

"You have no family anymore, little girl!" he spat. He unlocked the barred door in front of us and gave my body a hard shove. I fell on my ass and let out a pained groan. "Welcome to hell!" he snarled as he slammed the door closed and stomped away.

As I sat on the floor sobbing, I glanced around the cell. The walls were made of dark, rough stone. A metal toilet hung on the back wall while a long metal shelf that was meant to be a bed sat to the right of the toilet, a small metal sink to the left. I walked to the black metal bars at the front of the cell and gripped them tightly.

"Somebody help me! Please! I don't know anything! I promise!"

"Nobody is going to help you," a weak male voice said from the cell to my left. "It's best if you save your energy and your voice."

"Oh my god!" I yelled, frantically moving closer to the source of the voice. "Are you American too?"

"Yeah. I saw them bring you in just now. Pardon the poor joke, but what are you in for?"

"I got separated from my family and went down an alley to find a shortcut back to the hotel. A guy grabbed me and said I saw something I shouldn't have, but I didn't see anything. I swear!"

"You'll find they don't much care what you tell them. My name is James. And you are?"

"Anne."

"Nice to meet you. So, what brought you and your family to St. Petersburg?"

"My dad had business here and brought the whole family for a last-minute summer vacation for my sister and me. Mister, I'm scared." I sniffed. "What are they going to do to me here?"

He sighed. "They'll probably wait a couple of days and then have you try to contact your parents so they can demand ransom for your release. And I really hope your parents can pay it."

"Why? What will happen if they can't pay?"

"Let's not think about that. If I were you, I'd keep quiet and do whatever they tell you."

"Thank you, James. How long have you been here?"

"I honestly don't know. What day is it?"

"August twentieth."

"Already? I've been here almost two months."

"Your family couldn't pay the ransom?"

"Nobody can help me," he whispered.

"Why? What happened?"

"That's a story for another day. They'll be coming with food soon. We should be quiet. They don't like when prisoners talk to each other."

I stepped away from the bars. A few moments later, a man came down the corridor with a wheeled cart and handed me a bowl of a grayish-looking porridge and a plastic spoon through the small opening in the door's center. It almost tasted like mashed potatoes and had the consistency of watery paste. However, I'd eaten much worse in nicer prison cells.

The dungeon was silent after the meal. I decided to lie on my bunk and relax. It was encouraging that James had been so quick to introduce himself. Hopefully, that was a good sign. Eventually I fell asleep, awoken only by the occasional scream down the hall.

The next day Jackson came to my cell to "rough me up" as part of the ruse to scare the poor American tourist so she'd confess what she saw. Just when I thought we laid it on too thick, James yelled to leave me alone. Jackson responded by shouting several obscenities and threats before leaving me to sob and cry as loud as I could. Not long after, James asked if I was okay. I sat in the corner of my cell closest to him for a while so he could offer me words of comfort. So far, so good.

"You're lucky we don't make you work off your ransom in one of our whorehouses!" Jackson yelled as he dragged me back to my cell after we made a show of forcing me upstairs to make the ransom call to my parents later that day. The moment the door shut, I screamed at the top of my lungs for five minutes until I heard him.

"Anne, you need to calm down. Screaming won't help. It just shows them that they're getting to you," James said in a low voice.

"I need to get out of here," I sobbed. "I can't be here anymore. I need to find a way out."

"It's not that simple," he whispered sadly.

Jackson visited my cell a few times the next day to continue my "interrogations". In reality, I pinched and poked my wrists to create bruises while we moved around the cell. He slapped his bare arms or chest and I screamed, cried, and swore I knew nothing. When James yelled at him to stop, I nodded and he passed me a small piece of paper and a pencil before strolling out of my cell.

"Mind your business, scum!" he hissed, kicking the bars of James's cell as he passed by.

"Anne?" he asked quietly after the metal door closed. "Are you okay?"

"We've got to get out of here," I sniffed

"As nice as that sounds, I don't think that's possible."

"What if I could get his keys?"

"How?"

"Those last few slaps were so hard his keys almost dropped from his pocket. I could try to grab them."

"Do you really think you could?" His voice perked up a little.

"Yes, but I'd need help once we got them. Where do we even go if we get out of here?"

"Where do you want to go?

"The American Embassy I guess? But I don't know how to get there."

"I can't," he answered. "That would be almost worse than this place."

"Why?"

"Let's just say there was a misunderstanding and I'm a wanted man back home."

"Then what we do? I just want to get home to my family!" I cried.

"If I could get my hands on a cell phone, I know people who could help get us stateside."

"Really? You'd help me?"

"I need to get home, too. I have loose ends I need to tie up."

"Okay, it's a deal. I'll work on getting his keys," I whispered.

A guard on patrol yelled at us to shut up, ending our conversation. That night I left a note on my tray for Yani. The guard who picked up my half eaten dinner bowed his head and shoved it into his pocket.

The next morning, Nikolai, Yani's underboss, dragged me upstairs. Seeing him worried me. Was there news from Lucas? Icy fear raced through my veins as I climbed the stairs and headed to the office. Yani sat at his desk, looking through a file folder when I entered. The serious expression on his face made my stomach clench.

"Felton has been in touch," he said the moment the door closed. "You're needed in Venezuela. As soon as you're done here, you're to report to Caracas."

What. The. Fuck. "How did he know to contact you?" I did my best to keep my voice calm.

He shrugged. "One day the CIA is an enemy and the next day they're a friend. Today they are friends."

"That might be the case, but he didn't know I was here. I'm not here on CIA business."

"You're not? Then why are you—"

"It's best that you not know. But he's the one person I didn't want knowing my location."

"I'm sorry, Bianca. I had no idea."

"It's okay. But the timing is actually perfect. James is ready. I need Petyr to drop his keys in my cell the next time he visits."

"Consider it done," he replied. "Is there anything else you need from me?"

"Not unless you have any spies on the Italians," I answered, half joking.

"Which region?"

"Southern. The Sardis out of Bari."

He raised his eyebrows. "Anything specific you're looking for?"

"Any movements on Massimo Sardi, Marco, his enforcer, or his nephew, Gianni Martinetti?"

"I'll see what I can find out. Info out of the south has been limited. Massimo has been keeping things very close to the vest lately. I'm sure you know he's obsessed with finding the CIA sniper, even more so now that Gianni is missing."

"I'd heard about the bounty he placed on the sniper," I said, my voice neutral. "Five million dead, ten million alive."

"It's doubled."

I swallowed hard. "It's what?"

"Rumor has it the sniper has something to do with the kidnapping, so he's doubled it."

The air in my lungs froze. I'd never confirmed or denied my identity to him, but I also knew he wouldn't turn me in. However, he was putting himself at great risk.

"Wow. That's impressive."

He nodded quietly. "It is. Well, I'll let Petyr know you're ready to move and we'll make sure the coast is clear for you."

"Thank you, Yani. I know Prodigy appreciates all your help."

"Anything for a friend," he answered gruffly and nodded, dismissing me. "Bianca?" he called softly as I reached for the door.

"Yeah?"

"Once you leave here, get the hell out of Europe and back to the States as fast as you can. That kind of money makes people do crazy things."

"Don't I know it," I muttered.

Jackson was waiting for me in the hall when I left the office. My face apparently showed my worry because his brows creased as soon as our eyes met. Without another word, he led me to the same room we spoke before.

He watched me closely. "What's wrong?"

"What I'm about to say is merely a statement of fact and not an accusation," I said before taking a deep breath. "Felton knows I'm here, and he wasn't supposed to."

"Fuck," he muttered. "Nobody said anything to me, so I'm guessing he found out through unofficial channels. Okay, keep to your plan. I'll do my best to keep you safe until it's time for you to leave."

"Yani's probably going to tell you that we're a go. I just told him James is ready."

"Understood."

I knew Jackson wasn't the one who informed on me to Felton. We'd been through a lot of shit together, the kind that made or broke a person. The breach put his own assignment at risk if it was found he helped me with my unsanctioned actions, which didn't help. All I could hope for was for Barton to intervene if it was ever found out. That was a worry for another day. After handing me my two cell phones and making sure they were hidden on my body, he led me back to the stairs. He gave me a quick pep talk, reminding me I was almost done.

James picked up on my quiet mood and asked a few times if I was okay and encouraged me not to give up. My answers were always short, saying I was just tired and that I would still look for a way to escape. Finally, he let me be and I laid on my bed and just stared at the ceiling.

Massimo blaming me for the kidnapping wasn't surprising, but it was confusing. Doubling the bounty would no doubt ramp up the search for me, but the minute I was captured it would be pretty damn obvious I didn't have John. Everyone knew the man was psychotic, but what was he hoping to accomplish? I sighed and after sending Lucas a text message that I'd be traveling for the next few days and mostly unavailable to talk, I turned off both phones and tried to get some rest.

I woke up early and stretched my muscles to prepare for the day ahead, knowing it would be long and exhausting. Jackson stomped down the hall and threw the door open as he yelled for me to wake up. I dug my fingers into my neck to create fresh bruises, nodding at Jackson when I saw his discomfort and he turned away. I let out a strangled cry and moved my hand away as a cue to him that it was safe to turn around. As he passed me the keys, he nodded once and I mirrored the action. Our time as a couple was long over, but I knew he'd always be there for me if I ever needed him. We then got to work playing our final charade, cursing, yelling, and at one point making it sound like he had me pinned against the wall. Finally, he yelled a few more insults before leaving.

One key on the small ring he handed me was marked with red paint while the others had markings of different colors. Once he was gone, I tried the red key and my door swung open. Standing in front of James's cell, I tried to keep my face blank as I looked at the man who came so close to destroying Ari's life. He was cowered in the corner, but straightened when he saw me. His black hair and beard were both filthy and overgrown and his clothes were tattered and hung from his body. When I opened his door, his blue eyes snapped to life.

"Are you an angel come to take me to heaven?" he whispered.

"I'm Anne. It's nice to finally meet you face to face, James."

He stumbled toward me and fell forward as he hugged me tightly. "Thank you," he breathed into my neck.

"We have to go. I don't know when he's going to realize he doesn't have his keys. Come on."

He put his arm around my shoulders to steady himself as we trudged down the hall and upstairs. I kept an eye out to make sure we weren't spotted as he gripped the wall. It had been about fifteen minutes since we escaped, giving us another fifteen minutes to get out of the building. He directed us down the correct path, and after I dropped the keys near the door, we made it out with about five minutes to spare.

We walked down the alley as quickly as possible and after it felt like we were far enough away, we finally stopped to rest and breathe the fresh air. Leaning against a wall, I turned my head skyward and shut my eyes. Feeling his gaze on me, I opened my eyes and gave him a small, nervous smile.

"Thank you," he rasped. "I truly thought I would die in there."

"We aren't out of the woods yet. We're still a long way from home."

"Leave that to me."

Chapter 4

The Ballsy Belle

Larissa

I SAT AT THE table in my hotel room and pored over the floor plans for the hundredth time that evening. I'd already spent plenty of time going through them with James. This time, however, I was looking as someone intending to protect and defend.

The journey back to Seattle was long and eye-opening. As it turned out, James was not only extremely rich but also well connected. One of those connections met the private plane he chartered on the tarmac in Copenhagen with an envelope containing our new travel documents and a magazine. I kept my face blank at the picture of Ari and Patrick's engagement news on the front cover. He read the story once we were back in the air, growing more enraged with each paragraph. His version was pure fiction and made me wonder just how much of it he actually believed so he could live with what he'd done to his supposed true love.

Ari was his ex-girlfriend, he explained, who was now in an abusive relationship with Patrick. He'd tried to help her leave him, but there was a misunderstanding and that's why he was on the run. According to him, Patrick had connections, and that's how he wound up in Yani's dungeon. After reading the article myself, I asked him about the accusations mentioned in the article and he told me it was a case of mistaken identity. Someone else kidnapped and attacked her. When he found out she was missing, he searched for her on his own and found her near death in her house. Patrick was pissed that James rescued her, and the next thing he knew he was captured by Yani's men in Toronto and shipped off to Russia. Now that he was free, he was even more determined to get her away from Patrick, who he described as a monster.

We spent the entire day looking through the floor plans of the hotel hosting Ari and Patrick's engagement party the next day. The plan was for us to get to the ballroom through a service entrance. I'd stolen a couple of uniforms so we'd look like servers at the party. At the right time, I'd create a diversion, allowing him to snatch her and make a quick getaway.

The problem was the ballroom, and the hotel, were logistical nightmares. Not only was the room near several exits, but the building was very close to the highway, giving him an easy escape. Luckily, Georgia and her team would've figured out the same and planed their security accordingly.

I put the documents away and rested my eyes. After spending the entire day staring at blueprints and going over the plan several times, I was exhausted. James gave me a disposable phone in Denver, which I used to send descriptions of our uniforms to Georgia. I'd limited communications since we left St. Petersburg, reporting our locations as we traveled and any vital information. It was almost midnight when I finally crawled into bed. Tomorrow would be a very long day, no matter what happened.

The next morning, I snuck out of my room and jogged down to the waterfront. I'd kept radio silent during the trip to Seattle and I was desperate to talk to Lucas. After dashing across the street near the aquarium, I plopped down on a bench and watched the birds scamper around, looking for food.

"Please tell me you're not still in Russia," he begged the moment the call connected.

"No, I'm in Seattle. And Yani already told me about the bounty being doubled."

"How did he know it was you? And how do you know he's not going to rat you out?"

"I'm sure Massimo blasted my picture all over to everyone when he doubled it. Saldivar recognized me on sight when I was in Cuba. I'd be willing to guess most of my identities are pretty much toast. Thankfully, I'm certain Yani won't tell anyone I was there."

"How can you be so sure?"

"Because I was there for a mutual friend and ratting me out would not only derail that help, but it would also put him at risk if it was discovered he let me go. Besides, I have a bigger problem. Felton knew I was there."

"What the fuck?"

"Probably my fault. I used one of my older identities. I'm supposed to be in Caracas as soon as I'm done with this case."

"Listen to me very carefully," His voice was tense, as if he was trying to stay calm. "Two of Massimo's men were recently spotted in the Dominican Republic. It could be nothing, but that's too close for my comfort. It's important that you delay your arrival for as long as you can. Have you talked to Felton?"

"No, I haven't had the chance. The last time we spoke was the fourth of July, before I left for Verona. All I told him was I had a personal matter, so he didn't even know I was in Italy until I left Venice. I'm not sure how he found me in St. Petersburg, but I got to Seattle with an identity he doesn't know about. Hopefully, that buys me some time."

"How much longer are you there?"

"I should be done here by tonight. I'll call you as soon as I'm done so we can figure out my next steps. Have you heard anything else?"

"Nothing you don't already know. Be careful while you're doing your super-secret spy shit, yeah?"

I smiled. "Always."

James knocked on my door not long after I got back to my room. We found a pizza place a couple of blocks from the hotel and chatted about our families over lunch. His father, who recently died of cancer, founded the security company he now led. The way he spoke about his family, including his two brothers who also worked for the company, was sweet. If I hadn't seen the pictures and spoken to Ari myself, I'd almost find it hard to believe he was the same man plotting to kidnap his victim a second time.

A few hours later, we reported to the hotel kitchen to set up for the party. As I placed tablecloths, I took in the ballroom. The floor to ceiling windows were two stories high with a view of the beautiful atrium in the lobby. Large crystal chandeliers hung from the ceiling, bathing the room in a soft light that was enhanced by the cream-colored walls. I continued my work, hopping and stepping around the workers placing wood laminate over the plush blue carpet for what I was told would be the dance floor.

After a while, we all met in the center of the ballroom. The event coordinator, a very tall, skinny, and loud woman, screeched at all of us we were to work quickly, quietly and with the most positive attitude that was humanly possible. The event was much larger than I'd realized with the ballroom and foyer reserved for the event. Three smaller meeting rooms reserved for media and security would be used, and we were strictly forbidden to enter all three. I had a pretty good idea that the FBI was set up in the larger of the two rooms located nearest to the elevator. Once the meeting wrapped up, James signaled for me to follow him.

I tried to keep up as he led me to the basement. "Where are we going?"

"The utility room," he answered, producing a ring full of keys from his pocket. "Our best bet for a diversion is to cut the power. When the party starts, you'll come down here. I'll text you and then you'll press the master control button. The moment the lights go out, get out of here. I mean it. Take the stairs and get out of this hotel as fast as you can."

"Are you sure?"

"You've already done so much for me. I can't thank you enough for enduring everything you did in that hellhole. If not for you, I'd still be rotting in a cell. This plan probably sounds completely insane to you. I'm basically kidnapping her in order to rescue her, and that's why I'm keeping your involvement to a minimum. After you leave here, go home and live your life to the fullest. You're a very kind person, and I'll always be grateful for all the help you gave me."

"I'll never be able to thank you enough for all your kind words that helped keep me going," I replied. "There's no way I would've made it through without you. You really were a bright light in all that darkness." Dear god, the words turned my stomach as they came out of my mouth. This couldn't be over soon enough.

He checked his watch. "We should head back upstairs. I want to watch the security team when it moves into place. Plus, we need to change into our uniforms."

The moment I reached my room to change, I grabbed my FBI phone and sent a text outlining his plan. I changed into my uniform, a fitted white button-down shirt and black dress pants, and met him in the hall. We rode in the elevator in silence and gave each other a small nod as we went our separate ways. I headed to the kitchen and busied myself with the other staff as they prepared the meal.

A couple of hours later, I pushed a serving cart down the hallway behind the ballroom and waited for the signal. When the door opened, it was showtime and I routed plates to guest tables. After my cart was empty I stood by the exit and watched Ari scan the room as she clutched Patrick's hand. Our eyes met briefly before I left. It was time to help the madman.

I breezed through the door of the utility room, thankful it would all be over very soon. Ari would have her peace, and I could finally talk to Lucas for more than a few minutes. I played solitaire on the phone James gave me until a text appeared, telling me it was time. Once the control switch was flipped, the room was dark for only a few seconds before the emergency lighting turned on. I dropped the keys by the door and left, following the row of small orange lights at the bottom of the wall until I got to my rendezvous point. The door opened just as I reached for it, causing my stomach to lurch until I saw the person on the other side.

I blinked. "Agent Kenmore? What are you doing all the way here in Seattle?"

Brian Kenmore was a rookie field agent sent to Arizona to bring me back to headquarters three years earlier. Unfortunately for him, he'd pissed off his logistics tech and she got her revenge by sending him into the field with only a few resources and even fewer details about how to find me. When he arrived at the bar I was working at as my cover, he'd damn near divulged my identity and as a result I cornered him in the back and gave him several hard lessons on how to treat the logistics team and how field agents should behave. Regrettably, that lesson included me injecting him with a very powerful laxative. Normally that would've been enough punishment, but the poor bastard hit his head in the bathroom later that night and wound up hospitalized with a concussion. I'd heard he now treated his co-workers and the logistics crew with a lot more respect.

"Agent Kane sent me. He and Agent Kaplan felt it would be a good idea if you had a familiar face escorting you out, since there's so many people from other agencies running around," he explained with a small smile.

After a loud sound in his earpiece, he ushered me up the stairs. We reached the first floor and followed several darkened corridors until we got to the parking garage of the hotel. He directed me to a plain white van at the far side of the floor and turned to leave.

"Wait," I said, lightly tugging on his arm. "I'm sorry about what happened in Arizona. That was uncalled for and I feel bad that you wound up in the hospital."

He bowed his head and chuckled. "I accept, but I also deserved it. It's what I get for being a cocky little shit who thought I knew it all. I'm thankful that you took me down a peg or two. And yes, I bought Melanie an enormous box of chocolates when I got back."

"Stay safe, Agent," I instructed with a smile. "And thank you for the escort."

He nodded and walked away as I climbed into the rear of the van. I greeted the two agents inside and grabbed the headphones I was given and sat down.

"Your backpack is behind the driver's seat," the young man next to me whispered, pointing to the corner. "I'm Agent Hudson and this is Agent Pearson."

I nodded and waved to Pearson, an older woman who was typing furiously as she watched the monitors like a hawk. I grabbed my backpack and turned on both my phones. There were no messages needing my attention, so I stayed a little longer to make sure James was captured.

"Suspect is believed to be in the service hallway with a captive. Agents are sweeping the hallway. Standby," a voice announced through the headset.

With my eyes closed, I said a silent prayer. This had to work.

"She's in the hallway near the second door on the southeast corner," Agent Pearson said. "Tracker is still active."

"Copy. Agents entering southeast section of the corridor now."

We all heard a commotion and multiple voices yelling over the comm line.

"Holy shit! She's kicking his ass!" a random agent yelled.

"Repeat that?" Hudson asked, his eyebrows raised.

"Copy. Suspect is down. Captive was kicking him...in the abdomen and crotch when agents arrived on scene. Suspect is in custody."

I snapped my hand over my mouth to keep my laughter quiet, and the agents smiled. We listened to the chatter as Georgia arrived. She read him his rights and sent him on his way to a secure location so he could be removed from the hotel in secret. Because the other suspect was still free in Toronto, it was decided James's arrest wouldn't be made public until after his extradition. I leaned my head back and exhaled slowly. It was over. I removed my headphones when suddenly a frantic voice boomed through the comm line.

"Medic needed, southeast corner. Captive has collapsed and is unconscious."

I threw the pen in my hand. "Shit!"

Hudson held up his hand to quiet me and ordered an ambulance to the closest exit. I grabbed my backpack and after finding out which hospital she was headed to, ran out of the van. My involvement in the case was over, but I had to make sure she was okay. For my own peace of mind.

A few hours later, I came down the southeast staircase of Seattle Metro Hospital and crept into their ER. I rounded the corner and quietly slid the glass door of the exam room open and pulled the curtain back. Ari gasped, causing Patrick's head to snap around toward the door.

"Please don't make a sound," I pleaded softly. "I'm not supposed to be here. I just wanted to make sure you were okay."

She grinned. "We got him, Sara. I'm more than okay."

"You have no idea how glad I am to hear that."

"That thing you wanted me to look into," she said and then paused. "He was never in Lisbon. Whoever told you that is lying."

My skin chilled. "But I saw a video of him walking into the café."

She shook her head. "It's fake. A pretty good one, but still a fake. My source told me to take a closer look at Marianna Chambers."

"Marianna? What does she have to do with it?"

"I don't know. That's just what I was told. "

"Thank you for looking into it for me."

"Please be careful. I can't thank you enough for what you did for us," Patrick murmured, offering me his hand.

I gave my head a shake to stop the tears in my eyes. "Ari's info was thanks enough."

Minutes later I strolled out into the cool Seattle air. My heart was hammering in my chest as I searched for somewhere quiet to get a drink. I settled for a small café near the hospital and after ordering a giant coffee, dialed the red phone.

"Hey," Lucas answered.

"I have amazing news. I've got a lead on John."

"What?"

"He was never in Lisbon. The video was a fake. We've been looking in the wrong place the whole time."

"Fuck! Please tell me that you have more than just that. Something I can do something with."

"As a matter of fact, I do. I need you to find me everything you can about Marianna Chambers."

"Why does that name sound familiar?"

"She led the Cuba operation I went on." I leaned back in my chair and rolled my neck. "My source said we need to look into her."

"I'm on it. Are you secure where you are?"

"Yeah. The beauty of an unofficial assignment is I don't have to do any paperwork or debrief. I'm using an identity that nobody knows about, so I should be okay for the night."

"How the hell did you get another identity?"

"The fugitive sociopath I helped escape from a Russian dungeon bought it for me in Denmark."

"Well, that's better than a crappy t-shirt."

I took a long drink of coffee. "How long do you think it will take to dig up the info?"

"I should have something within twenty-four hours. Anything else you need?"

"A location on Marcus Vargas if you really want to impress me," I joked.

"I do love a challenge. Okay, hang tight. I'm on it."

"Thanks. Please give Nonna and Zia hugs from me."

We hung up, and I dialed again. It was after midnight, but I needed his help to stay off the grid. Barton sounded groggy when he answered. "Lissa? What's up?"

"I'm sorry to be calling so late, but I have a problem. Felton tracked me while I was in the field."

"What the hell?"

"He called me in on a case. I'm supposed to be on my way to Caracas. It's crucial that you stall him for me. If he calls and asks, please tell him you haven't been in contact with me. You know nothing about St. Petersburg and have no idea why I went there."

"Done. I don't know where you are and I haven't talked to you lately. But I'll be expecting an explanation at some point."

"Done. You're a lifesaver. Thank you."

"We'll talk more when I'm awake. Good night."

I found a hotel for the night and got a few hours of sleep once I finally got my brain to quiet down. It was still dark outside when I woke up, so I went for a jog along the waterfront. I was standing at the pier watching a ferry cross the Puget Sound when my red phone rang.

"She's in Miami," Lucas announced. "I just sent you the file. It makes for some interesting reading."

"Oh my god," I whispered. "Thank you. I'll make sure I read it on the plane."

"Good. While you're there, stop off at South Beach and have a talk with Marcus."

"I will."

"Keep me posted and don't do anything crazy."

"I'll keep you posted, but I can't promise I'll stay sane once I see her."

"Okay, don't do anything crazy that will get you killed," he clarified. "Now go find him and bring him home."

I raced back to the hotel to pack. An hour later, I walked into SeaTac airport and found the first plane to Miami. I read through the file on the plane, poring over every single detail until I had a plan in my head when we landed.

"Enjoy your stay in Miami," the flight attendant said with a bright smile as I exited the plane.

"Oh, I most certainly will."

Miami Slice

Larissa

MIAMI WAS HOT, EVEN for September. Marianna had a nice house in Coconut Grove, a neighborhood in the southern part of the city. On the outside, it looked like a simple, single story white stucco house with a small backyard. A quick trip around the perimeter showed me the perfect window to gain entry. I watched her drive her red SUV down the street and pulled my rental into traffic, thankful for the car's air conditioning.

According to Lucas's information, she owned both a condo close to CIA headquarters in Langley and the house in Florida. It didn't look like she was in an active case based on her activity for the past few days. Her mornings began at the gym near her house and then most of her day was spent visiting various restaurants and shops in Little Havana. In the evening, she spent a few hours at an upscale Latin American restaurant where she sat at the bar and chatted with the bartender until about nine each night. I wasn't a huge fan of the fried plantains, but their house made chorizo more than made up for it.

When she left her house on the third day, I crept out of the trees behind the house and went to the backyard. After remotely disarming the security system, I slid through the window and strolled down the hall. While the exterior of the house looked older, the interior had been remodeled. The kitchen had a sleek, modern look that boasted the most current appliances. The house was decorated with simple pictures and other items. Notably, there were no pictures of friends or family anywhere.

I unpacked my knapsack and got to work. Once everything was set out to my liking, I helped myself to the leftovers she brought home the night before. The empanada was soggy, but the grilled corn salad tasted amazing. After lunch, I spent a couple hours looking through her computer and found that she had quite the addiction to online auctions and a large collection of illegally downloaded movies on her hard drive.

About half an hour before she was scheduled to arrive home, I moved to my hiding spot inside her closet. When I heard the front door close and the sounds of her footsteps in the hall, my body tingled. She entered the bedroom and after spending a few moments in the bathroom, I knew her next stop was the closet so she could place her clothes in the hamper next to me. The door opened with a soft click. Her clothes had just dropped from her hand when I pounced, grabbing her firmly by the throat and shoving my Colt in her mouth when she gasped. She was wearing a black sports bra and boy shorts, making it easy to tell she had no hidden weapons.

"Good evening, Ms. Chambers." I led her to the dining room. "We have several things to discuss. Why don't you take a seat?"

Her eyes shone with tears as I secured her arms to the chair with zip ties. I may have secured the one around her right arm too tightly based on her wince. Whoops. Once she was secure, I sat facing her on the dining table, propping both my feet on the arms of the chair.

"That's better. I'll remind you that there's no point in screaming since you have no neighbors, and also it would just make things even harder for you. Ready? Let's get started."

"Stephanie, I'm sorry, but I don't know the meaning behind this," she pleaded, shaking like a leaf.

"The meaning behind this is you drop the bullshit and tell me how long you've known my true identity."

Her brows came together. "Your true identity? I don't know what you mean. You're Stephanie Yates. Aren't you?"

"Okay, hard way it is." I grabbed the black case next to me and unzipped it slowly. Her eyes widened when she saw the contents. I grabbed a blue marker out of the case and leaned closer. She tried to jolt away as I drew a line on both her forearms and each thigh.

"Stephanie, honestly. I don't know what you're talking about."

"When I was a kid, I really enjoyed watching medical shows on TV," I began, ignoring her dramatic gasps and whimpers. "I especially loved watching surgeons. They really seemed to know their stuff. I learned later, however, these shows are hardly realistic. Take scalpels, for example. The way these shows make it sound, there's only one kind. You always hear them asking for a 'ten blade' for every single surgery."

I pointed to the case in my lap. "It turns out scalpels come in all shapes and sizes. Size ten is one of the most common for general surgeries and then there are other sizes and styles. There's also special, thicker blades designed specifically for performing autopsies." I picked up the knife with a curved tip and held it up. "This one, for example, is a twelve blade. Doctors use it to lance abscesses. It's one of my favorites since it has such a fine point. I have a few other favorites. The forty is almost like a carving knife, but that's because coroners need a thicker blade to cut through dead skin once rigor has set in and whatnot."

"What are you going to do?" she whispered.

"So, this is how it's going to work." I started braiding my hair. "I'm going to ask you questions. If you lie, and I'll know if you are,

I cut. The more lies you tell, the more cuts I make. Now, I'm sure you're wondering the purpose of the blue lines. Those show the approximate location of the major artery in each of your limbs. My cuts will start far away from those lines and move closer. And trust me when I say you really don't want me to hit one of those arteries."

Her eyes widened when I grabbed a pair of latex gloves on the table. "Don't want my hands to get slippery from all the blood now, do we?" I folded my hands in my lap and squared my shoulders. "Shall we begin? What's my name?"

"I only know you as Stephanie Yates. Please. There has to be some kind of mistake." When the twelve blade traveled down the length of her left arm and left a red streak, she gasped and cried for several seconds.

I scooted closer until my face was inches away from hers. "Wanna try again?"

Her eyes narrowed to slits. "You're Larissa Donovan."

"There we go! That wasn't so hard, was it?" I twiddled the blade between my fingers. "So since we're learning each other's names, let's say we have a discussion about Marisol Saldivar."

Her eyes widened a fraction, but her face went blank. "What do you want to know? I've only heard of her in passing."

I grabbed the sixteen blade, a longer and thicker blade, and drew a thin slice across her right thigh. She hissed, muttering obscenities under her breath.

"Let's say we stop dancing around each other, shall we? I know you're Marisol, and I know that Ernesto Saldivar was your cousin. What I'd like to know is whose idea was it to send me to Cuba, where he just happened to find me and tried to collect on Massimo's bounty." The color drained from her face as she closed her eyes. I smiled. "That's right, bitch. You have your connections and I have mine. Start talking."

"Massimo forced me. He has my mother and sister and told me if I didn't get you down there, he'd kill them both," she admitted, her voice cracking.

"Was the mission even real?"

"Yes. Nevara had to be returned to her father, and I knew she was betrothed to Ernesto. He's always at the compound, so it wouldn't have been hard for him to nab you."

"It was still risky, though. You had to guarantee Felton would sign off on it. Is that why you pushed it through behind his back?"

"Partially. Felton knew what was going on. That's why he was so opposed to you going."

"Bullshit!" I screamed, slicing another cut into her arm.

She cried out and shook her head. "You can slice me up all you want, but it doesn't change that he knew exactly what was going to happen."

"Then why did he agree to it in the end, huh? Explain that to me if he knew."

"Because he was told if he didn't sign off on it, I'd kill you."

I clutched the sixteen blade in my hand and held it above the blue line on her right thigh. "And who told him that?"

"Massimo," she whispered.

My pulse raced and I felt lightheaded. It wasn't until she gasped that I realized the blade in my hand was resting on her skin. I shook my head and sat back on the table. "Do you mean to tell me that my CIA handler has been working with the mob boss who's been trying to kill me? Is that what you're saying? Choose your next words carefully."

"How much do you know about Felton Lynch?"

"He fucking raised me after Massimo had my parents murdered. I've known him for over twenty years, and at no time has he ever given the impression he worked for that psychotic shitbag."

"I'm sure you've heard the rumors about him over the years. He's not a nice man. He's cold, manipulative, secretive. The reality is, he has a checkered past and there aren't many in the US who know that much about him."

"Well, why don't you enlighten me, since you seem to know so much about him?" I challenged, leaning forward.

"He's worked for Massimo and the Sardi family for years."

"You're telling me the man who raised me, the same man who taught me how to defend myself from the family that killed my parents, has worked for that same family all this time?"

"Is it that hard to believe? After all, who worked with Massimo's nephew at the CIA? Who the hell do you think recruited him out of the Army to begin with?"

I hadn't mentioned John on purpose. If, and only if, she stonewalled about Cuba, did I plan to hit her with the fact I knew she was involved in his kidnapping.

"What can you tell me about his nephew? I hear you might know a thing or two about his disappearance."

"Why should I tell you anything? Will it save my mother and sister if I do?"

I shook my head. "You and I both know they're already dead."

"So why should I tell you?"

I pulled a pistol out of my knapsack, and she gasped when she saw the suppressor. "Because telling me the truth is the difference between a quick and painless death by this or you bleeding out on your dining room floor while I watch and eat more leftovers out of your fridge. I will say that restaurant your boyfriend works at makes some pretty damn good food."

"That's not much of an incentive for me, is it?"

"Probably not, but him taking the fall for your murder might be."

"You wouldn't."

"You wanna take that chance?"

"I was on his plane when he left Tampa," she finally admitted, letting out a shaky breath. "I drugged his scotch and redirected the flight.".

"On whose orders?"

"Felton's."

Everything in my brain scattered, but I kept my face calm. "Where?"

"Boston."

"And why should I believe this?"

"Look into Felton's travel. I swear. I know he's taken time off work and gone back there in the last few weeks."

"Why? Why would he take him?"

"All Felton said was that he knew too much and he had to keep him quiet. I asked why he didn't just kill him and he said he had other plans. He never told me what those plans were, I swear."

I leaned my head back and said a prayer. She swore under her breath in Spanish, but seemed resigned to her fate. After picking up the recorder sitting next to me on the table, I showed it to her and pressed the stop button. I stared at her, pondering my next move. She fidgeted in her chair as the seconds ticked past.

"Well, thank you for this conversation, Marisol. It's been truly eye opening. I'll be looking into everything, and if I find out you've been lying, that boyfriend of yours will rot in prison for the rest of his life. You also better fucking pray that I find John alive or I'll do far worse than send him to prison. Any last words?"

She shook her head, eyes glistening. "I'm sorry, Larissa. For everything."

"I'm not," I replied with a small shrug before grabbing the sixteen blade in one hand and the larger twenty-four blade in the other.

Her eyes widened as both hands came down and sliced through the blue lines on her thighs. She screamed as blood gushed onto the floor, which became garbled once I slashed her throat. After several seconds of watching her choke on her blood, I fired a single suppressed shot into her forehead. Enjoying quiet, I took my time cleaning the blood from my scalpels and wiping down the case.

"Your boyfriend is safe. For now," I promised, placing the bullet casing on the table.

My mind continued to percolate as I walked to my rental car around the corner. She was right about Felton being a manipulative control freak who didn't show emotion, but he was still the man who took me in that horrible night. Groaning, I turned in the opposite direction of my hotel. I needed answers, and I wasn't getting any sleep until I had them. Unfortunately, the only way to get them was half an hour away in South Beach.

The lights were on in the small brown stucco house at the end of the cul-de-sac. I looked at the house and shook my head. It hardly looked like the home of a world-renowned computer hacker who could track a person's itinerary down to how many seconds early or late their plane or train arrived or departed.

Marcus Vargas, the owner of the house, was understandably paranoid. I was amazed Lucas actually tracked him to a physical address. Ownership of the house had been hidden underneath several fake identities, which made sense as he was often a target for law enforcement. He'd recently been forced into hiding after attempting to track Ari, not realizing she was on a watch list.

I watched the house from across the street. The motion sensors on all the windows and doors made sneaking in impossible, as did the security cameras. After what felt like forever, the luck I needed wandered out from behind the house and lit up a joint. The unsuspecting intern, a short young lady with bright green hair, stood back from the streetlight and stared up at the sky. When she bent down to tie her shoe, I jumped out from behind the tree and grabbed her. She gasped, causing me to place my hand over her mouth and spin her around to face me.

"I promise I'm not here to hurt you," I whispered. "I just need to talk to Marcus. You're going to bring me inside. I'm going to get the info I need from him, and then I'm going to leave. Okay?"

She nodded, her eyes were glassy but fearful. "You promise you're not going to hurt anyone?"

"You have my word." Everyone would most likely be taken in for questioning, but nobody would be hurt.

She gestured for me to follow her to the back door. At her direction, I lingered outside the range of the security camera until she signaled for me to rush the door and come inside. I gently grasped the back of her neck and led her down the hall.

"What the fuck?" the spiky-haired blond kid on the couch yelled as he looked up from his laptop.

The man seated at the large desk in the far end of the room glanced up from the array of monitors before him. He shot up in his seat once our eyes met. I raised my eyebrows, not expecting him to be so tall and buff. He ran his hand through his curly dark blond hair. "I...um, please don't hurt my interns. Just let them go and we can talk. Or...whatever you've come to do. I promise they won't tell anyone anything. P-please."

"Marcus, relax." Raising my hands, I showed I was unarmed. "I just need some info. I would've called or gone through the proper channels, but I was in the area and in a bit of a time crunch. I'm trying to find someone who was abducted a couple of months ago."

He narrowed his dark brown eyes. "Who are you?"

"My primary identities are Sara Lynch and Bianca Monroe. More recently, I used Erin King and Stephanie Yates."

"Are you with law enforcement?"

Always the million dollar question. "Yes, but this case is personal. I need an expert, and I know you're the best, so I'm begging you."

"Does anyone else know you're here?"

"My brother, but he's very far away," I answered. I handed him both cell phones, which were turned off.

"Where the hell did you get this sexy little thing?" he asked, glancing at the red phone. "She's a beauty."

"It's how I keep in touch with my family in hiding."

He stared at me after returning both phones. "And why does an American intelligence agent have a fully encrypted phone that no agency on this side of the world currently has?"

"I promised your intern no harm would come to any of you. If I answer that question, I'll break that promise, Marcus. Please. I just need some info and then I'll be out of your hair and you'll never see or hear from me again."

He nodded. "Follow me. What info do you need?"

"The first thing I need is for you to track the transponder for VNZ6072 on June nineteenth. It left Tampa, and the manifest says it arrived in Lisbon, but I'm told that's not where it really went."

"I love a challenge," he mused and started typing. My eyes fluttered shut as he worked, enjoying a few minutes of quiet after what happened in Coconut Grove. "Jackpot! It landed in Boston and then went to Miami."

"Of course. Bitch had to fly home afterward," I muttered. "Thank you for checking. I have a couple other things for you to check if you wouldn't mind."

"What else have you got for me?"

"I need travel records for Felton Lynch," I paused, taking a deep breath and swallowing back the bile in my throat.

His fingers flew across his keyboard, and after a brief time, he turned the monitor toward me. My heart sank as I saw the long list of flights from Dulles to Boston. The trips were pretty regular, occurring every couple weeks, and I would've been willing to bet the flights coincided with the long weekends he took off work the past couple of months.

"Fuck," I muttered. "Is there any way I can get a screenshot of this or something?"

"Yes, you can take pictures, but only with your red phone."

"Does anything else stick out to you on his travel?"

He scanned the screen. "A flight from Boston to Caracas three days ago."

"I was afraid you'd say that." I gazed at the screen. "Can you get me a list of everyone who flew into Caracas and all other major airports within a hundred-mile radius in the past two weeks? I need to send those names to my brother so he can check them out for me."

"Give me his email address. But warn him that the file will be encrypted. It will only be accessible for 24 hours and after that, it'll destroy itself."

"Deal."

"I honestly can't thank you enough," I yawned twenty minutes later after he emailed the file to Lucas.

Shaking Marcus's hand and assuring him I'd keep everything I was told a secret made me feel like shit. I wasn't going to share any of the info they gave me, but I was still going to lead the FBI right to him. I had a feeling Barton would make sure he got a sweetheart deal that would have him out and back online within six months. No matter how much the intelligence community complained about Marcus, they were one of his best customers.

I nearly fell asleep driving back to the hotel, but made it back with just enough energy to collapse in the center of the bed. A text message from Lucas was waiting for me when I woke up, telling me he was running the list of names and planned to have more info by that night.

For once, I was thankful he didn't call. My brain was too jumbled to talk. I glanced out the window and sipped my coffee. The trip was educational, but a lot more than I bargained for. I knew one thing for certain: I had to get to Boston. Fast. Everything else could wait until I found John. Then I'd worry about those responsible.

Proof wasn't the issue; I had more than enough to open an investigation. What I needed was answers. Why did Felton take him and why did Massimo tell the world I did it? The two were connected, but there were so many questions. A new text from Lucas telling me he'd already found two Sardi family associates on the list. It served as a reminder that the walls were closing in on me and I needed to be fast and invisible. Dialing my silver phone, I leaned against the balcony of my hotel room.

"I hope I didn't wake you," I greeted in a low voice. "I need help."

Chapter 6

Origin Stories

Larissa

"Yolanda, people are going to think I kidnapped you unless you blink and stop white knuckling your cup," I whispered, pouring syrup over my pancakes.

She blinked, and her eyes widened. "I'm sorry. I'm just...Are you sure?"

"Not a hundred percent. This is all based on the word of a corrupt officer who baited me to go on a mission so her cousin could kill me. The info I got from Marcus corroborates a lot of it, though."

We sat in a diner somewhere in North Carolina while I told her everything I knew about John's disappearance. I felt bad for getting her involved, but I needed help and I needed it kept secret. Luckily, before she quit to stay at home with their two children, Barton's wife, Yolanda, was a highly respected analyst with the NSA for almost fifteen years.

"So, walk me through this," she began. "According to Marianna, Felton has worked for Massimo Sardi and his family for years. He was forced to send you on this mission where you were supposed to be captured or killed, and if he didn't, she was going to kill you. Am I right so far?"

"Yeah. Her cousin was waiting to intercept me in Cuba and collect the bounty."

"And Felton worked with John at the CIA, who's also Massimo's nephew. And, according to her, she was ordered to kidnap John by Felton."

"Correct."

"That's where you've lost me," she sighed, shaking her head. "Why would he do that?"

"That's the million-dollar question. I don't know. He knows it'll get him killed if Massimo ever finds out."

She checked her watch. "We should get on the road soon. My mom is watching the kids because Barton's in New York, but he's back tonight. I didn't exactly tell him about this little trip. So, what's the plan?"

"First thing I need to do is find John. I was able to get Marcus to help me, and he tracked his plane to Boston."

"So you need to get to Boston."

I shook my head. "Not yet. I wouldn't even know where to look. Also, there's no way I'm going by myself. I need reinforcements."

"Where will you find reinforcements?"

"New York. And I need to ask a favor."

"What do you need?"

"First, I need a completely clean identity. All of mine are known to Felton, and he's most likely got them flagged. I got a new one while I did that special favor for Georgia, but I need something more secure than that. Next, I need to see if there's any way you can get me a list of some of Seamus's old associates."

"I'll see what I can find," she replied. "What are you going to do?"

"I'm going to get out of this car in Richmond and lie low until I hear from you, and then your involvement in this will be done."

"Lissa."

"No, Yo. It's too risky."

"All right," she sighed. "But you have to promise me you won't do anything crazy. No vigilante shit."

"I promise. The minute I have more proof, I'm calling Barton. Knowing Felton, he's probably got John holed up in some ungodly place with one of his cronies keeping watch. No way in hell I'm going in alone."

I took a nap and woke up just outside Richmond, where Yolanda dropped me off in the heart of downtown. Deciding to clear my head for a while, I spent the rest of the day hitting various tourist places and just walking around before settling into a hotel for the night.

"It's about fucking time you called," Lucas yelled when he answered the phone the next morning. "It's been almost a week. Where the fuck are you?"

"I'm in Richmond," I yawned, still in bed. "Sorry I didn't call before I left Miami, but I had to make a quick exit. I won't go into all the details, but the most important thing I learned is John's plane was diverted to Boston."

"Jesus, you've been busy. Do I even want to know how you got that lead?"

"Probably not. I will say that I learned some very interesting and disturbing things, but I'll deal with them later. I honestly don't care about anything else until I find him."

"Then why aren't you in Boston?"

"I'm waiting on a clean identity and the names of a couple of contacts. I need reinforcements, and I have a good idea where to find them."

"Where? You're making me nervous."

"Back to where it all began, Lucas. New York."

"Are you fucking insane?" he roared. "That's the heart of Genovese country!"

"Which is why I'm not reaching out to any Italians and nobody will know I'm there."

"What are you up to?"

"Just know that I know what I'm doing."

"Christ, no wonder you and John are perfect for each other," he muttered. "Both of you are fucking crazy. Are you sure you don't need any help on my end? Are these contacts trustworthy?"

"As trustworthy as they get. Listen, I need to go. I'll call you as soon as I have something to report."

"For the love of god, be careful."

I tossed the phone on the bed next to me. According to Marianna, Felton didn't plan to kill John. I knew all too well that accidents happened, however. It had been three months, and for all I knew, the circumstances could've changed. Plus, I knew some of his associates, and none of them were people I'd trust to care for a feral animal, let alone a mobster's nephew.

It took two days, but Yolanda came through with the documents for my new identity and the name of two of my dad's closest associates. Included in the envelope was a small amount of cash, which I used to buy a bus ticket to New York. Not the most luxurious way to travel, but there were too many buses for anyone to check them all.

Fall was in the air when I climbed off the bus nearly seven hours later. The air was warm, but the wind carried a slight chill. It was nighttime, and the city was indeed wide awake and full of life. I double checked the address of my first contact and thanked whatever forces in the universe aligned enough for my bus stop to be close to my destination.

Eddie O'Rourke, according to the file, accompanied Seamus on several collection runs while they were both part of the Westies. He was built like a brick shithouse, standing well over six feet tall and sporting an extremely muscular build in the pictures. He left the gang at the same time as my dad, choosing to become a cop. The fact he was associated with the Irish mob nearly kept him out of the police academy, but ultimately his knowledge of rival gangs made him too great an asset to gang unit.

He was still only a beat cop after nearly thirty years with the NYPD, and a corrupt one at that. It was well known he accepted bribes to "protect" local businesses and harassed them when they refused to pay, so it was no surprise when I found him inside a corner market with the clerk's head pressed against the counter. He was still muscular, judging by how he manhandled his victim. The only difference was his once thick brown hair was gone and he was completely bald.

"I'm gonna ask you again. Did you see who broke the window across the street at the laundromat?" he growled, shoving the kid's head forward.

"I...I," a young Asian man who looked a little older than nineteen stammered.

As if sensing he was being watched, his head snapped up. His dark green eyes narrowed and his face transformed into a nasty sneer. "Store's closed, honey. You'll need to go somewhere else to buy your bubble gum. Run along."

"So glad to hear it. That makes this easier," I replied with a sweet smile. "FBI. Let's just say I'm not here for bubblegum. *Honey.*"

"Fuckin' fed, huh? Let's see some ID."

"Hands up first," I ordered. "Last thing I'm gonna do is give the clichéd corrupt cop a chance to shoot me."

"Cute, babe." He let up the clerk and held up his hands.

"Yeah, absolutely fucking charming," I replied, brandishing my credentials, followed by my gun.

"Whoa!" he yelled. "Take it easy."

"So, this is how it's going to work. You and I are going to leave and go somewhere private to talk. Otherwise, I'll gladly bring you in and you can spend those eighteen months you've been counting down to retirement with Internal Affairs up your ass."

"And why would I go somewhere private with you, huh? For all I know that badge is fake, and you're some psycho hired by my ex-wife."

Without batting an eye, I flipped my badge up and showed him the one picture I had of Seamus hidden inside. His eyes widened. "What the fuck?" he whispered, taking a step closer.

"Glad we're on the same page. Let's go."

Fifteen minutes later, he led me inside his crappy apartment. When I heard him lock the first of three deadbolts, I whipped around and drew my gun. He stepped away from the door and held up his hands. "Easy! It's New York." He breathed deeply and stared at me for a moment. "Now, can you please tell me who you are and why you have a picture of Seamus Donovan? Are you who I think you are?"

"He was my father."

He blew out a breath. "Larissa? Jesus Christ! Where the hell have you been all these years?"

"It's a long story, one that I really don't have time to tell right now. The bottom line is I need help, so I've been trying to get a hold of my dad's friends."

"Honestly, I have little contact with anyone from the old gang. I'm not sure how much I can help you. I hope I'm not the only one of your dad's associates you've found."

"You were the first one on the list," I confessed. "I'm just...I don't have many options right now."

"Well, if nothing else, I can offer an ear and maybe give you some advice. I know I probably look like a scumbag cop on the take to you, but I owe my life to your dad. That man saved my ass more times than I can count."

Leaning against the wall, I let myself relax as he talked about Seamus. I remembered a few of my dad's friends from what he called "the old days". Eddie's name sounded familiar, but I didn't remember him ever visiting my parents' house.

"Sorry if I seem overly paranoid," I said, smiling faintly. "Occupational hazard."

"So, you're really with the FBI?"

"Almost six years now."

He nodded. "Sorry, I'm just still wrapping my head around the fact you're standing in front of me. Everyone thought you died in the fire with your mom."

He ordered a pizza, and we compared stories from our respective jobs. I gave him an extremely watered-down version of the past few years of my life. After dinner, we sat around the table in his tiny kitchen and stared at each other.

As if sensing my apprehension, he placed both hands palm down on the table. "So, what do you need help with?"

"My boyfriend was kidnapped on a chartered flight to Lisbon. He never made it there. I confirmed his plane was diverted to Boston instead."

He stared at the fake wood grain on the table between us. "Do you know who took him?"

"Does the name Felton Lynch mean anything to you?"

His eyes widened. "Larissa, please tell me you have no connection to him. That man is dangerous."

"He raised me."

"Son of a bitch!" he muttered and shot to his feet. He stomped into the hallway, where a small, cheap desk sat covered in stacks of papers. I heard him rummaging around and cursing under his breath. He returned shortly with an old business card and his cell phone.

"Eddie? Who are you calling?"

He held up a finger as he waited for the call to connect. "Hey, it's O'Rourke. Call me as soon as you get this message, no matter what time it is. It's about Seamus."

I watched him closely. "What's going on?"

"You're going to stay here tonight until he calls me back. I can't let you back out there knowing that shithead Lynch is involved."

"And who's 'he'?"

"Someone with enough money and connections to get you and, hopefully your boyfriend out of Felton's grasp. I don't want to alarm you, but most people who cross him wind up dead."

"I know that all too well."

"What do you mean?"

"I took an assignment in Portland a couple of years ago, and it wound up being a trap set up by the Sardi family. I'd always wondered how they found me, and now I think I know."

"Felton?"

I nodded. "Apparently, he's been working for the family for years."

"Fucking two-faced rat."

"Were he and my dad close? Felton always told me they were close friends. What can you tell me about them back in the day? Or even my parents, for that matter?"

He left the room again and I heard him rummaging around in what sounded like a drawer. After a few minutes and a stream of curse words, he returned carrying a small cardboard box full of pictures. He grabbed a small stack and thumbed through them.

"There they are," he mumbled, a hint of a smile on his face as he passed me the small picture. "This was taken about a year before they died."

I inhaled sharply and my eyes watered. Everything was destroyed in the fire, so there were very few mementos for me to remember them by. The picture looked like it was taken at a party while they talked to someone outside of the frame. My mother's eyes sparkled, and she had a wide smile on her face. Seamus had his arm wrapped tightly around her waist with one hand and a beer in the other. His chin rested on top of her head, and he looked completely at ease.

"They look so happy and in love here," I whispered.

He smiled sadly. "I don't know how much you know about their history, but it wasn't always the case. At first, we thought she was just some random female we hired as a stripper. Seamus always seemed to have a thing for her. In fact, his girlfriend at the time hated Sera's guts because he seemed to pay more attention to her."

"Really?"

"It wouldn't surprise me at all if Kiki had been the one who told everyone she was a spy. The night it all went down was brutal. Mickey, our boss, knew Seamus wouldn't kill her, so I was supposed to be the one to do it. Seamus went fucking bananas. Pulled a gun on both of us and said if anyone touched her, they were dead. He took her out of there and the story was he put her to work at his house as a maid. Mickey sent a couple of guys to his house to collect her, and Seamus fucked them up pretty bad. The next thing we knew they were married. Here's a picture from the party we had after he told us."

I examined the picture and they certainly looked very awkward around each other. The smile on my mom's face was very strained as she gripped his arm tightly. My dad's face wasn't as tense. His smile seemed genuine, but there was a trace of anxiety and worry as well. My eyes traveled to the light green dress my mom wore and noticed a small bump.

"She was pregnant with you when they got married," he said, confirming my unspoken thoughts. "There had been rumors about the two of them for months before she was found out, so it made sense why he was so protective and married her so quickly."

I handed the picture back to him. "Where did Felton fit into everything back then?"

"He and your dad knew each other back in Ireland. I guess Seamus even spent a summer or two at Felton's grandparents' house before the Donovans moved to the States. When they reconnected, they were thick as thieves. He used to razz Felton a lot for working for the CIA, but whenever anyone said we shouldn't trust him, Seamus always vouched for him. I guess Felton was informing on smaller Irish groups and kept them out of our shit back in Dublin. And then it all changed."

"What happened?"

He sighed. "Sera. Their breakup was ugly, with all the accusations and name calling. And then it got even worse after he married Karina."

"Surprise, surprise," I muttered. At his raised eyebrows, I shrugged. "Let's just say whenever he wasn't around, she made it abundantly clear she didn't want me around."

"Karina never liked kids, never wanted them. That's why they didn't have any. And you two loved to hate each other.

"Really?"

"I think you were probably three or four when they got married. We had a small party for them, same as we did for your parents. Karina was the center of attention, so she was happy.

That is, until you got into her makeup bag and drew all over the tablecloth with her eyeliner."

"Now I know why she refused to teach me how to put on make-up when I was a teenager," I laughed.

"Yeah, probably. She ripped the eyeliner out of your hand and started screaming at you. Your mother went ballistic, of course. She ran over to pull you away, but you'd already kicked Karina in the shin and ran to your dad. The shouting match they got into was epic."

He shared more pictures and stories of my parents and our life together before they died. The next thing we knew it was almost one in the morning. He apologized for only having a couch for me to sleep on, but I joked I'd recently spent a couple weeks in a Russian prison cell and he simply laughed. I couldn't help the small giggle once he closed his bedroom door, since I was pretty sure he thought I was joking.

The stories about my parents were fascinating. For a time, they were real people and not just fading memories. It was great to hear Eddie tell me about the time my mother told one of the resident drunks at the strip club she'd break all his fingers if he didn't quit grabbing her ass, or when my dad took him out drinking and they wound up in a Mexican restaurant in Philadelphia with no memory of how they got there.

My thoughts strayed to Felton. I was no closer to unraveling the truth about his identity or involvement, but the more I learned about him the more nervous I got. He'd always said he and my dad were close, but I never knew their friendship started all the way back in Ireland when they were kids, nor did I know they'd ever had a falling out. If all the stories were true, he'd lived quite a life: Irish mob informant, possibly corrupt CIA officer, and lord only knew what else. I'd never given it much thought until now, but it was entirely possible his life was spent even more in the shadows than my own.

Chapter 7

Il Mio Incubo

Larissa

Alexandria, Virginia

October 7, Twenty three years ago

I HID UNDER MY *dad's car, paralyzed with fear. My mom told me to run and find him, but the man in the other car was there and something about him scared me. I never saw his face, but I could tell he was mad. They spoke softly so I couldn't hear, but I could tell they didn't like each other.*

My dad's voice suddenly got loud. "She knows what a slimy monster you are and didn't want you anywhere near either of them. So, out of the love and respect I have for my wife, I agreed to keep her secret."

"Well, now I know, and you can bet that I'll be a part of her life. You won't keep her from me. Period," the other man argued.

My dad laughed and asked the other man another question. When I heard my mom's name, I stretched my neck to hear more. What did my mom have to do with their fight? Who was this man and why was he a monster?

"You can't keep her from me," the other said.

His voice made me nervous. It reminded me of the big kid on the playground at school who wanted my basketball the other day. When I wouldn't give it to him, he shoved me down and took it from me.

This man sounded just as mad, like he wanted to hurt my dad if he didn't get what he wanted.

"Did you really think?" he suddenly yelled and then lowered his voice.

My heartbeat got really fast. I wanted to yell out, tell my dad I was there, and we needed to run away and go help Mommy. She needed us, but more importantly, we needed to get away from this man who wanted to hurt him. I opened my mouth, but I was suddenly my body froze and a weird whooshing sound blared in my ears. I heard both men yelling, but I couldn't hear what was said. All I knew was we both needed to get away now.

The angry man's voice suddenly became crystal clear. "That's the idea." Suddenly, a loud boom rang out.

My eyes snapped open as I turned my head into the pillow to muffle my gasp. I rolled onto my back and inhaled deeply to calm my rapid heartbeat. Dreams about that night weren't unusual, especially since the anniversary of their deaths was about a month away. This time, however, the conversation between my dad and the mystery shooter seemed more intense and detailed. Seamus mentioned my mom, but where did she fit into this? Was she who the other man wanted to see? Whose life was he determined to be a part of? I rubbed my eyes and tried to clear my mental fog. Was that conversation just a vivid dream, or was I remembering an extra detail from that night?

I glanced around the room and remembered I was on Eddie's couch. The room was quiet, but I could hear him talking in the bedroom. When he quietly opened his door, I burrowed my head between the pillow and the couch to look like I was still asleep.

"Look, I swear on my life. It's her. You need to hurry your ass up and get over here," he whispered.

I kept my face blank and breathing soft. My fingers moved to my gun hidden under the pillow. Silly, silly Eddie. He'd learn soon enough what happened to those who tried to double cross me. The door closed again and I heard his voice in the other room. Sliding out from under the blanket, I crept around, checking the kitchen and bathroom windows for an escape route.

A little while later, he emerged from his room in jeans and an old black t-shirt. He paused by the couch but continued into the kitchen. When the smell of coffee and breakfast foods wafted into the room, I couldn't help when my stomach growled.

I strolled into the kitchen not long after. "Good morning."

"Mornin'," he replied as he poured coffee into a large mug and took a sip. He opened the cupboard above his head. "Help yourself."

"Thanks."

"I heard from my friend," he announced, stirring the food on the stove. "Didn't believe me when I told him you were here. He said he'd be here in an hour to see for himself."

"I see."

"Lissi, I promise you can trust him. He's another friend of your dad's."

"Like Felton was?"

"I get why you're suspicious and I don't blame you," he said with a sigh. "But I promise you, he's a friend and he can get you and hopefully your boyfriend out of the shit storm you're in."

"Then why won't you tell me his name?"

"Because he asked that I didn't. He's almost more paranoid than you are, and for several damn good reasons. He wants to see you with his own eyes and then he'll tell you his name."

"For your sake, you better be telling the truth."

"I swear on my daughter's life. Look, if it makes you feel better, hold my ass at gunpoint while we wait. In the meantime, breakfast is ready if you feel like eating."

I pointed to the stove. "Take a bite first."

A small smile formed on his lips as he grabbed a fork. "Your dad didn't believe in killing before breakfast." He scooped a forkful into his mouth. "And I'd never defile my mother's corned beef hash recipe by drugging it."

We sat around the small table in the kitchen as we ate. I kept the pistol on my lap, which didn't dissuade him from making jokes and small talk during the meal. "Are you this paranoid with your boyfriend?"

"Well, he did drug and kidnap me, so I was for a little while."

"Sounds like a match made in heaven."

I laughed. "As crazy as it sounds, it is. And I got my revenge. Probably a bit of overkill, but I think he got the message pretty loud and clear."

"What did you do?"

"Booby trapped his property and blew up his weapons cache. Put most of his men in the hospital. And then shot him with a bean bag round."

"Jesus Christ!" His eyes were like saucers. "You FBI broads are crazy!"

"In my defense, after he drugged me, I woke up three days later in Italy."

"Yeah, that's pretty dirty."

A loud knock at the door interrupted us. Our heads snapped toward the sound and he slowly stood. I grabbed my gun and moved to stand next to the fridge, where I could see the door.

"Easy," he hissed, holding up his hands before unlocking the door.

I watched as he whispered to the visitor. After a couple of minutes, he nodded and opened the door wider. A tall, slender man entered and glanced around the room. When his dark blue eyes met mine, his eyebrows shot up when I raised my gun and aimed at his head.

"Larissa, wait!" Eddie shouted. "Please."

The man held up his hands. "Lissi, I mean you no harm."

I studied his appearance. He wore a black tailored suit that looked extremely expensive. His light brown hair was mixed with gray and expertly styled. There was something familiar about the warmth in his eyes and smile.

"Who are you?"

"My name is Callum Flannery," he answered. "You may remember me."

My brain flashed to the memory of my parents' close friend. "Uncle Cal?"

He exhaled. "Yes, Princess. It's me."

My eyes filled with tears. "How do I know it's really you?"

"I last saw you when you and your parents came to my house for dinner. We tried to get you to stay in the living room so we could talk privately, so I let you play video games."

"Which game?"

"Tetris," he answered with a smile.

Satisfied, I nodded and lowered my gun. Both men relaxed their posture. Cal's eyes were full of tears when he pulled me into a hug. "Where have you been all these years?"

"Felton," Eddie spat.

"What?" His voice was barely a whisper.

"You two should go somewhere and catch up," Eddie suggested. "I've got a meeting I need to get to, and she should probably be somewhere more secure than this shithole."

"Thank you for calling me, friend," Cal said quietly as he shook his hand.

"Thank you for the couch and the memories," I said as I hugged Eddie. "It felt good to see their pictures and hear about them."

"You be safe out there, kid," he chuckled. "I hope you're able to find your boyfriend."

"Boyfriend?" Cal inquired mildly.

"I'll explain when we get where we're going."

An hour later, we sat in the executive suite in one of Cal's law offices in Lower Manhattan. He was a senior partner for a law firm with offices in New York, Boston, and Washington, D.C. His base office was in Boston, but he'd been in town for the past couple of weeks for a private divorce.

"Fucking Felton," he muttered as he sat behind his desk and fidgeted with his pen. "If anything happened to your parents, you were supposed to be sent to me."

"I was?"

"That was what they wanted, what we'd agreed to. Unfortunately, we never had time to formalize it in a will before they died. I doubt it would have mattered, anyway. By the time I learned Felton had you, it was too late. He'd already found a judge to grant him temporary custody."

"That's my fault," I said, my voice cracking. "The night everything...happened. I panicked after Dad was shot and I just ran. After a while I got disoriented and when I figured out where I was, Felton's house was the closest. I'm sorry."

He tossed the pen and hurried around his desk to pull me into a hug. "Don't you ever think you have to apologize for anything that happened that night. You were a scared six-year-old girl who'd lost both her parents. There isn't a single thing you did wrong, Lissi."

"But if I hadn't gone to his house, maybe this wouldn't have happened."

"Don't you worry about it. I planned to challenge him for custody, but then my family started getting all sorts of threats. I wanted to fight for you, I really did, but when someone broke into my mother's house and held her at knifepoint, I knew there was no way he would ever let you go. I wound up moving my mom and I to Boston in the dead of the night."

"I'm sorry."

He held up his hand. "Let's stop worrying about the past and focus on your problem right now. What's the story with your boyfriend?"

"Long story short, and believe me I'm leaving a lot out when I say that, Felton has him. I've recently come across information that shows he has ties to the mob, and a former CIA officer told me she took part in John's abduction. She snuck aboard his chartered plane and diverted it to Boston."

"Boston? Why there?"

"I have no idea, and I don't even know where to even look. The CIA officer told me he didn't plan to kill him, but I also know the fucked up people Felton associates himself with and what they're capable of."

"Have you talked to anyone at the FBI about this?"

"I don't have any proof. The CIA officer is dead, and Felton's travel information came from a hacker who's already wanted," I answered.

Cal stared at his computer screen for a few minutes and started typing. His brows furrowed and his fingers moved faster. He cursed under his breath, only to smile soon after. The printer behind him sprang to life, and he grabbed the single sheet of paper that emerged from the machine.

"Call the FBI and tell them to look at these buildings," he instructed as he handed me the sheet. "Chances are he's in one of them."

I studied the list. "Why? Who do they belong to?"

"You."

"Me??"

"I'm not sure if you knew, but your dad had several properties from Boston to D.C. He sold off most of them, but the rest are being held in a trust for you that is payable at age thirty."

"Is this the same one his brother knew about?"

"No. That's a separate one that was funded through, shall we say, ill-gotten gains. The intent with that trust was in case you ever needed to go into hiding. He wanted you to have access to funds without the US government knowing about it. That's why he gave the info to Titus. This second trust was funded through legal means. You may not have known about it, but you can't tell me Felton didn't. The best place to hide something is where nobody knows it exists."

"Excellent point."

I grabbed the silver phone out of my knapsack. It was barely nine o'clock, so Barton would be in the office. I just prayed he'd be willing to make things happen with the small amount of information I had.

"Lissa?" he answered.

"Barton, I don't know where to even begin, but I have a situation, and I need your help."

"What's going on?"

"I need to report a kidnapping, and I have a list of likely locations."

"Okay," he drawled. "How about a list of suspects?"

"It's complicated. I know who's responsible, but I need time to get the evidence to prove it. I have a list of addresses that need to be checked out. That should be enough for a warrant."

"Give me the list. I'll see what I can do."

My shoulders relaxed. "Thank you. If you find anything, I'm going to need you to reactivate me without Felton knowing about it."

"Once this is all over, you're going to sit your ass down and explain everything, Larissa. This is some crazy shit you're asking me to do."

"It's just the tip of the iceberg, Barton. But I promise I'll tell you everything once this is all over."

Eight hours later, I stepped out of a black van dressed in full tactical gear courtesy of the FBI. I adjusted my bulletproof vest and strolled through the lobby of the office building commandeered by the operation. A logistics tech handed me a radio, and I adjusted the earpieces on my way to the small conference room across the lobby. Thomas McManus, the lead agent from the Boston field office, was just getting ready to brief everyone on the operation.

"Here's what we know," he announced, causing the room to fall silent. "Thermal imaging shows nine people inside the building next door. Seven appear to be guards on regular patrols. One person has been seen traveling through several rooms on the second floor. The last person is in a room on the northeast corner of the building on the first floor. He's been seated in the center of the room and hasn't moved, so we believe that is our hostage."

Hostage. For so many years, the word was just another type of target, a faceless person I was assigned to rescue and protect so they could return to their life. Once safe, they flitted out of my life and were never seen again. Until that moment. The realization turned my stomach and I inhaled sharply.

"Agent, are you okay?" Barton whispered in my ear.

Blowing out a slow breath, I nodded, unsure if I believed that. I folded my shaking hands together, and when that didn't work, I put them in my pockets. Sweat dotted my forehead and the back of my neck, but I forced myself to focus on McManus. When my heart echoed in my ears, I studied the thermal image of the man in the chair. I felt a warm hand on my shoulder and turned to my boss. His eyes widened.

My stomach churned and bile rose in my throat. Shaking my head, I covered my mouth and raced from the room. The hall never seemed longer as my feet carried me to the bathroom only three doors down. My shoulder ached in protest when I hit the door, followed by my knees when I slid to the floor and emptied my stomach into the closest toilet.

After several unpleasant minutes, my stomach was thankfully empty, and I stumbled from the stall. The cool water from the sink felt like heaven against my lips as I drank it from my hand and felt even better when I splashed it on my face. Bracing my hands against the counter, I lowered my head and let my stomach continue to war with itself. At the sound of two footsteps, I looked up and my eyes met Barton's in the mirror.

"Are you okay?" he murmured.

"I could *say* I am, current events to the contrary," I replied before taking another deep breath.

"That's probably the closest I'll get to you admitting you're not okay. I'll take it." He leaned against the wall. "I've known you for five years. I've watched you approach each case cool, calm, and collected. No matter how stressful, no matter the stakes, you're always the levelheaded one who focuses on getting the job done. But today..."

"The picture," I blurted out. "It's the first time I've seen a glimmer of hope that he's alive. But it's not just a glimmer. There's a faceless person in there in red and orange and other colors. But this time it's not a faceless person. He matters to me."

"Yes, he does."

"I'm probably one of the most qualified people to sit behind the scope and help get him out of there, and I should be turning cartwheels in the hallway that you're finally trusting me to do it."

"But?"

I brought my hand to my face and choked back a sob. "This isn't just another person who goes home to his family if this goes as planned. If it goes as planned, he's coming home with *me*. He's my family. But that also means if it goes bad…"

"It's okay to be scared. I'd be worried if you weren't."

"Good, because I'm fucking petrified," I choked out. "In the past, if those colors went out, I'd beat myself up about the loss, but I'd recover. If his colors go out…I promised people I'd bring him home. If his colors go away, I'm afraid I will, too."

His eyes softened. "I'm not going to tell you what to do, because this is an impossible situation. But I will say that there's nothing wrong with stepping back if it's all too much, Agent. We have backup sharpshooters on the scene."

I stared at him in the mirror as I weighed his words and my options. It was lucky Barton even considered allowing a rifle in my hand, considering the circumstances. I was grateful that I'd regained his trust and wanted to prove he wasn't wrong. But still I hesitated. Could I do my best to clear my head? Would it be enough to get the job done?

"Yes," I whispered. "Please call a backup."

He blinked. "Are you absolutely sure?"

"I could probably clear my head enough to do what I need to do, but I refuse to accept 'probably'. For any job. I'm too close to this one, Barton."

Nodding, he stepped into the hallway and I heard his voice in my earpiece requesting a backup to the conference room the sharpshooter team was set to meet. Closing my eyes, I let my shoulders sag. When the chatter in my ear picked up with various updates, I lowered the volume on the earpiece and pulled it free.

"All set," Barton announced.

"I'd like to be part of the ground team."

"I think we can make space for you once the first floor is cleared. Stay close to the command center and you can go in with Ground Two."

I took my time in the bathroom and it was only once my stomach was completely settled that I wandered back to the command center. By then I'd grabbed a bureau windbreaker, switched out my comms, and grabbed extra ammo for my pistol. Barton and McManus were crowded around a monitor, watching what looked like camera feeds from the sharpshooters. Knowing it wouldn't be a good idea to linger, I made my way to where the second ground team was waiting to be deployed. I made small talk with a couple of agents, but it still felt like time had slowed to a crawl as we waited for our turn.

At last, McManus's voice came through our channel. "First floor is secure. Ground two proceed to entry and secure second floor."

I steadied my nerves and exhaled slowly as I pulled my gun from the holster and followed my fellow agents.

I'm coming, baby. Hold tight...

$\cdot\ \cdot\ \bullet\ \cdot\ \bullet\ \cdot\ \bullet\ \cdot\ \cdot$

John

It was a lazy afternoon in our bedroom back in Verona. A song played in an odd key, with lyrics crooning about the foolish things desire made people do. I kept my eyes closed and enjoyed feeling her close to me.

She stilled. "This song is kind of depressing, don't you think?"

My eyes snapped open, and I smiled up at her. "Can't really say I ever gave it much thought. And I'm really enjoying the view too much to think about it right now."

"Liar. Your eyes were closed."

I laughed and ran my hands over her bare legs. She was straddling my lap as I rested against the headboard of our bed. She inspected the part, looking for the slightest imperfection. My fingers teased the back of her knees, causing a small smile on her face that quickly turned to a look of annoyance.

"My eyes were closed because I was picturing all the things I'm going to do to you once you're done cleaning your damn gun."

She rolled her eyes. "This would go a lot quicker if you'd helped like you said you were going to do."

She reassembled the pistol in record time. After inspecting it to make sure everything was to her liking, she placed it on my night table next to my phone, which was still playing the strange song I couldn't place.

"Happy now?" She slid off her latex gloves and tossed them on the table.

I grabbed her hands and pulled her to me until she was lying on my chest. "I am now."

She smiled and sat upright. I ran my fingers across her legs again, this time lightly tickling the skin. She laughed and leaned forward, placing her hand on my bare chest to steady herself above me. "And I would've been done a lot sooner if you hadn't kept tickling me."

"I've made a new rule. You can lie on me all you want while you clean your gun, but from now on, you have to be naked." My hand moved under her black tank top and softly caressed the smooth skin underneath.

She lowered her mouth to mine. Our lips barely met before she stopped and stared out the open balcony door. "Storm's coming," she whispered. Her gaze found mine and she looked worried.

I found myself suddenly filled with dread. "Liss?"

"Wait for me."

"What?"

She placed her hand on my chest. "Hold on and wait for me, Gianni. I'll always come for you."

"I don't understand, baby."

"Hold on and wait for me," she whispered.

I gasped awake at the sound of a loud bang and yelling, causing near blinding pain to radiate through my body. No matter how hard I shut my eyes or tried to talk myself down, I couldn't calm the panic rising in my chest. It was more than just stagnant air or anxiety that made it harder and harder to breathe. For the first time since I'd woken up in this house of horrors, I was worried.

Felton had been MIA for a while, so Franz ran things unchecked and unrestrained. The sick bastard's last beating was the most brutal yet. I knew I had multiple broken ribs, so the constant shortness of breath led me to believe I had a collapsed lung. That was also the least of my problems, I suspected, since my body felt weaker with each passing day.

Sleep was a welcome break from the pain when it came. Eyes closed, I tried to return to my dream to deflect the pain just a bit longer. I was at home in Verona, in my bedroom, with the curtains open. There had been a light breeze and a soft voice that said a storm was coming. I saw a pair of beautiful pale blue eyes that contained a fire like no other. Larissa.

"Hold on and wait for me, Gianni. I'll always come for you."

I squeezed my eyes shut, desperate to get back to her. Felton signed her death warrant the minute he called my uncle. I hadn't heard a shred of news, not that I expected to. For all I knew, she was already dead and was telling me she was coming to bring me to heaven or hell with her. Who was I kidding? Assassins didn't go to heaven.

"I'm coming, baby," I whispered. "Hopefully, you have a nice spot in hell for the two of us."

The door flew open with a loud crash and I opened my eyes, ready to accept my fate. Franz ran toward me carrying a large pistol and a large gash on his scalp. His normally dark, dead eyes now blazed with a crazed fury.

"We've got company," he announced with an evil smile. "Looks like it's time to cut bait and head back to shore."

The next few seconds passed in a blur. He raised the gun to my face and pulled the hammer back. I shut my eyes, preparing for the end and welcoming it, since it meant I'd finally be with her. Then, the sound of the door opening and an earsplitting boom filled the room. Warm liquid dowsed my face and body, and I opened my eyes. A redheaded woman with braided hair was bent over the arm of my chair as she cut the rope around my wrist. She freed the other arm before looking at me. I gasped as my eyes were met with the same beautiful pair of pale blue eyes I saw in my dreams.

How was it possible? Was she my guardian angel come to escort me onward? She looked at me with grave concern, but managed a small smile.

"Did you miss me?"

Chapter 8

Vital Signs

Larissa

"X5 REQUESTING STATUS ON the second floor," I said, running toward the stairs immediately to my left.

"Hostage is still in the first room of the northeast corner. Be advised the suspect is heading down the hall toward that room."

"Copy. X5 moving up northeast stairs with T1 to secure hostage."

"Copy, X5. Proceed with caution," HQ replied.

I'd picked X5 as my call sign on purpose. It was the same one John used when he infiltrated my job in Prague three years ago. Once he was free I knew he'd have a good laugh about it. T1, a petite woman with short black hair, followed me closely up the stairs. Both our guns were drawn, ready to shoot. I pushed forward despite my heart thundering in my ears. There would be time to let all this sink in and fall apart later.

"X5 and T1, top of the stairs is clear. Suspect is about ten feet away from the hostage room," M3, a sniper reported.

"Fuck! Copy, M3." I raced up the stairs, ignoring my partner's protests to slow down.

The hallway on the second floor was dimly lit. As we rounded the corner, a stocky figure approached the last door. He smirked as soon as he saw me, and my blood ran cold instantly when I recognized him. Franz was a sick fuck who thrived on torture. I'd been a student of his teachings when I was home on breaks in college. Our training came to a sudden but much welcomed stop when Felton caught him snooping in my bedroom. He kicked Franz out and told him to never come back or he'd make sure the Bratva found him. Realizing this was the person Felton left to handle John made my blood boil.

I stood my ground at the top of the stairs and aimed for his head. "FBI! Drop the gun and get your hands up!"

The laugh that echoed down the hall gave me chills. "I don't think so, love," he taunted before firing at me.

I took cover, but raced after him once the door shut. T1 called after me. She had my back, but it barely registered. The look in his eyes told me all I needed to know. Felton's demand that John be kept alive now meant absolutely nothing to him.

The heavily dented door flew open with one kick. The dim light from the hallway was enough for me to see Franz with his gun in John's face and an evil gleam in his eyes. I fired without a second thought, taking comfort in the sound of the bullet hitting its target.

His body had barely dropped to the floor when I raced into the room and cut the ropes around John's wrists. It wasn't until both ropes were cut free that I allowed myself to look at him. The darkness made it hard to see all of his face, but what I saw shattered my heart. His face was covered in bruises, filth, and an overgrown beard full of debris that I didn't even want to think about. I couldn't see the luster in his eyes, but when they met mine, I gave him a small smile.

"Did you miss me?" I whispered, trying to keep my emotions in check.

He tried to speak, but his head slumped forward and the rest of his body went limp. I put my hands out to catch him before he fell and felt around his neck for a pulse. After finding a very weak one, I realized how cold his skin was. Trying not to panic, I brought my face down to his and listened to his breathing.

"X5 status. Suspect is eliminated. Hostage is down. Repeat. Hostage is down! Request EMT's STAT!"

"Holy shit! He's alive?" T1 yelled as she ran into the room.

"Barely. Pulse is very weak and there's no breath sounds."

"Fuck, he has a collapsed lung." She felt along his ribcage. "Oh no," she added.

"What?"

With a head shake, she spoke into her headset. "T1 status. Advise EMTs that the hostage has four broken ribs on the right side and a collapsed lung. Suspect possible internal bleeding and head trauma. Advise medical chopper to hospital. Patient is unconscious with a weak pulse and should be considered in critical condition."

"What do you need me to do?"

"See if you can find a light switch. They're going to need to see."

I felt along the wall as she continued to assess his condition. After what seemed like an eternity, I found the switch and light flooded the room. Something caught my eye, and I stopped dead in my tracks. Feeling completely numb, I took in the dozens of pictures that decorated the two walls in front of me. They looked like they were taken in the weeks after his abduction, except for the wall in front of his chair that contained dozens of pictures of me, Lucas, Nonna, Elena, and Paolo outside of Venice. A picture of Lucas hugging me as I cried sat eye level with the chair. Tears welled in my eyes as I shook my head and watched him over my shoulder. Knowing we were all being watched and he couldn't protect us would've been absolute hell for him.

"Make way!" a voice yelled as two EMTs entered the room.

I stepped closer and watched as they took his vitals. He was ghostly pale and emaciated, a far cry from his usual muscular build and olive complexion. His ribcage on the right side looked misshapen, almost flattened. The left side was a collection of deep, angry bruises. One of the EMTs placed a needle into his right side and I knew that meant they were trying to re-inflate the lung. I continued my watch, silently willing them to hurry so they could get him out of this hellhole.

At last, they got him on the gurney, and we were on our way. I followed closely, helping bring him down the stairs and soon I was running after them as they hustled him to the helicopter waiting in the vacant parking lot across the street. Barton called after me, but I ignored him.

"I'm coming with him," I demanded as they loaded him inside.

"Patient and EMTs only," the short and curvy redheaded paramedic countered, gesturing me to move back with her hand.

"He's a material witness. I'm coming with him come hell or high water. I promise I'll stay out of the way."

She nodded reluctantly and climbed inside. I followed behind and sat on the floor next to his feet. Once the building was no longer in my line of sight, my shoulders slumped and I let out a long breath. Turning my full attention back to the chaos before me, I watched every move the staff made as they worked to stabilize him. When the heart monitor sounded an alert and his body seized, I clutched the shelf nearby and tried to control my rising panic. Once the seizure stopped, I watched as they worked to restart his heart. When the monitor beeped once again, I looked down so nobody would notice the tears in my eyes.

We finally arrived at the hospital's helipad, and I hustled out of the way so they could rush him to the elevator. In a matter of seconds, the cold metal doors opened, and he was whisked away.

My hand traced the length of the doors, desperately trying to calm the fear flooding my veins. I lowered my head and took several deep breaths. He was free, I reminded myself. With my eyes closed, I forced myself to focus on that one simple fact as my pulse finally slowed. Just as I felt like I could face sitting in an uncomfortable chair downstairs and the endless waiting for an update, I saw a piece of debris stuck to the sole of my boot. The air in my lungs completely evaporated when I turned it over and saw a bloody gauze pad stuck to the sole.

The last bit of control over my emotions snapped. John wasn't a faceless hostage who might thank me in his prayers once he returned to his home. He was the love of my life who was surrounded by doctors trying to keep him alive several stories below my feet. No longer holding back, I slumped against the wall near the stairwell and sobbed. The helicopter pilot ran to me and asked if I was hurt and offered me a gentle pat on the shoulder after I explained the situation. I forced myself to focus on the moon in the cloudless night sky, and in a little while, I counted the stars until it felt easier to breathe. A blast of icy wind served as the perfect reminder that I ought to get my ass off the roof. Wiping my eyes, I pulled my hair out of the braid before yanking open the door to the stairwell and heading inside.

• • • • • • • • • •

"Lissa?" a voice softly sounded in my ear. "Good morning."

Yolanda's light brown eyes looked back at me once I woke up. I sat up from the small couch I'd been sleeping on and she pulled me into a tight hug. It was amazing how strong she was for such a petite woman.

"What time is it?" I mumbled, glancing around the waiting room for a clock.

"Just after six. Have you heard anything?"

I shook my head. "He's been in surgery for a while now."

"How are you doing?"

"I'm okay, as long as he's alive. That's about all I can share with you right now."

"Oh, honey." She sat down on the other end of the couch and handed me the bag in her hand. "I know it's the furthest thing from your mind, but you need to eat."

I perused the bag and grabbed the breakfast sandwich inside. "Where's Barton?"

"He was asleep when I got to the hotel. When I talked to him just before my plane, he'd just left the scene. He said it was pretty messed up."

"I wouldn't know," I replied numbly. "My only focus was making sure the EMTs were who they said they were and getting him the hell out of there."

The door to the waiting room opened and a haggard looking elderly man in scrubs came in. "Are you here for the John Doe?"

I nodded, petrified of what news this man was bringing me. "Please tell me he's okay."

He sat on the coffee table in front of us. "I heard you accompanied him here, so you saw what terrible shape he was in. He had a collapsed lung and internal bleeding from a ruptured spleen and a liver laceration. Also, he has a pretty bad concussion from several head contusions. His heart stopped three times, but luckily we were able to get it back each time we shocked it."

"Oh, god," I whispered, my voice cracking. Yolanda clutched my hand.

"We stopped the bleeding, but we had to remove his spleen. He's unconscious and on a ventilator. He's not out of the woods by any means, but if he shows improvements within the next forty-eight hours, I'd say he has a damn good chance."

"When can I see him?" I sniffed, quickly swiping the tears from my eyes.

"We're going to move him to the ICU in about an hour, and then you can see him."

"He's a material witness. I need to have two guards watching him at all times until I can make arrangements with the US Marshals Office."

"I'll see to it immediately," he said as he stood up.

Barton came off the elevator on my way to the ICU. The hospital security guards stood outside John's room, so I followed him to a small conference room down the hall.

"You look like hell," I stated, closing the door.

"So do you. Have you even slept?"

I sat at a small table in the room. "A little. How bad was the scene?"

Shaking his head, he took a seat. "Are you sure you want to know? It was pretty damn bad."

"I need to know, Barton."

He sighed and scrolled through his cell phone for a short time before handing it to me. My stomach turned as I scrolled through a gruesome assortment of torture rooms. A metal bed frame and a car battery, a hose tossed on the floor in the background. The warehouse's industrial freezer had been turned on and used, as shown by the pair of handcuffs attached to a shelf low to the floor. When I saw the picture of the room full of broken mirrors and blood on the floor, I felt sick. The last room contained several chains that hung from the ceiling, a shelf full of batons, whips and knives not far away. My hand flew to my mouth to muffle my sobs as I thrust the phone in his hand.

"I told you it was bad," he said quietly.

"It wasn't that I didn't believe you. I had to see for myself, see the hell he went through for three goddamned months."

"Who did this to him?"

"Before I tell you, you need to pick up that phone and have the DOJ send some marshals here to guard his room for the length of his stay. Next, as soon as he's stable, I need him transferred to the hospital at Lejeune and placed under maximum security."

"What the hell? On what grounds?"

"Because he's a material witness against the CIA officer who's responsible for his kidnapping, incarceration and torture for the last three fucking months. If we want to keep him alive, we have to keep him away from the D.C. area. I know people at Lejeune. He'll be safe there."

My eyes fell shut and I rested my head against the chair as he requested the marshals to arrive as soon as possible. Next, he called Melanie and put her working out the logistics for his transfer. My eyes snapped open when he tossed his phone on the table.

"Who?" he demanded, standing up.

"Felton fucking Lynch did this to him."

His eyes widened and he fell back into the seat. With his eyes closed, he took a deep breath. "That's a very serious accusation. You know I'm going to need proof."

"I have it, and I will get it to you right away. I have a recording of the CIA officer who diverted John's plane to Boston, which is corroborated by a copy of the transponder records of his plane. I also have Felton's travel records that show multiple trips to Boston."

"Jesus fucking Christ," he muttered, shaking his head. "Why? Why'd he do it?"

"That part I don't know. According to the recording I have, he's been working for the Sardi family for years. I don't have proof of that, but I have enough to prove that he was the mastermind behind the kidnapping."

"Do you know where he is?"

"Caracas, according to the travel records I have."

"Isn't that where you were supposed to go after you finished in Russia?"

I nodded. "I was, and based on the six Sardi family members who flew into the area in the last week, I'd say I would've been arriving into a trap if I'd gone."

"Lissa," he began uneasily. "This is the same man who raised you. What the hell happened?"

"I have no idea. I refused to think about the reasons behind it until I found John. Now that he's safe, all I can think about right now is trying to figure out exactly how bad this is and how I get us out of this mess."

"You need to get some rest. You look like you haven't slept in weeks."

"I haven't. I got a lead on finding him while I was still in Seattle finishing up our deal, and I've been chasing down leads ever since."

"He's safe now. You can relax."

"But not out of the woods," I countered.

"And unless you're a medical doctor, that's out of your control. Let the medical experts take care of him while the marshals watch the room and you get some damn sleep."

"I'm not leaving him."

"I never said you had to. There's a recliner in his room. Probably not the most comfortable, but I'm sure it'll do."

"I've slept in worse," I yawned. "Are the marshals here yet?"

He nodded. "I got a text about ten minutes ago when they arrived. Let's get you back to his room so you can see him and get some rest."

Halfway down the hall, I paused. "By chance, do you know what happened to Callum Flannery? He was the guy with me when I first got to the command center."

"He was taken to the Boston field office to give his statement. I'll make sure someone lets him know you're here so he can get in touch."

"Thank you, Barton. For everything," I said softly outside John's room. "And please tell Yolanda that I appreciate all her help, too."

"I have a feeling she probably helped you a lot more than either of you will ever tell me," he replied with a small smile. "Get some sleep, Agent. You look like shit."

He left and after nodding at the two marshals outside, I slid open the glass door to John's room. As soon as I saw him, all my guilt and sorrow made it hard to breathe. The parts of his face not covered by the beard were clean, but it did little to improve his ashen skin, sunken cheeks and the dark circles under his eyes. Various cuts and burns were scattered all over his arms and peeked out from under his hospital gown, the worst of which were bandaged. I sank into the chair next to his bed and took his hand in mine.

"God, I am so sorry he did this to you," I sobbed. "I'm still trying to understand everything, but I promise he'll get everything he deserves."

I stared at his chest, watching it slowly move as the ventilator breathed for him. My eyes traveled down his arm, taking in all the wounds, stopping at the bandage around his wrist. After seeing the pictures of the rooms, I couldn't even imagine the hell he went through. Releasing his hand, I leaned against mine and went back to watching the monitors, refusing to surrender to sleep until I read the information on each machine. When my eyes grew heavy, the last thing I heard was the constant beeping of the heart monitor reminding me that despite not being out of the woods, he was still alive.

Chapter 9

Critical Mass

Larissa

I WOKE UP FACE down on John's bed with my hand still over his. My neck was sore when I sat up in the chair. Massaging the tense muscles, I read each monitor, and then leaned my head back in the chair to take in the sunrise.

"Good morning," I whispered, giving his hand a gentle squeeze, happy that he made it through the night. It was a minor victory, but still a victory.

"Ah, you're awake. Good morning," a tall, heavyset woman with short, black hair greeted me as she entered the room. "I'm Dr. Parker, and I've been assigned to Mr. Morrow's care. I didn't catch your name."

"Agent Taylor Wallace, FBI," I answered, shaking her hand and nodding at the nurse behind her.

John was hospitalized under the name Lawrence Morrow as an additional precaution. Both our identities were so secure that an access code and a fingerprint were required to even view the files. Since Barton was the only one who possessed both the code and the fingerprint, I felt better about our safety for the time being. I wouldn't feel John was totally secure until he was moved to the base, but the doctors had yet to tell us he was stable enough to transfer.

"His lung function has improved and his stats are looking bet-ter," Dr. Parker stated as she listened to his chest. "The neurologist will come by later to check on him, but for now the slight improve-ments I'm seeing in less than twenty-four hours are encouraging."

"That's great news. Thank you, Doctor," I responded, exhaling slowly.

She gave me a small nod and headed for the door. I saw her shoot a curious look my way before exiting to the hallway. Shrug-ging, I gazed out the window at the partly cloudy sky. An FBI agent holding the hand of the person she was guarding no doubt led to a lot of questions, but I didn't have it in me to care. I rubbed my eyes and turned back to him, stifling a yawn.

"I'd say scoot over so I could get some proper rest, but I guess that would be rude because of the coma and all," I joked. "And I'm sure that would only make Dr. Parker even more suspicious. Too bad you aren't awake to help me stir up the rumor mill."

"Agent Wallace? There was a man who came in earlier to talk to you, but you were still sleeping. He said when you woke up to meet him in the hospital chapel," a nurse announced from the doorway.

I nodded my head in thanks and then turned back to the bed. "That's probably Cal. I better go see what he wants. Try not to start any trouble while I'm gone."

The chapel was across from the gift shop on the first floor. Electric candelabras adorned the plain white walls. The altar at the front was white marble and stood before the dark wood paneling. The windows were all stained glass in beautiful shades of blue. I stopped at the door and admired the large stained glass window above the altar before walking any further. Cal sat in one of the plain wooden chairs to the right. Our eyes met briefly before I lit a candle and bowed my head. After I finished my silent prayer, I made the sign of the cross and turned back to him.

"I never saw you as the overly religious type," he said as I took the seat next to him.

"He survived the night after all the shit that psychopath put him through. It's the least I could do."

"I saw the marshals posted outside his room."

"He's a material witness, which puts him under maximum security," I replied. "I'm having him moved to North Carolina as soon as he's stable enough."

"What's in North Carolina?"

"A shit ton of Marines who would have no problem wasting anyone who came after him."

"What about you?"

I sighed. "I need answers. The first one being why Felton would kidnap him. It makes no sense. If he's worked so closely with the Sardis, why would he kidnap Massimo's nephew? He had to know that would be a death sentence. So why do it?"

"It doesn't make sense, but I realized long ago Felton sometimes does crazy things nobody else understands. I think that's why your dad ultimately walked away from him."

"He did?"

He nodded. "About a year before he died. He never told me why, and I didn't ask. We just never spoke of it."

"That's odd. Felton always said they were the best of friends. Then again, it's not like I knew any differently. I only ever saw him a few times when I was a kid."

"Seamus kept it very quiet. All he ever said to me was Felton wouldn't be coming around anymore, and that was that. Everything was quiet for a few months, so I never gave it any thought."

"What happened after those few months of quiet?"

"Your parents wanted to register you for school, and suddenly your dad came to me in need of a birth certificate for you," he answered.

"You get fake documents for people?"

"Not exactly," he hedged. "I knew a few people, friends of my brother. Nolan was in the gang with your dad."

I leaned back in my chair and stared at the stained-glass window above the altar as I mulled things over. There had been something gnawing at my brain ever since I left Miami. Sometimes it sounded completely insane. However, other times, it made perfect sense. The only reason two seemingly unrelated things would intertwine as they had. I hadn't voiced my suspicion to anyone, mostly because I'd been caught up in John's rescue, but also because I was terrified of the answer. Since Cal knew more about my parents than anyone else, he was one of the few people who would give me an honest answer about my theory.

"What can you tell me about Soren Luccetti?"

His brows furrowed. "Why?"

"Just curious."

"All I know is what I heard from Nolan and Seamus the few times they talked about him. He was a hit man for the Sardi family."

"Really?"

"One of the best. Knives were his specialty. They said it was almost as beautiful as it was disturbing the way he sliced people up, like a sick form of art. They also said he was like a ghost. Nobody ever saw him until it was too late. He was everywhere and nowhere all at once."

"Well, that would explain why he taught me how to use a knife," I muttered to myself, shaking my head.

"What?"

"What if I told you Seamus wasn't my father? How shocked would you be?"

"I would say I suspected as much when he told me he didn't want to use your real birth certificate for school. Are you telling me Soren is your real dad?"

"Confirmed by a DNA test from his known son in Italy."

His eyes widened. "Holy shit."

"Let me ask you an even crazier question, Cal. What if that ghost has been hiding in plain sight for the last thirty-plus years? As an officer of the CIA."

He stared at me dumbstruck for a short time before connecting the dots. "Felton?" His voice was barely louder than a whisper. "Are you saying Soren is Felton?"

"When John was kidnapped, Massimo responded by telling everyone I was responsible and doubled the bounty on me. At first, it didn't make sense. Why pin it on me when I had nothing to do with it? But what if Massimo knew Felton was the one who had John?"

"If he's really your father, it would explain why Sera insisted on keeping you away from him," he answered after a few moments. "It could also explain why he and your dad had their falling out. Maybe Felton figured everything out and tried to force the issue?"

"It makes sense. John's grandmother told me that my mother was adamant that Soren never learned he was my father. What doesn't make sense is why he would greenlight me going on the case that started all this? When I was sent to Portland to keep John under surveillance. He knew who John was, which means he had to know that the case was a setup from the start. Why would he put his daughter in danger?"

"I don't know, but what I do know is you need a plan. Fast. Massimo gunning for you is one thing, but that shit in Venezuela with Felton sounds dodgy, too. I'm worried about you."

"I need to call Barton and see if he's found out anything. I also need to get more proof about Felton if I'm going to bring him down."

"I hate to leave, but I have a meeting," he said, glancing at his watch. He pulled me into a hug. "You let me know if you need anything. And I mean anything. Promise me."

"I promise." He handed me my knapsack that had been sitting on the floor. "I can't thank you enough for everything you've done. I'm forever in your debt."

"That's where you're wrong, Lissi. I should've been there to help you all along, and I'm sorry that shithead took that away from me. I now understand why, but that doesn't change the fact I should've been there."

We spoke for a few more minutes and then he left. My eyes closed and I savored the quiet of the chapel. Gone was my fear of not finding John, but in its place there were a ton of questions about where things went from there. I grabbed my silver phone out of my knapsack and dialed.

"I was just about to call you," Barton greeted.

"Sounds like a perfect reason for you to come over here to talk."

"How is he?"

"He survived the night. The doctor said she saw some progress, so she's optimistic. You can see for yourself when you get here."

"You okay? Why the sudden rush?"

"I was talking to Cal and I realized a couple of things I need to run by you. Things that I'd rather not discuss over the phone."

"I can be there in half an hour. Yolanda will be back at the hotel later with the kids, so I can only stay for a short time.

"Fair enough. I'll see you soon."

We hung up, and I had just grabbed my knapsack and exited the chapel when my phone rang. The caller ID said it was an unknown caller, which wasn't out of the ordinary for numbers from FBI extensions. I pressed the button, thinking it was Barton.

"What's up?" I answered.

"Hello, Miss Donovan. I didn't realize you answered your work phone so informally," a deep, heavily accented voice replied.

My heart stuttered and I froze, stopping just inside the entrance to the chapel. Massimo Sardi. I leaned against the wall and tried not to panic. Why was he calling me now? How did he get the number for this phone when it was supposed to be secured by the FBI? I choked down my initial shock and focused on what was important: finding out what he wanted and not giving away any information about John's current condition.

"Well, Signore Sardi, I apologize. I didn't realize the psychotic mob boss who hates me so much he lied and told everyone that I kidnapped his nephew would call me," I retorted.

"Watch your tone, young lady," he warned. "I've killed greater men for lesser crimes than your flippant attitude."

"And I've killed lesser men for greater crimes, starting with your brother. To what do I owe the dubious honor of your call?"

He chuckled, causing the hair on my neck to stand up. "You are certainly a feisty one. I can see why you amuse Gianni so much. Word has reached me about your recent personal struggles with my nephew. I must confess my annoyance that you were so quick to blame me."

I rolled my eyes. Talking to this man was maddening. "Such an interesting way to phrase that someone kidnapped him and rather than try to find him, you pin the blame on me. One would almost think you didn't want him found."

"That mouth of yours is going to be your downfall, child," he bit out. "Your arrogance blinds you to all else. My accusation against you was to impress upon the real culprit how much they might want to re-think their decision to act against my family."

"You knew he was my father."

"Without going into too many boring details, I've known for almost as long as you. One of my associates got a hold of the test results Gianni procured. As I'm sure you'd like to express anger that I never told you, that blame would be misplaced."

"Look," I sighed. "With all due respect, which is none, why don't you get to the point? Did you call me just because you could? How did you even get this number?"

"How I got this number is not important. The reason for my call is to advise you that you are currently not being hunted by my family or associates."

"Sorry if I don't send you a thank you card. I seem to be fresh out of postage stamps. Do I even want to know who your new target is?"

"Well, your father was the spineless man I've always known him to be. It was bad enough that he kidnapped Gianni and was foolish enough to think he could exchange him for your safety. But then he had to make it worse by lying to me. You see, he thought he could double cross me by telling me you were in New York City. He then tried to sneak you into another country, so you'd be harder to find once I realized his deception."

"Is that why your men were seen traveling to that region? I thought they all just decided to vacation together."

He chuckled. "That would be the reason, Miss Donovan. Once I realized his treachery, I sent men there to monitor you as an insurance policy. I'll admit that I misjudged you, however, since you never arrived. It seems you have your resources as well."

"You make it sound like the man gives two shits about me. If he cared so much that he lied to protect me, why'd he sell me out to your brother two years ago?"

"I'm afraid I'm not privy to that information. You would have to ask him yourself."

"God, I understand why John hates talking to you so much," I muttered. "So, to recap, you called to tell me you knew Felton had kidnapped John all along and you blamed me for it to scare him. Oh, and that he's a lying scumbag. Does that about sum it up?"

"And you're just as annoying as that fucking brother of yours," he growled. "I called to tell you my family and associates will not be pursuing you until your father has been dealt with."

"Forgive me if I don't believe a single word that comes out of your mouth. But your claim has been duly noted. Congrats on finding a two-bit hacker to find my phone number, by the way."

"Miss Donovan, I really don't care for your attitude, nor do I care if you believe me or not. I'm afraid I really must go, but I look forward to crossing paths with you again sometime soon. Good day."

Chapter 10

The Sins of the Father

Larissa

"You look like you've seen a ghost," Barton observed as he entered the room.

As soon as Massimo ended our call, I turned off the phone and raced upstairs to make sure John was okay. The chances were slim that he knew our location, but I had to see with my own eyes that nobody had been sent to hurt him or take him away from me again. Once I saw he was still in bed and unconscious, I sat next to him with his hand in mine and watched the ventilator breathe for him.

I handed Barton the FBI issued phone. "Massimo just called me."

His face paled. "What did he say?"

"To say Felton is his target right now because he knew he was behind John's abduction."

"Does he even know his nephew has been rescued?"

I laughed humorlessly. "He didn't ask."

"That's messed up."

"It is, but sadly you get used to it. The only reason John is the family's heir is because Massimo has no sons and John is the oldest grandson on both sides of the family. If he ever found a way to carry on his legacy without John, he'd kill him because he feels John allowed himself to be tainted by me."

He shook his head. "Jesus Christ. Well, I'm here now. What did you want to talk about?"

"I need to know when we can move him. Reading between the lines, that call was a warning. He's going after Felton, but I'm sure he's still looking for the perfect time to strike at me, too. I'll be damned if he gets caught up in all this."

"The logistics on our end are a go. I'll talk to his doctor and see if he's stable enough. Once she gives the green light, he'll be moved within twenty-four hours."

"Thank you."

"What else do you need?"

"Aside from a week-long nap?" I joked, giving him a small smile. "In all seriousness, the first thing I need is a new phone, and apparently it should be more secure than that one. The next thing I need is a bit more complicated. I need a DNA test."

His head snapped up and he gaped. "On whom?"

"Felton and myself."

"What the fuck?"

"I told you it was complicated." I handed him a thumb drive. "This is a copy of a recording of the CIA officer confessing to diverting John's plane to Boston at Felton's behest. She also told me he'd been working for the Sardi family for years. I'll work on getting you proof of that in the next couple of days. All you need is that DNA test and you've got a pretty ironclad case against him."

He paled. "Are you saying what I think you're saying?"

"I am," I whispered, refusing to say the words. "I'll send you the travel information I got that shows he made several trips to Boston after the abduction. It should be enough for you to take to Hannah Myers-Nelson, Felton's boss, and get her to release his DNA sample for analysis. Like I said, I'll have more for you in a couple of days."

"Where are you getting the evidence?"

"From my brother."

His brows came together. "Who's your brother?"

"Not now. Someday, but I just can't right now." The torrent of information I unearthed was beyond overwhelming. I desperately needed some time free of chaos so I could fully wrap my head around everything. Unfortunately, I knew that wasn't going to happen soon.

He nodded and clapped his hand on my shoulder. "When you're ready. You've been through enough. Is there anything else you need from me?"

"Not right now. Once John is safe and we have the DNA results, we can try to figure out what the hell to do. In the meantime, I should probably call my brother and let him know what's going on."

"I'll be in touch. You're not handling all this alone anymore. Get some rest. You look like you're about to drop."

I nodded silently and murmured a goodbye, keeping my eyes on John. His fingers felt a little warmer when I grasped his hand. Staring at all the tubes and wires connected to his body, I shook my head. "*Why* did he take you?" I whispered. "That's the part I can't understand."

The question played repeatedly in my mind. What reason would Felton have for kidnapping him? They had known each other and worked together for years, and while there was obviously a lot of animosity between the two, I never thought it would go to such an extreme. I watched him for a few more minutes before releasing his hand and pulling out my other phone. It would be very early on the island, but I knew he wouldn't care.

"Please tell me you have good news," Lucas answered, yawning.

"I found him."

"Oh my god! Where? How? Is he okay?"

"I'll tell you everything, but you have to promise not to tell Nonna just yet. He's not entirely out of the woods."

"Lissa?" His voice was shaky.

I spent the next few minutes telling him everything; from locating the building to the rescue operation to my plan to have him moved to North Carolina. Once I told him that Massimo called me, he lost his cool.

"What the fuck did he want?"

"The usual. To intimidate me and be an asshole. But right now there's a bigger issue. And I need you to promise me you'll stay calm."

"Fine," he muttered after a few seconds.

"This is going to sound like an odd question, but how did Felton act toward you when we were in Tampa? Did he do or say anything that seemed strange to you?"

"Not really. You saw most of my interactions with him."

"What about when I wasn't there? Were you ever alone with him?"

"No, John did everything he could to make sure that didn't happen. I wasn't even alone with him after he left," he answered slowly and then paused. "Why are you asking me about Felton?"

"He's the one who kidnapped him, Luc," I answered, my voice cracking.

"What?" His voice was faint. "Why?"

"I don't know why, but there's more. And this is where I really need you to stay calm. Can you please do that for me?"

"I'll try. That's all I can promise right now."

"There's a very strong possibility that Felton is Soren. I've already requested a DNA test to confirm it, and I should know in a couple of days at most, but apparently he's been working for Massimo for years."

Silence. All I could hear on the other end was his sharp intake of breath and his continued breathing for several minutes. I shut my eyes, wishing he was with me. For a split second, I hated the distance between us as he was left to digest the news alone.

"Lucas?"

He exhaled slowly. "I'm getting on a plane and coming to see you."

"No!"

"Yes, I am. He raised you as if you were his own, and now you're telling me the sick son of a bitch is our father? You need me. There's no way I'm staying here."

"Please calm down," I pleaded. "You can't leave the island, especially not right now. It's far too dangerous."

"I don't fucking care. I'll be damned if you're going to go through all this by yourself. I feel like shit for all that you've had to go through on your own already."

"Lucas, stop! I'll call Tavi and have him keep you there by force if necessary," I threatened, fully intending to call my head of security once I finished the call. "Your uncle is gunning for Felton and he doesn't care who he takes down with him. That's why I'm moving John, and I'll be damned if I let you put yourself in danger."

"So, am I supposed to just continue to sit around on my ass while you run yourself into the ground?"

"No, I need you to chase down some documents and send them to me so we can build the case against Felton."

He sighed, resigned. "What do you need?"

I went over all the information I needed him to gather. He filled me in on how everyone was doing on the island. Not surprisingly, Nonna had already taken over the kitchen at the main house while Elena spent a lot of time in the garden when she wasn't in the kitchen with her mother. It was nice to hear they were both settling into life on the island. When I asked Lucas how he was doing, he muttered he was fine. I smiled sadly, knowing just how angry he was with me in that moment and wanting nothing more for him to be there with me.

"Are you at least eating and sleeping?" he asked, attempting to change the subject. "Right now, I'm guessing you're sitting there in his room, staring at him and watching every monitor you can."

"I'm fine, Lucas. I eat when I'm hungry and I sleep when I'm tired."

"And John told me the same thing. You need to get up, get out of that room, and go outside."

"I'll go out and walk around soon."

"He told me that plenty of times, too. You'll go out and walk around as soon as you hang up this phone," he commanded gently. "And you two need a career change so I can stop worrying about both of you."

"I'm working on it."

"Go outside. And then go to a restaurant that's far enough from the hospital that you can't see the building and eat something that must be served on a plate and can't be boxed up to go. Keep me posted and call me when he wakes up."

"Fine," I groaned. "I'll go. Happy?"

"Yep. Love ya!"

"Love you too, asshat."

I hung up the phone and squeezed John's hand. "Lucas says hi. I'm sure you'll be happy to hear he's still an overbearing pain in the ass," I paused, sighing. "Who was thrilled to hear you've been found. We're not telling Nonna yet, though. You're going to have to wake up and tell her yourself. No pressure or anything, but the sooner, the better. You know how she hates to wait."

As it turned out, I didn't go outside to walk around. I watched him sleep for a while, and the next thing I knew, I woke up at the foot of his bed with my arm wrapped around his legs. Sitting up, I found a large shopping bag on the chair beside me and a styrofoam container full of baked ziti on the table. Yolanda left a note telling me to take it easy and she'd stop by the next morning. As I wolfed down the pasta, I looked through the shopping bag and found clothes and toiletries. After a long, hot shower in John's bathroom, I settled into the chair and watched the monitors before falling asleep.

• • • • • • • • • •

I turned off the shaver and surveyed my work. "Okay, I'm happy to announce you don't look like a mountain man anymore."

It had been two days, and John's lungs had improved enough to remove the ventilator. Both Dr. Parker and the neurologist agreed it was safe to move him, and his transfer to Camp Lejeune was finally scheduled for the following morning. I'd asked when he would wake up and Dr. Parker told me he might regain consciousness before the trip, but it might take another day or two.

Now that the tube was out of his mouth, I decided to shave the nasty, overgrown beard. The neurologist had shaved small patches of hair on the back of his head during surgery, so I cut his hair as well. His skin was still sickly pale, but he looked more like the man I loved.

I caressed his now bare cheek. "I know you'll probably be pissed, but in the long run you'll thank me. I'm pretty sure you had a family of squirrels living in that beard," I joked and then sighed. "And to be honest, I would love nothing more for you to wake up and start bitching. Please wake up, baby. I need you and I miss you."

Sitting at the edge of the bed, I scrolled through the documents Lucas emailed me, hoping they would help build the case against Felton. Barton called that morning to tell me he'd be stopping by to talk and share the DNA results. After nearly two days of minimal contact with anyone other than doctors and nurses, I was eager for his arrival.

"Whoa!" Yolanda exclaimed as she walked into the room, followed by Barton. "You've been busy."

"They took him off the ventilator this morning and I couldn't stand it any longer," I replied, giving her a hug. "Where are the kids?"

"My sister lives in Cambridge. She took them to the aquarium," Barton answered. "How are you doing?"

"Ready to get him out of here."

"Larissa, how are *you* doing?"

"I'm fine, Barton."

He rolled his eyes and handed me a manila envelope. "Here are the DNA results."

My hands shook as I took the parcel. I turned it over in my hands a few times before pulling out the sheet of paper inside. My stomach sank like a stone as I read the statement declaring that Felton Jacob Lynch was my father with 99.999% certainty.

"You're going to want to make a copy of this," I said in a flat tone, handing him the paper. "It's confirmed."

"Shit," he sighed. "This was probably the one time I didn't want you to be right."

"I had no desire to be right either, but it actually helps your case. And I have more evidence for you: the DNA results showing I'm the sister of Soren Luccetti's known and documented son. I also sent documents that show the transponder of the plane John chartered was the same one Marianna diverted. And then a list of phone calls and bank transfers between Felton and Massimo, along with proof of the phone numbers and bank accounts belonging to each."

He thumbed through the documents on his phone. "How the hell did you get all this?"

"The plane info came from Marcus. As for the rest, let's just say my brother is quite resourceful."

"I guess all we need to do now is figure out where he's hiding."

"Well, you can go back to looking for him after we all have lunch," Yolanda said brightly. "Lissa, you've camped out in this room long enough. It's a nice, sunny day and we're going outside to enjoy it."

"I wish I could go with you guys, but I need to get go back to the office and turn all this in," he replied, holding up his phone.

"We don't have to go. I can stay here," I offered. My voice died in my throat when she shot me a glare.

"Nice try, missy. We're going. Now."

"Fine, I'll go outside," I mock whined as I grabbed John's hoodie from my knapsack. "But only because you're making me."

Barton bent down low to give his wife a kiss before he left. She giggled as he held her close and whispered in her ear. I smiled as I watched them before turning back to the bed behind me.

"This could be us if you'd just hurry and wake up," I joked, gently kissing his forehead. "I'll be back. I love you."

It was a sunny and cool September day in Boston. We ate lunch outside at a restaurant near the hospital and after both agreeing we wouldn't talk about the FBI, Felton or anything else related to all the drama going on, we had a great time. She told me about how big the kids were getting, and I told her a few stories about my time in Ireland and Verona. Afterward, she headed off to meet Barton's sister while I took a short walk.

I stood on the footbridge over the pond in Boston Common and watched the surrounding scenery. The leaves started changing colors, the orange, red, and yellow leaves creating a beautiful contrast to the greenery. I watched the squirrels scamper around the grass and along the trees as they hunted for food and wrestled with each other. After a while, I sat on a vacant bench and turned the item that had been clutched in my hand for the last half hour over and over as if it would give me help with the debate that raged in my head. A couple of seconds later, I said a silent prayer in my head and dialed the disposable phone.

"This is Field Officer Felton Lynch. To whom am I speaking?" he answered briskly.

I drew a deep breath and exhaled slowly. "This is Special Agent Larissa Donovan, FBI. Am I speaking to Felton Lynch or Soren Luccetti?"

"You're speaking to Felton Lynch, the CIA field officer who is wondering why the fuck my employee didn't report to Venezuela as instructed," he bit out.

"Yeah, sorry about that. I didn't think it would be a good idea to go, what with the hit squad waiting for me and all. Instead, I took a couple of side trips. Had some pretty good Cuban food at Marianna's place, reconnected with some of my dad's friends in New York, and then picked up a really important parcel in one of *my* buildings in Boston."

"Sweetheart, I—,"

"Not. Another. Fucking. Word. You lost the right to call me that the minute you sold me out to the fucking family who killed my parents."

"Seamus Donovan was never one of your parents," he snarled. "I raised you."

"And you weren't supposed to, were you? You see, I've had some very interesting conversations the past couple weeks. It turns out you've carved out quite the life for yourself, Mr. Luccetti."

"Larissa, I understand you're upset."

I laughed. "I was upset when Gio conned the FBI into sending me into a trap. Then I found Franz about to kill John, and now all I can say is you better goddamn hope that Massimo finds you before I do. He seemed pretty pissed when I talked to him."

"You spoke to Massimo?"

"He saw fit to hack my FBI phone and send me his regards. Apparently, he's going to take a break from trying to kill me and focus his attention on you. This not being my first trip to that dance, however, I know he wouldn't be upset if I wound up as collateral damage."

"Please listen to me," he pleaded. "You are going to need my help if you want to have any hope of getting out of this shit with him alive."

"This coming from the asshole who served me up on a platter in Portland? And don't get me started on Cuba. Why would I even think about trusting you?"

"I haven't been proud of my actions for quite some time now, Larissa. And I promise to explain everything to you soon, but if you want to have even the slightest chance, you need me."

I crossed the street and stood at the corner near the hospital entrance. The sunlight was fading, the first blushes of orange and pink creeping into the horizon. Felton's voice buzzed like an annoying bug, but I wasn't listening. Getting upstairs and checking on John was all I cared about.

"I'll think about it," I snapped and hung up.

Turning off the phone, I headed inside, stopping at the cafeteria for a sandwich before making my way to the twelfth floor.

I nodded at the two marshals at the door and murmured a quick hello before entering his room.

He looked like he was sleeping peacefully. I was disappointed he wasn't awake, but the fact he was breathing on his own and his face had more color was more than enough for me. I sighed and sat next to him on the bed. After the conversations with both Massimo and Felton, I was overwhelmed and exhausted. I had no idea what was in store from either of them, and I was too tired to think about it. At that moment, there was only one thing I needed.

"You need to wake up soon, baby," I whispered, gripping his hand in both of mine. "With all the shit that's going on, I need you to open your eyes. I need to know you're going to be okay."

His hand weakly held on to mine, startling me. My eyes snapped up to his face and his deep brown eyes were staring back at me. He blinked a few times before he inhaled deeply and gave my hand a squeeze.

"So," he rasped quietly. "Did I miss anything?"

Chapter 11

Need

John

"I NEED YOU."

Over the years, I grew to loathe that goddamned phrase. It had been used countless times to manipulate me to do what others wanted. My uncles needed me to kill people for them so they could show off their power and authority. The vapid eye candy that liked to think of themselves as my girlfriends needed my attention, my family's reputation, and/or my bank account for various reasons to get them ahead. Was it a cynical way to look at the world? Sure. After so many years and so many people "needing" me to advance their own personal gains, however, I never thought there would be anyone or anything to make me think that would ever change.

"I *need you.*"

The words started as a faint buzzing through the fog as I tried to open my eyes and figure out what the hell was going on. My eyes wouldn't budge, which only added to the mystery. Was I alive? Dead? The last thing I remembered was the redheaded angel with blue eyes who reminded me of Larissa. I needed to believe it was her, but by then I didn't know what was real or what was in my head. When her mouth moved, all I heard was silence before everything went black.

The faint buzzing of the words I hated so much continued, but for once, they didn't anger me. Why? I usually ignored the person as soon as they said it. This time I couldn't. I had to know the source and the reason. Who needed me, and why?

My body felt heavier and what few voices I heard sounded as if they were under water. My body soon felt lighter and the voices clearer, almost as if I was moving closer to the surface. The desire to know who needed me persisted, and then suddenly a lone voice completely broke through the darkness.

"You need to wake up soon, baby," she whispered. She held my hand in both of hers. "With all the shit that's going on, I need you to open your eyes. I need to know you're going to be okay."

A feeling of warmth started in my heart and spread throughout my body. Larissa was here, alive. In that moment, I knew I hadn't imagined her in that dark room, but was still afraid she'd slip away. I grasped her hand and opened my eyes, finally seeing the same heavenly pale blue ones that brought so much light and joy to the drab existence I led before she entered my world.

"So, did I miss anything?" My voice was rough on my throat.

"Oh my god," she gasped, standing up.

I tightened my grip to keep her from moving too far away, and her eyes filled with tears. Her lower lip trembled as she stared at me, and I tried to pull her close. When she sobbed, I couldn't take it anymore and tugged on her arm as hard as I could. She collapsed onto the bed next to me and when her head rested against my chest, I embraced her. My body protested, but I didn't care.

"Hey," I whispered.

Her hand moved to mine, which she clutched as she cried. After a while, she sat up and offered me a tearful smile. I reached up and gently wiped the tears away with my thumb. She cupped my face with both hands and brought her lips to mine for a slow, tender kiss. As soon as our lips met, my heart felt like it would burst. I wanted so badly to hold her again, but the pain in my sides couldn't be ignored any longer.

"Hey," she murmured. "How do you feel?"

She looked exhausted. The dark circles under her eyes were deep and her skin was extremely pale against her dark red hair. Wait. "Where's Lucas? And Nonna? Why is your hair red?"

"Slow down," she answered, sitting by my side and pressing the call button on the bed. "I'll answer your questions once the doctors examine you."

The doctors came in several minutes later and soon I was poked, prodded, and asked an endless barrage of questions. When she wasn't pacing around the room, she leaned against the windowsill and watched everyone closely. After a short while, she stopped fidgeting with her hair and started tapping her collarbone with her thumb. Shit, that meant her anxiety was nearing its limit. The last time she did that was on the way to Massimo's estate before the ball. Soon she'd start biting and peeling her fingernails. I answered all the doctors' questions as quickly as I could, and motioned her to me as soon as they left the room.

"Before you bruise your collarbone any more or destroy your nails, how about you tell me what's wrong?"

She let out a long breath. "A lot of shit has happened. I'm not sure where to begin, and I don't want to stress you out while you're still recovering."

"Let's start with what day it is and where are Lucas and Nonna."

"It's September seventeenth. Our family is safe. We didn't know who was behind your disappearance, so I moved them as a precaution. The only people who know their location are myself and my private security team."

The middle of September. He'd kept me in that hellhole for three months. The brief flash of anger I felt was quickly overshadowed by the relief that everyone was safe. "What happened?"

"Lucas and I had a suspicion Massimo knew something was up. Several of his men were spotted in Verona, which was bad enough. But then Marco was spotted too close to Venice for either of our liking. For all we knew, it was a way for him to smoke me out again, so I sent them away. Lucas, Nonna, Zia Elena…all three are where nobody can find them or use them against us."

"Zia?" My heart soared at the way she referred to the family as ours.

"Elena's orders," she replied. "After I left Venice, things took an interesting turn. I'll spare you all the details, but when all was said and done, Marianna died a traitor's death and I found you."

"Do I want to know?"

She shook her head. "That story stays between me and my scalpels."

The cold look in her eyes told me enough. She'd let her killer out to play, and the monster had one hell of a time. I'd heard stories about her surgical precision and how disturbingly brutal it was when she used a blade to do the job. She was right. I didn't want to know.

"The FBI ran a DNA test and confirmed Felton's true identity as Soren Luccetti," she stated hollowly.

I took her hand in mine, hating the pained expression on her face. It was a shock when I made the connection, so I couldn't even imagine how hard it had been to realize the man who had raised her was actually her father. However, the way she worded her statement told me it would be wise not to refer to him in any way that reminded her of that.

"That should help their case," I offered lamely, unsure what else to say.

"He took you because you figured out who he was, didn't he?"

I nodded slowly. "That night he and I got into the fight at the hospital. When you came out of your room, he and Lucas had the same looks on their faces. And then I may have opened my big, fat mouth and told him I knew things he didn't want anyone else to know."

"When Massimo told me that Felton tried to leverage you for my safety, I figured that was the reason."

"What do you mean he told you?"

"He hacked my phone to tell me he was focusing on Felton for now and would leave me alone," she explained with a small shrug of her shoulder. "I don't believe it for a second, of course."

"Good. Have you heard anything from Felton?"

"I called him on a burner phone and he offered to help me kill Massimo. I hung up on him."

"So they're concentrating on each other right now?" I smiled when she nodded. "While they focus on killing each other, we can use that time to come up with a plan. The sooner, the better."

"No, you need to focus on recovering from the shit my disgusting sperm donor put you through," she replied. She looked down and shook her head. "I'm so sorry he did all this to you."

I pulled her closer until her face hovered above mine. "Baby, listen to me. You never apologize for him. Ever. He's a sick, manipulative son of a bitch, and that's not your fault. That has nothing to do with you. Okay?"

She nodded, and I kissed her forehead. That she even felt the need to apologize for that asshole made my blood boil. I looked at her beautiful, tear-stained face and kissed her again. I saw the small paper bag on the table by the bed.

"Grab your food and come sit with me," I told her. "You need to eat something."

As she grabbed the bag, I scooted over. When she saw me grimace, she hurried to the chair next to the bed. "You're still sore. The last thing you need is me taking up space in the bed."

I grabbed the bag out of her hands and tucked it under my arm. "No, what I need is you close to me. Come and sit. Please."

She rolled her eyes and sat down on the bed. I chuckled at the glare she shot me and handed her the bag. She ate her sandwich quietly and the moment she finished, I wrapped my arm around her and pulled her backwards until she finally relaxed.

"When was the last time you had a decent meal?"

"Barton's wife, Yolanda, took me out to lunch today."

"When was the last time you had three decent meals in a row? And a full night's sleep?"

"The night before I left for Russia. So, that was," she paused. "Early August I think? I've been busy."

"Larissa!"

"What? I've been traveling, and it's not like Yani has a gourmet chef cooking the food for the people in his dungeon."

"Wait. What??"

My stomach dropped. A dungeon? What the fuck? And did she mean Yani Petracova? The same Yani who ran part of the fucking Russian mafia? Just what the hell did she get herself into in the three months I was gone?

Her eyes widened. "Um, I wasn't going to tell you that story until tomorrow. I meant to save it for the plane ride."

My eyes narrowed. "And where are we going?"

"Um, Camp Lejeune?"

"Why?"

"Because you're a material witness against a rogue CIA officer," she answered, the annoyance in her voice growing.

"Liss."

"Did you really think I would leave you in a civilian hospital? Fuck no! You're being placed under maximum security in a place where I actually know the people and if I have to leave, I know you'll be safe while you recover."

"Okay," I replied, hugging her gently. "I'm sorry. I've been comatose, so I didn't know the plan. That works for me."

I held her close and a little while later, she leaned her head against my shoulder. Her comment about leaving worried me, but I didn't want to bring it up and risk upsetting her again. The thought of being away from her made my heart ache and filled me with worry. She needed to lie low while Felton and Massimo battled each other.

"Just got you back and I'll be damned if I'm losing you again," she muttered.

"I know the feeling," I whispered, kissing her forehead. I said the same thing to her nearly six months earlier. She'd given me hell for the comment, begging me to let her leave. Back then, the likelihood of her saying those same words to me seemed impossible. Hearing them in that moment only bolstered my determination to never let her go.

"When Lucas called and told me you were missing, it felt like my heart had been ripped out," she admitted quietly, her eyes tearing up again. "My mind kept coming up with all these horrible images."

"Mine did, too. I saw so many terrifying things in my head that I actually dreaded falling asleep. And then seeing all those pictures and knowing he'd been watching all of you," I paused. "It was a nightmare. He told me that my family was looking for me at first, but then made it sound like the search was called off."

She swiped her eyes angrily. "Never. The only thing that kept all of us going was chasing down every lead and refusing to give up."

"I always admired your stubborn streak," I joked, squeezing her hand.

"One of my better qualities."

"Thank you for never giving up on me."

She smiled. "I'm always going to love you and need you in my life. Nothing is ever going to change that."

I gave her a slow, tender kiss, wishing I could do more. After three months, it didn't feel like I could hold or kiss her enough to heal either of us. Once this was all over, I vowed to myself we'd get the hell away from this life and start over. A life free of fucked up family ties, psychotic mobsters, and constantly worrying about living to see the next day.

"I'm not going anywhere, baby. Ever."

She smiled and rested her hand over my heart. Neither of us wanted to go to sleep yet, so I turned on the TV and we watched old movies for a while. Nonna's favorite movie, *A Streetcar Named Desire*, came on. She giggled when I told her about my grandmother's crush on Marlon Brando, but wasn't amused when I suggested the name Stella as one of her aliases.

By the time the credits rolled, she was sound asleep with her head resting in my lap. To my surprise, my own eyes felt heavy. I turned off the TV and lights, but the instant the room was dark, a tidal wave of anxiety tore through me. I was immediately back in the pitch black room where I'd spent my nights in agony while Franz slept comfortably and dreamed of ways to terrorize me. Quickly hitting the button on the remote, the light and sounds

from the TV returned, giving me immediate relief. Now too agitated to rest, I gazed at the walls and watched her for a while before
I could finally relax and let sleep overtake me.

I was nearly blinded the next morning by the first sunrise I'd
seen since before leaving Tampa. The sleeping beauty in my lap
snored softly as I brushed the hair back from her face. She looked
good with the red hair, but her natural dark brown was my favorite.
I really wanted to hear the story that led to the color change, even
if the amount of danger she'd placed herself in scared the shit out
of me.

"She shouldn't be sleeping in your bed," the bitchy nurse
sneered the moment she entered the room.

"Considering she's my wife and the woman who rescued me,
I'm going to let her sleep wherever the hell she wants," I snapped.
"Now, what do you need?"

She clenched her jaw but said nothing as she checked my vitals.
The paper cup with my medications was practically slammed into
the palm of my hand. With one last glare at both of us, she spun
on her heel and stomped out.

"Your wife, huh?" a gravelly voice asked from the door.

A very tall, thin redheaded man stood in the doorway. Based on
the wrinkles around his dark blue eyes and the white hair lightly
peppered amongst the red, he appeared to be in his mid-forties.
He narrowed his eyes and stared at me expectantly.

"I was speaking in the future tense. Who the hell are you?"

"I'm FBI Field Team Lead Barton Kane," he replied as he strolled
into the room. "Lissa's handler. You must be John."

"I am. I'll be honest, I'm not sure how to describe where I fit
into her life right now."

He nodded at her as she slept. "She does that with a lot of people. There are people who keep things close to the vest, and then there's her."

"Doesn't help I had to screw things up a couple times along the way."

"That's what I've heard."

I ran my fingers through her hair and brought my hand down protectively over her shoulder. "Look, if you're here as some sort of protective, fatherly thing..."

"I'd say she has enough fatherly 'things' going on right now, wouldn't you? I work with her, but I also consider her a friend. An important friend. You know how strong she is, what she's survived. You also know the amazing amount of shit she's been through in the past few years."

"I do, and if it were up to me, I'd get her out of it if I could. Judging by her exhaustion and the few things I've heard that she's done and been through the last three months, I'd love nothing more than to have her on the first plane going as far away from here as possible. Unfortunately, the trouble we're in would follow, and that would put more lives at risk."

"Glad we both understand the situation," he declared. "But I'm still going to advise you to not add to her complications. Whether or not she realizes it, she has a lot of friends at the Bureau who wouldn't take too kindly to her being hurt again."

"Message received loud and clear, Agent Kane. I promise I'm not here to hurt her. I know I have in the past, and it did a lot of damage. But the bottom line is I love her, and if I have to spend the rest of my life making it up to her, I will."

He smiled. "I believe you. And I'm hoping we can find Felton, so that's one less complication for you two. I really don't like the idea of a rogue CIA officer on the loose. Even if he is her..."

My hand shot up. "Please don't say it. Their connection is a very sore subject. She might look like she's asleep, but I don't want to risk her hearing it and going batshit. Unfortunately, he's not the one to worry about."

"Yes. Massimo is a whole other set of problems."

"Don't I know it. I'm hoping I can get her to lie low once we get to the base. She needs to rest and then we need to figure out where to go from here, but we'll see. We both know she's going to do what she wants to do."

"All too well," he chuckled. "Transport will be here in a couple hours to take you both to the airport."

"She's coming with me?"

"Yes. She's the agent assigned to oversee the transfer until custody is signed over to the base commander at Lejeune," he answered and then smiled. "After that, it's up to you to get her to sit still long enough to get some rest. Good luck."

"Thanks."

He glanced at his watch. "I'll be back before Transport gets here. I have a coffee date with my better half," he said before motioning toward her. "See if you can get yours to eat something when she wakes up. You don't want to be on a plane with her if she's hungry."

He left and as I looked down at her still peaceful face, her words from the previous night echoed in my ears. Not only did she love me, she needed me. For so long I'd hated that phrase, but hearing it from her gave me hope. I knew our relationship was far from being completely fixed, but I certainly felt more optimistic now.

She stirred. Her eyes slowly opened, widening slightly when they met mine. She looked around the room, blinking slowly.

"Good morning."

"Morning," she mumbled, yawning. "What time is it?"

"Just after seven. Barton has already been by and said he'd be back before Transport got here. He also said you aren't allowed on the plane unless you eat something."

"Something tells me you may have put your own spin on that, Mr. Martinetti," she giggled. "How did you sleep?"

"I slept okay."

"After how long?"

Dammit, there was no hiding or sugarcoating anything with her. Not when we shared all too similar pasts and not when she knew me as well as I knew her. She sat up and took her hand in mine before giving me a gentle smile. I didn't want to admit the fear and anxiety I felt over the simple act of turning off a light and the TV, but I knew too many people who suffered in silence.

"Three hours," I admitted, not meeting her eyes.

"I'm sorry, baby. Please wake me up next time, okay? I'm here for you. Always. If you want to talk about it, or if you want to talk about anything but what happened. Just say the word and I'm there. And there are plenty of people you can talk to at Lejeune if you want."

I nodded, ready to change the subject. "You should probably get something to eat soon. Barton seemed pretty adamant about not letting you fly if you're hungry."

"I'll make a deal with you, soldier. I'll eat breakfast if you call Nonna before we leave."

"Oh god, please no! I will do just about anything you want if you'll talk to her. Please. You know how she gets."

"As a matter of fact, I do. She scolded me for crying in her pasta dough. I almost got thrown out of the kitchen that day. And don't even get me started on how much food she shoved into both Lucas and me."

"You cooked with Nonna?"

"I did," she said. "Just the basics, mostly fettuccini and spaghetti noodles. We were going to work on a few others, but then we had to leave."

"She actually let you work in the kitchen with her? That's huge."

"Lucas likened it to getting a blessing from the Pope," she answered, rolling her eyes. She leaned forward and gave me a quick peck on the lips. "But you're still going to call her. I'm going to grab some food. Back in a jiff!"

I couldn't help but laugh when she hopped off the bed and dashed out of the room. Jokes aside, the fact Nonna invited her into the kitchen didn't surprise me. That woman took a shining to her from the moment they met, so much so that she told me on several occasions I damn well better make an honest woman of her. Little did she know I knew I'd marry her back in that ballroom in Bari.

Now we just needed to stay alive to make it a reality.

· · · ● · ● · · ·

"I used to smuggle flash drives and recording devices out of embassies and military bases," she huffed as she walked into the room and pulled a hidden paper bag out from under her jacket. "Now I'm smuggling food into a hospital."

"See, now you're torturing me because now all I can think of is frisking you."

"Eat your sandwich."

We arrived at the military base two days earlier, where I was placed in a special wing of the hospital. Four guards were posted at the door, and several other security measures were in place. I could see why she insisted on this base; it was nearly impenetrable.

I still had mixed feelings about being moved, especially when she told me where I'd be staying once released from the hospital in a few days. My anxiety nearly tripled when her old drill sergeant, Connor Menton, entered the room. He was one scary bastard. The last time we spoke, he held me at gunpoint after seeing how messed up she was after she escaped from Portland. I successfully convinced him to go into hiding and hoped our paths never crossed again.

The scary bastard hugged her and only released her after scolding her for looking like she hadn't slept in weeks. She laughed and they spoke privately for a moment. As they chatted, he glanced at me a few times and nodded. He patted her arm and then approached my bed. My eyes met hers, and she gave me a small smile.

"Heard you've been through some shit." He sat down next to the bed. "I've seen my fair share of shit, and I want you to know if you ever need someone to talk to, I'm more than happy to listen. And if you're ever tired of talking, I'm more than happy to enjoy the silence, too. Morning jog is at 0400 and we go to the shooting range every Thursday at 0900. Chow times are at 0600, 1200 and 1800. She tells me you're a pretty damn good cook, so you'll be cooking dinner at least once a week. When I cook, you're on dish duty. Questions?"

"No, sir."

"Jesus, you two and the 'sir' shit," he muttered. "The name's Connor. Calling me 'sir' makes me want to—"

"Connor!" she barked from the corner of the room.

He whipped his head over his shoulder. "Scoot. Go outside and get some sun, Lynch. You're too damn pale."

She made a face but left. "It's raining. And that's not my name!" she called back.

Connor and I spoke for a while. He told me about several of his experiences in Vietnam, and some stories he heard from his fellow soldiers and former students. I said little aside from the occasional nod, but it helped. The idea of staying at his house still scared the shit out of me, but at least I wasn't convinced he'd shoot me the second I came through the front door. She returned not long after he left with milkshakes for both of us.

On the way to North Carolina, she told me the full story about the deal she made with Barton, the couple from Seattle she helped for Georgia, and her trip to Russia. Yani wasn't known to be a very generous man and to hear he allowed her safe passage was surprising, but not nearly as much as learning how she stumbled into the one lead she needed in order to find me.

"You know, it could be argued that fate intervened when you helped her. What was her name? Annie?"

"Ari," she corrected. "And it was luck. Pure dumb luck that I helped a former hacker who had enough connections to figure things out."

"We're probably going to be in our nineties sitting on the couch in the rec room at the nursing home still debating this, you know. And I'm sure one of us will have forgotten to put our teeth in, too."

She laughed. "Assuming you survive long enough to make it to your nineties. And who's to say I haven't run off with one of the sexy male nurses at the nursing home by then? You know how much of a sucker I am for a hot guy in uniform."

"See, you've never seen me in uniform. As soon as you do, you know you'll never look at any other guy ever again."

Our laughter was cut short by a loud knock on the door. We both looked up to find Barton entering the room. I raised my eyebrows and noted the look of worry on her face.

"Agent Kane, what a surprise," I greeted with a smile until seeing the grave look on his face.

"Barton, what's wrong?"

"Lissa, can we talk privately for a moment? Maybe out in the hall?"

"Does it need to be private? You can discuss it in front of John."

"I'm afraid it's a security matter."

She looked uneasy. "Okay."

I squeezed her hand before she followed him to the hallway. I watched her face as he started talking and froze when I saw it pale and her arms drop to her sides. He said something else, which caused her to shake her head. He nodded and then left after patting her on the shoulder.

"Baby, what's wrong?"

"One of Felton's co-workers was found murdered in his house. Her name was Ginnie Matthews, and I'd worked with her several times over the years when he was in the field. The last time I talked to her was when I asked her to look for leads on your disappearance."

"Do they think Felton did it?"

"That's what it's looking like. Nobody can find him, so it's entirely possible. But that wasn't all," she answered, her voice hollow.

"Liss?"

She wiped her eyes. "Do you remember my friend Jake when we were in Portland? After I left, they moved to Georgia. Their house burned down."

My heart dropped. I helped Jake and his then fiancée go into hiding so my uncle wouldn't use them against her, but not before he beat the shit out of me. I hadn't even known where they settled once they left.

"Oh my god. Are they okay?"

She shook her head. "His wife got out just fine, but Jake was injured while he was getting their two-year-old son out. He's in the hospital with smoke inhalation and some nasty burns."

I gently pulled her closer, and she sat down on the bed. "I'm sorry. Do they have any leads?"

"All they know right now is it was definitely arson."

I noticed the conflicted expression on her face as she stared at the wall. She leaned back on the bed and closed her eyes. Clasping her hand so she knew I had her, we laid together quietly. After a while, she wrapped her arm around me and softly snored. I held her as close as my sore body would allow, worried about how she'd react once she fully digested the news.

She was leaning against the wall, staring out the window when I woke up a while later. The rain continued tapping against the glass, something she'd always found soothing. Looking at her face, however, she was anything but calm.

"You okay?"

She jumped and quickly swept her fingers under her eyes. "Not really."

"Something tells me I'm not going to like what you're about to say."

She approached the bed and took my hand, allowing me to pull her closer. "Probably not." She took a deep breath. "I'm going to disappear for a while. Throw everyone off, just in case anyone's tracking me. And also get some answers."

"To what questions?"

"See what I can find out about both cases, see if there's been any sign of Felton. Plus, I'm going to call in a couple favors."

I leaned against my pillow and watched her closely. She gripped my hand, and my eyes met hers. "I want you to stay," I stated, covering her hand with mine. "I want to be mad and say you're crazy for leaving. I want to beg you to stay here where you'll be safe. But I'd rather not fight when I know your mind is already made up."

"I want to stay, too, baby. But I need to find out what's going on. Ginnie's murder isn't surprising. She and Felton were colleagues and pretty good friends. The fire at Jake's house is another story. He has no involvement in any of this aside from being a friend of mine."

"I get why you want to do this, but there isn't a single thing you can say that will make me be okay with it. You've nearly gotten yourself killed every time we've gone our separate ways. The idea of you leaving again scares the shit out of me."

"I'm sorry," she whispered.

I pressed her forehead to mine. "This is the last time. Promise me this is the *last* time you walk away from me, Larissa."

"I promise."

We agreed to use disposable phones to keep in touch, calling each other every few days. Once I recovered, the plan was for me to head to D.C. and we'd figure out what to do next. She gave me the numbers of a few of her friends in case I needed anything and she couldn't be reached. We went over everything several times until we were both exhausted. She stretched out on her side next to me. The hospital staff gave up on keeping her out of the bed. After giving me a tender kiss goodnight, she leaned her head on my shoulder and soon we were both asleep.

The next morning was very subdued. Neither of us spoke much as we ate breakfast and she packed. We took a shower together and held each other long enough for our fingers to be pruned, but not nearly long enough to ease the ache in my chest.

"I still owe you a night you'll never forget, you know," I teased, leaning against the bathroom doorway as she dried her hair.

"We should probably take care of our psychotic relatives before worrying about that."

I walked behind her and wrapped my hands around her waist. "And when this is all over, I'm marrying you."

"Assuming we survive."

I spun her around, gently pushing her chin until she gazed into my eyes. "We will. After all the shit we've been through, I'll be damned if those two assholes are going to win. And besides, once I'm all better, you know you won't be able to say no to me anyway."

"There's the cocky bastard I know and love."

She helped me back into bed, and soon things were quiet between us again. A friend of hers would drive her to Wilmington, where she'd make her way to New York to talk to a couple of Seamus's friends.

"I still don't like this," I sighed as we laid together.

"I know."

"Don't do anything crazy."

She rolled her eyes. "The last crazy thing I did was blow up your gate and that was like six months ago."

"What do you call infiltrating a Russian dungeon and going on the lam with a fugitive you helped escape?"

"A deal to avoid prosecution."

"You're impossible."

"And you love that about me."

I covered her mouth with mine. She gasped a little in surprise, but then relaxed and placed her hand on my chest. I deepened the kiss, ignoring the ache in my sides. She moaned softly when my tongue teased hers and pulled me closer.

"Sorry if I hurt you," she whispered a moment later, breathless.

"You leaving this room is going to hurt far worse than any of my injuries."

"John."

"Last time, Larissa. We both agreed this is the last time."

"I swear."

"I need you alive and in one piece."

"I need you, too. If there's one thing I learned from all of this, it's just how much I love and need you."

A sharp knock on the door interrupted my reply. I looked up as a very petite Black woman entered the room. She introduced herself as Barton's wife, Yolanda, and firmly shook my hand. Based on the stories I heard about her, she was an amazing friend who had provided a lot of help over the past few weeks. The three of us chatted briefly while Liss gathered her bags, and all too soon she gave me a hug.

"Play nice with Connor and the other Marines," she joked.

"Stay safe. That's an order. I'll see you soon."

"Soon."

After telling each other we loved the other one last time, she hustled out of the room. Yolanda wrapped an arm around her shoulder as she rubbed her eyes, and they were gone. A cold emptiness entered my body the moment she left, as if a piece of my heart was ripped away. I collected myself and immediately knew what I had to do.

I dialed one of the disposable cell phones she left me. As it rang, my resolve hardened. I failed her the last time, but I'd never make that mistake again. My girl needed me. I heard the call connect and spoke before the other person said a single word.

"We need to talk."

Chapter 12

The Irish Council

Larissa

Walking out of that hospital room was one of the hardest things I'd ever done. The crack in my heart widened with every step. Yolanda wrapped her arm around me as we left, hustling me down the hall the moment she heard me sniff. Once we were in her car, the tears flowed freely as I sobbed into her shoulder for several minutes.

"You'll see him again soon," she soothed, patting my back.

"I know. I'm just getting sick of all this, you know? So ready for this shit to be over."

"Let's hope this trip will put you one step closer to that. How much does he know about the meeting?"

"Just that I'm meeting Eddie and Cal," I answered, taking a deep breath. "He'd be pissed if he knew the truth."

"You realize that he's going to know the truth anyway, so you're just delaying him being pissed, right?"

"Not helping, Yo," I said, laughing slightly.

No, I hadn't told him the whole story behind my decision to leave. Part of the reason was to keep him safe in case I was followed. And while I wanted to get more information about Ginnie's murder and the fire at Jake's house, I could've easily got updates if I'd stayed with him in North Carolina. The real reason I left was to call in favors long overdue.

In my defense, not telling him the whole plan was for his own good. He was understandably suspicious of Eddie and Cal when he first heard about them. My plan to go to New York didn't make him any happier, so I let him think it was a meeting just to see if either of them could help.

I paced behind the car as I dialed the disposable phone. We stopped at a coffee shop close to the base so I could make the call while Yolanda grabbed a coffee. We spoke briefly, only long enough to agree to meet at Cal's law firm in Midtown in two days.

Once we were back on the road, Yolanda told me what was known about the fire and the murder. Roberto Cantu, a Sardi family associate, was the primary person of interest for the fire at Jake's house. His rental car was found abandoned a mile away, the same as his hotel room. They had no idea where he went, to which I suggested they monitor Genovese hangouts in New York.

"Felton is the suspect in Ginnie's murder," she stated with no emotion. "Or at least the evidence at the scene was good enough to make him the suspect."

"What did they find?"

"Crumpled piece of paper in her hand with his fingerprints all over it. The paper was a copy of your DNA results. They also found several strands of his hair on her and his skin under her fingernails."

"Fuck," I muttered, closing my eyes.

The Felton Lynch I thought I knew, the man who raised me, told me he'd only ever killed when it was necessary for an assignment. I recognized and accepted that he'd always been cool and detached, but never imagined him killing in cold blood. I muttered under my breath, reminding myself this was the same man who fooled everyone, including the CIA, into thinking he was an ordinary man for close to thirty years. It was another reminder that he was capable of the same brutality committed by those I'd been sent out on various assignments to stop.

"Lissa?" she asked several minutes later.

"And nobody has any idea where he is."

"None."

"And nobody will until he's ready to show his hand. I'd be willing to bet he's still in D.C., but lord only knows how many hiding spots he has. Tell Barton to get eyes on Georgia's place and the surrounding area. He'll be keeping an eye on her. And Melanie."

"You think he's waiting for you to come back to D.C.."

"It was only a matter of time before I had to. I still haven't even given my official statement about John's rescue in Boston."

We fell silent and I gazed out the window. The scenery flew by at a dizzying pace, but my anxiety about getting to New York as quickly as possible made it feel like we were moving at a snail's crawl. Staring straight ahead, I focused on what needed to be done once I got there. I was hopeful it would go well, but I didn't know that for sure.

After a long and quiet trip, my bus arrived in Manhattan the next morning. I kept to myself and most people avoided the girl dressed all in black who kept her hoodie over her face and stared out the window the entire sixteen hours we were on the road. John would've given me a ration of crap for not sleeping, but after three months of near constant chaos and stress, the ability to sit and think about next to nothing for a short time was more relaxing than any amount of sleep. I simply peered out the window and watched the world go by, admiring the fall colors and the deep blue of the ocean.

Cal and Eddie tried to get me to stay at their respective places, but I turned them down and opted for a small hotel. A special guest was supposed to be at our meeting the next day, and I needed to make sure they arrived with no problems. As I fielded a second call from Eddie asking me to meet him at a diner by his house for dinner, I perched on the counter of the kitchenette in my room and watched the street below from the small window.

From my view on the second floor, a familiar face crossed the street with a casual gait that I knew all too well. Once across the street, they stopped and looked around, taking in the surroundings as if they hadn't seen them in a very long time. A puff of smoke rose from a newly lit cigarette and the figure entered the pool hall on the corner. My phone chimed, and my body relaxed. My contact inside the pool hall would watch and make sure my guest came to no harm.

The next morning, I dashed around the tiny bathroom hoping to get out the door on time. I wore a long-sleeved, dark gray wrap dress that stopped just above my knees and, after pulling on my black knee length stiletto boots and grabbing my jacket, I was out the door.

"Erin King to see Cal," I announced briskly at the reception desk.

I was shown into a small conference room around the corner, where a man in a dark blue suit stood in front of a wall of windows facing the skyline. As if sensing my presence, he turned. I hadn't seen him in nearly ten months, not since Christmas. His hair now had more gray than light brown and a few more wrinkles lined his face, but his pale blue eyes softened as soon as he saw me. He smiled and quickly crossed the room and extended his arms.

"There she is," he murmured, hugging me.

"Hey, Titus."

Part of me felt bad for not keeping in contact with him after I left Ireland. One reason was because I knew his reaction to John kidnapping me wouldn't have been great. However, once my true parentage was discovered, I feared his reaction when he learned I wasn't his blood relative. He was brash, grouchy, and sometimes a downright mean son of a bitch who helped me recover from one of the darkest periods of my life. The idea of losing him was just too painful.

"What is it?"

I studied his face, now etched with concern. Something in his voice raised a suspicion that made me feel foolish for not thinking of it sooner. My eyes closed, and I exhaled slowly. "Did you know? About my dad?"

He hung his head. "Lissi."

"You knew."

"I knew. Shortly before he died, he called me. That's when he gave me the info about your trust fund. He told me everything."

My eyes burned. "And you never thought to tell me? You didn't think that was something I needed to know?"

"Listen to me, Larissa. Yes, my brother told me everything. He told me he wasn't your father. And then he told me how he stole from the Irish mob to set up a thirty million dollar trust fund for you."

"And also a ten million dollar trust fund for you with his legal money," Cal interjected as he entered the conference room. He didn't seem surprised to see my guest, nodding at Titus before he continued. "He also made a deal to inform on the mob to avoid prosecution so he could come home to you and your mother every night."

"It didn't matter to him. It never did. You were always his little fire," Titus added, hugging me again. "And I assure you it sure as hell never mattered to me."

Closing my eyes, I let his words wash over me. In that moment, I felt foolish for doubting he'd accept me. He'd never treated me as anything other than his kin, freely telling me about the trust fund I never knew I had and helping me to find the light when I came back to Ireland still mired in the dark. His arm tightened around me once more before he turned to the door of the conference room.

"Definitely a pleasant surprise, Titus. Hope you've been doing well. Lissi, good to see you," Cal beamed, pulling me into a hug as soon as Titus released me. "How's the boyfriend?"

"Boyfriend?" Titus barked. "Please tell me it's not that Italian shithead!"

"Please tell me the Italian shithead is the same one whose house you blew up?" Eddie chuckled as he wandered into the room. He nodded to Cal and stopped short when he saw Titus.

"I didn't blow up his house," I hissed. "Just one of his gates and the building holding his weapons."

Titus's eyes were like saucers. "You did what?"

"Later," I whispered.

Cal closed the conference room door and we all sat around the table. He clapped both Eddie and Titus on the shoulders as he passed them and took his own seat. "So what's going on?"

"In short, a cluster fuck," I answered, motioning toward my uncle. "I'm sure you guys are wondering why I asked Titus to come. I need help."

"Tell us everything," he said. "All of it, no matter how minor it is."

I drew a deep breath and started at the beginning, my disastrous assignment in Portland. For the next hour, I spared no detail. From Gio's death to the discovery that Soren spent the last thirty years masquerading as Felton Lynch, I brought all three men up to speed on the entire situation. Cal remained quiet, as he knew some of the more explosive details. Eddie sat dumbstruck as he absorbed everything. Titus, on the other hand, was absolutely enraged.

"That fucking traitorous bastard!" he thundered, pounding his fist on the table. "He was like a brother to Seamus! Those two were practically inseparable until his family moved away!"

Eddie turned to Cal. "Was Soren the one you told me about?

"Yes, he was," he answered. "He killed Mickey's brother."

"Jesus! That fucker carved up Phillip like a bloody Thanksgiving turkey!"

Cal held up his hand. "So we need to come up with a plan. My guess is eventually Massimo will head here to deal with Felton, and then Lissi."

"Right. First priority is protection. I'll have three of my best men on a plane tomorrow morning. I won't leave here until I know she's protected," Titus stated.

"Titus, you don't have to," I began.

"Stop right there, missy," he growled, pointing a gnarled finger at me. "I don't care how many people you've killed or how many ways you can kill a man with your bare hands. I made a promise to my brother to protect you with my life. You will always have at least one person watching you. End of story."

I rolled my eyes. "We'll see."

"Yes, we certainly shall," he shot back. "I'll also have a crew head over so they're here and ready when that sick bastard shows up."

Resigned, I sighed deeply. "Thank you."

"I'll talk to my contacts in the gang task force," Eddie offered. "See if they've heard anything. If not, they'll want to know we might have some shit headed our way."

Titus looked up from his phone. "Either of you know a place where a dozen men could lie low temporarily?"

I smirked. "What, Fiona doesn't have room for them?"

"How do you know—"

"I have my ways, namely the Madison Hotel. I watched you head over to the pool hall last night and figured it was to say hello to your favorite bar owner. Your room might even be a couple of doors down from mine. Second floor, right? I am a spy, after all."

"And a damn good one."

The four of us spoke for a while longer, making plans and formulating back-up plans and contingencies. We each had additional leg work and phone calls to make once the meeting was over. I was to call Barton and let him know about the impending arrivals from Ireland. A bunch of my uncle's crew would make him more than anxious. Titus wasn't a mobster per se, but he had a lot of connections, and his business dealings were anything but legal.

"So I think it's important that we route all communications about this through me," Cal cut in. "That way, it just looks like client communications. And since Lissa's trust fund is about to become active, it's absolutely believable."

"Good thinking," Eddie replied. He dug into his wallet and tossed a single dollar bill on the table. "I'll even pay the retainer."

We all laughed. Eddie checked his watch and announced his need to get back to the precinct. He gave me a hug and shook Cal's and Titus's hands. Titus whispered something in his ear, and after a few moments, Eddie nodded and whispered his reply. After promising to be in touch, he left.

Titus put his arm around my shoulder. "Got time for lunch with an old man?"

"As long as you have her back here by four," Cal replied.

At my confused look, Titus's arm tensed. "Because you staying at the Madison Hotel isn't safe. You're staying at his condo."

"As if I could really object if you're both on the same side," I muttered. "Let's go, old man."

We went to the diner around the corner from the office. After ranting that I was too skinny, he ordered us both a milkshake while we waited for our food. We settled into an awkward silence, neither of us sure where to begin with all the questions and things that needed to be said.

He fidgeted with his straw. "So, you and the Italian shithead?"

"I know how thrilled you'd be if I would've fallen into Thomas's arms back in Doolin, but it was never going to happen. And I know you hate John, but we love each other. End of story."

"You're damn right I hate him! You nearly died because of him and his family. Twice."

"And when his uncle tried to drown me in the Adriatic, he dove in and saved me. I know you'll probably never trust him, and I don't expect you to understand what he and I have. But after everything we've been through, we're both still standing. Together."

"Why did you blow up his...whatever it was you blew up?"

"He drugged me and I woke up in Italy. Not the most romantic method of whisking me away. I'll admit, shooting him with the bean bag round might have been overkill."

"Jesus, you two are made for each other," he muttered, grinning slightly. "All right. The shithead can live for now. I promise I won't try to kill him if you ever bring him with you to visit. And you damn well better visit once all this is over."

"I promise I'll come visit. You'll just have to deal with being around him because leaving him at home won't be an option. He and that brother of mine are annoyingly overprotective."

"I seem to remember you accusing me of the same thing several times."

"Yeah, yeah, yeah," I grumbled, rolling my eyes.

His face turned serious. "How did you feel when you found out the truth about your dad? I won't apologize for keeping it from you, but I'm sure it was a very nasty shock."

"Seamus Donovan is my father. End of story. Felton might have raised me, and for that I'll be grateful, but I'll never forgive all the lies and other messed up shit he's done."

"The look in your eye and the steel in your voice right now is why it never mattered to any of us. You sounded exactly like Seamus did the night he told me everything. You may not be our blood, but you sure as shit are our kin. You're a Donovan, and nothing will ever change that."

"Did he know it was Felton?"

He sighed. "If he did, he certainly kept it quiet, and I can understand why. Soren Luccetti was a fucking butcher. If it were ever to get out that you were his kid, you would've had a target on your back. Worse, if he ever found out you were his, he would've tried to take you away because Felton's a possessive bastard. All I know is your mom got really spooked after your sixth birthday. I'm willing to bet that's when Felton figured out the truth and confronted her or Seamus. It all went to shit after that."

I picked at my fries in silent debate before I asked the question that had been gnawing at me for almost three years, ever since John spoke the name in a shitty warehouse in Portland. The same name my dad ordered me to keep secret and not tell another soul. "Who's Aednat?"

He tensed. "Where did you hear that name?"

"Tell me who she is first."

"Aednat Leary was Felton's maternal grandmother. Your dad spent a couple of summers at her house with Felton when we were kids. They wound up forming a very close bond. Probably the first woman to show him unconditional love since lord knows our drunk of a mum couldn't be bothered to care about us. Now, how do you know that name?"

"It's my middle name. My real one. The one my dad told me never to tell anyone."

He grinned. "That bastard knew the whole time Felton was your dad and hid you in plain sight. Fucking brilliant."

"What?"

"You look just like your mom and Seamus had blue eyes, so nobody ever had reason to suspect a thing. Knowing Seamus, he'd see it as giving the bastard the middle finger for cheating on Sera."

"Why didn't Seamus just turn him in? He could've easily had him locked up for spying on the CIA."

"Seamus was probably willing to leave well enough alone as long as the truth remained hidden. After you and your mom came into his world, all he wanted was a simple life. That's why he made the deal with the CIA to begin with," he answered. "He always was the more levelheaded between the two of us. I probably would've blown the fucker away long before he started sniffing around."

"If Felton had been working with the Sardis all this time, is it wrong of me to think he had something to do with their deaths?"

He stared at his glass. "That one I just don't know. Telling the Sardi boys would've almost guaranteed both yours and Sera's deaths. There's absolutely no way he would've put either of you at risk like that. He was damn near obsessed with your mum, and it's obvious how much he cares about you."

"Sometimes he had an odd way of showing it. I understand why he wanted me to know how to defend myself, but there wasn't a lot of warmth in that house. Sometimes I felt more like a burden than anything else."

"I'm not asking you to understand him. You never will. What I will say is Felton had an extremely messed up childhood and no doubt it messed up how he interacts with people. It doesn't excuse anything, but it helps to explain why he is the way he is."

I nodded silently. Felton always seemed unable to handle human emotions, whether it was his own or someone else's. I had to give him credit for at least trying when I was a kid. Looking back, all the training and activities he insisted on gave us something to have in common. That didn't fully explain some of the lingering questions I had about his actions over the past few years.

"The one thing I'll never understand is if he supposedly cared about me so much that he kidnapped John to bargain his life for mine, why the fuck was he so willing to serve me up to Gio three years ago?"

"We may never know. The only person who could tell you that would be Felton himself."

"Of course," I muttered.

"I'm sorry. This is one hell of a mess you've found yourself in."

"I have to believe I'll live long enough to see the end."

"If the three of us have anything to say about it, you will. I promise you that."

We sat and talked until his phone rang. The roll of his eyes told me it was Cal, and we needed to head back to his office. He was in no rush as we made our way down the street, strolling with his arm protectively around me. All too soon, we trudged through the lobby and back into the elevator to the fifty-sixth floor.

"Finn and Thomas will be here tomorrow night. Aiden should be along in a couple of days," he stated as he read a message on his phone.

"Really, Titus? You're sending Thomas? It wasn't bad enough you made the lad stay with his mom so he could babysit me for you in Doolin?"

His eyes narrowed and he clucked his tongue against the roof of his mouth. "So, lover boy *was* there spying on you before he made his move. Thomas thought he saw him around the village that morning and called me. Good thing I gave him his description or he would've shot the bastard when he brought you home that afternoon."

"Titus!"

"I could give two shits if lover boy likes him or not. It might be a good way to remind him of what he damn near lost. As for the other two, they're good lads, so please be gentle with them. If they give you any shit, they're just following my orders to keep you safe. One of them needs to know where you are at all times. Can you do that for me?"

"Not like I have much choice," I muttered.

"Not really, no." He leaned against the wall. "What's next for you? Are you heading back to wherever you have the shithead stashed?"

"TBD. I don't want to stay in one place for very long, so I'll wait until your men get here and then I'll probably hit the road again. I imagine your henchmen will report back regularly?"

"Yes, in that annoyingly overprotective manner you love so much," he quipped.

Cal invited Titus to join us for dinner, but he declined, saying he was meeting Fiona. After ordering me several times to not give his men any trouble, which included a long and specific list of things I wasn't allowed to do, he gave me a bone-crushing hug and left. Not long afterward, Cal and I used the private elevator to go down to the parking garage.

We arrived at the executive condo he used when he was in town. After showing me to the guest room, he excused himself to change and start cooking dinner. After changing into a pair of black yoga pants and one of John's old sweaters I stole from his closet before leaving Verona, I grabbed my FBI phone and dialed.

"How'd it go?" Barton answered.

"Don't be surprised if you hear chatter about an increase in Irish activity in the next couple of weeks. Titus is in."

"Is he sticking around? If so, that could be problematic since he still has a couple of federal warrants out on him."

"No, he's only here until my new security guards arrive and then he's heading back. Three days maximum," I answered. "Yolanda told me you were looking into witness protection."

"I'm looking at all the options. Anything and everything to bring this shit to an end."

"The only endgame for Massimo and Marco is death. None of us will be safe otherwise."

"What about Felton?"

I considered my answer. "Honestly? I don't know. Besides, witness protection is a moot point. If they kill me, I won't need it. If I survive, there's no way I'm sticking around."

"Let's just work on finding Felton first and then we'll go from there. How much longer are you in New York?"

"Three days at most," I answered. "Once my security arrives, I'm going to go to ground for a bit. Don't worry, I'll check in every couple days. If you need to get a hold of me, get a hold of Cal."

"I can't even begin to describe how much the idea of you going into hiding worries me."

"I know, but he's hiding out in D.C. waiting for me to come back, and I'm not ready for him to find me yet."

He sighed. "Be careful, Agent Donovan. That's a direct order."

"Understood, sir."

My next call was to Lucas, whose shitty mood only got worse when I told him my plan. After I pointed out it was the best I could do to throw Felton off, his grousing lessened only slightly. I gave him Cal's info and promised I'd be careful before hanging up.

I flopped on the bed and closed my eyes to stop the tears threatening to fall. It had been six weeks since I last saw my family, and talking to Lucas only drove home how much I missed them. This had to end soon. John and I had the next chapter of our lives to move on to, and a family waiting for us. I reminded myself to keep my eye on the prize: a new life where we didn't have to worry about someone trying to kill us.

"Lissi, dinner's ready!" Cal called from the kitchen.

"I'll be there in a minute," I called back, my red phone held to my ear.

"John's Auto Repair," the deep voice I'd grown to love so much answered.

"Well, thank god. I've got a Buick that isn't running right."

"Hey, baby. Where are you?"

"I'm at Cal's. Did you get all settled in?"

He was released from the hospital that morning, and would be staying at Cal's house as he finished his rehab. He'd been nervous at first about staying with the old man, but his anxiety eased after their conversation when we first arrived. I never pressed for details of the discussion, but I knew Connor was one of the best people to help him work through the after-effects of his time in captivity.

"Yep. I'm unpacked, and Connor's in the living room yelling at the football game," he answered.

"That's pretty normal for him. When it's your turn to make dinner, steaks, and Jameson will win him over every time."

"I'll keep that in mind."

"How are you feeling?"

"Still sore, though the lung seems to be better. Respiratory rehab and physical therapy start next week. Other than that, I'm good aside from being surrounded by a bunch of crazy Marines."

"I'm sure you'll win them over with that charming wit of yours," I giggled. "It sure worked on me."

"And here I thought it was my animal magnetism."

"That grew on me after a while, too." My voice lowered. "I miss you."

"I miss you, too. What have you been able to find out so far?"

"Felton's the prime suspect in Ginnie's murder. Cops are looking for one of your uncle's lackeys for questioning in Jake's case."

"What about the favor you were going to call in? Wasn't that why you were meeting with Cal and Eddie?"

"It went well. Very well," I answered vaguely.

"You gonna tell me the entire story now?"

"You're not going to like it."

"Why do you say that?"

"Because I met with Titus."

Dead silence. After what felt like a small lifetime, I heard a heavy sigh. "And you didn't tell me because?"

"Because I know how much you hate him and you'd freak the hell out if I told you before I left."

The two men shared a mutual and understandable hatred for one another. Apparently, John had helped to break up one of Titus's gun running operations a couple years before he retired from the CIA. My uncle escaped, and several months later he got his revenge when he burned down a restaurant that John bought. Since it's such a fucking small world, the debacle with John and I only ensured that hatred would probably never diminish.

"I don't hate him, not anymore," he breathed after a few moments. "He was there for you when I wasn't, took care of you. And I know he hates me because I hurt you."

"He's coming around. Said he won't try to shoot you when we come to visit."

"Well, that's comforting. What else did he say?"

"He's sending a crew to help in case shit with Massimo comes to a head. And he's also sending me three personal bodyguards."

"You sound so thrilled with that last part. Honestly, I'm glad to hear it."

"Of course you are," I grumbled.

"You're not coming back here, are you?"

"I need Felton to worry about where I am for a while, so no. When things don't go as planned for a long enough time, he gets impulsive. When he gets impulsive, he makes mistakes."

"Only when it comes to you."

"Only when it comes to me," I confirmed. "So call Cal if you need to get a hold of me right away. That way it looks like client communications, since he's the administrator of my trust fund."

He sighed. "Just so long as I know where to meet you when I'm out of here. You've handled this on your own long enough."

"I promise."

"As long as you're promising things…"

"Nice try, Gianni."

He laughed. "I love you, Larissa Donovan."

"I love you too."

"Soon, baby. This will all be over soon. I promise you."

With my eyes closed, I said a silent prayer that he was right.

Chapter 13

Home

Larissa

TV AND MOVIES MAKE going into hiding look like a staycation in a crappy hotel. No experience needed; just make sure you use cash and a disposable cell phone and you're golden. The reality is quite the opposite, of course, more like a cross between an extreme version of dress up and hide and seek. Only if someone catches you, you won't be the one counting and yelling "ready or not, here I come".

My uncle spent more years off the grid than me, which meant his men knew what the hell they were doing. I had mixed feelings about Titus sending three of his best men, but I knew how arguing about it would go. Thomas agreed to watch over Cal, much to my relief. The next day, I hit the road with Finn and Aiden.

We headed to Atlanta, where Jake was transferred to a burn unit better suited to treat his injuries. The bandages and burns on his arms, right shoulder and face looked scary, but he seemed in good spirits as he talked to the nurse pushing his wheelchair in the elevator. He smiled as he told her how much he looked forward to visiting an old friend in North Carolina once he was released. As he talked, he didn't notice the anonymous couple behind him, Aiden and me in disguise. The nurse wheeled him back to his room on the fourth floor, and I made a mental note to tell Connor the McGuire family would visit in the future.

From Atlanta, we bounced from city to city for the next few weeks. I checked in with Barton, Cal, John, and Lucas regularly, which basically meant I was calling one of them every night. We were on the road to Richmond when Barton officially called me back to FBI headquarters. The logistics for getting me back into the city felt extreme, but Barton was quick to point out Felton was still at large. We also learned he wasn't the only person looking for me.

Surprising no one, Massimo was headed stateside. Felton was his primary target, but I was also still on his radar. Several of his associates were also expected to travel stateside, though we didn't know how many. Upon hearing the news, my travel arrangements changed and two days later, I was snuck into Georgia's neighborhood in the cab of a garbage truck.

Georgia was in Seattle, so her house was empty. I didn't like the idea of using it, but Barton assured me that security measures were in place. The basement, used by Georgia's son before he left for college, was like a small apartment and quite comfortable.

"Any problems during the trip?" John greeted when I could finally call.

"None. All this prep almost feels like overkill now that I'm here. Even though I know it's not."

"Where are Titus's men?"

"Thomas is in Boston with Cal. Finn and Aiden are watching the house. How are you doing?"

"Down to one rehab session a week. I should be done and out of here soon."

He'd been out of the hospital for nearly six weeks since the rescue. The doctors were optimistic, but I was still nervous because his injuries were so damn bad. I felt horrible for not being there, as if I abandoned him when he needed me most. He reassured me several times he understood, but I knew I wouldn't feel better until we were together again.

"I'm glad," I whispered, trying to keep my voice from cracking.

"Soon, baby. And when I get there, I'm going to hold you and never let go."

"You better not," I said, wiping my eyes.

"Get some rest. I love you."

"I love you too."

We hung up and I curled up under the plush down comforter. It had been a long, tiring day and the next day wouldn't be any better. I was scheduled to be debriefed and record my formal statement about the events in Boston and what I knew about Felton Lynch and his crimes. All the documents Lucas sent were turned in as evidence, but it was now up to me to connect everything together. Eventually, John would also need to give his statement, something he hadn't been too keen to discuss the few times I brought it up. Refusing to give this mess any further thought, I rested my eyes and thought back to happier times with John in Verona.

I knew unraveling the mystery of Soren and how he turned into Felton would be long and difficult, but nothing prepared me for the mountain of file folders that awaited me when I walked into the meeting room that had been turned into the command center for the case. As if the volume of the evidence wasn't intimidating enough, Hannah Myers-Nelson, department head, and Felton's boss, sat at the table and watched my testimony with narrowed eyes. She watched me closely, as if scanning for any hint that I was trying to cover anything up. I held firm, returning her gaze with determination. I had nothing to hide. Well, aside from killing a rogue CIA officer in Miami.

And on it went for the next four days. Hannah's questioning started on the third day, asking about specific assignments Felton assigned me and the people I worked with. I learned several team members I worked with in various locations, including Osaka, Rome, and Prague, were now under investigation for possible criminal connections. After everything I knew about my assignment in Prague, I wasn't surprised. However, learning how often members of my team spied on me and reported my every movement to him left me speechless.

"You okay?" Barton asked as we finished up the fourth day of questioning.

"Just when I think I have my head wrapped around everything with this shit, something new and weirder pops up," I sighed, shaking my head.

"He's been doing this for the last thirty years. We've probably barely scratched the surface, and we already have enough to put him away for a couple of lifetimes."

"And tomorrow we'll probably learn something weirder, like he's actually from Jupiter or hoards off brand baseball cards."

He patted my shoulder. "Get some rest. I imagine we'll need it."

A few hours later, I was curled up on the bed in Georgia's basement eating mac and cheese and watching old movies on TV. I called Lucas and heard Nonna laughing hysterically in the background. He told me they'd had to visit the clinic because he fell at the farmer's market. I couldn't figure out why that would make her laugh so hard until she grabbed the phone and told me he was trying to pick up some tourist and fell off the pier, injuring his ankle when he landed on the beach below. She told me he was fine and after promising her both John and I were okay, she hung up.

Next, I called Titus, who sounded extremely distracted. When I pressed him, he assured me he was fine, but one of his suppliers was hassling him. To make matters worse, two of the wrestlers in his illegal fighting ring had been murdered. The last bit of news was a red flag to me, but he promised it was unrelated to my "Italian infestation" as he called it.

My last call was to John. Our calls were a nightly habit now that I was no longer traveling. We'd tell each other about our day, in my case, as much as I could, since most of it was confidential. His voice was the last one I heard before going to sleep, and while it wasn't the same as falling asleep in each other's arms, it was enough for the moment.

The next day was a Friday, and it seemed everyone was looking forward to the coming weekend. Even Hannah seemed subdued that morning and drank more than a few cups of coffee. I took little comfort in the knowledge this case was weighing on us all, and there was still so much more to unearth. It had been a long week and everyone was tired of the topic of Felton Lynch, so we all agreed to wrap up early. Barton and Hannah left not long after we adjourned, but I stuck around and started working on my Boston statement. I was nearly done when Georgia called.

"I leave for a couple weeks and the weather goes completely crazy!" she said.

"They're predicting snow in the next few days."

"I saw that. Had I known, I would've just headed for San Diego."

"So, you're back in town finally?"

"I am, but I don't know for how long. You still staying at the house?"

"Yep."

"Well, grab some wine on your way home and we'll make a night of it," she offered. "How much longer do you think you'll be?"

I glanced at the clock on my laptop. "I could probably be there in about an hour. Sound good?"

"It's a date!"

Of course, there was a line at the grocery store, but that was my fault. On my way to the wine aisle, I wandered over to the frozen food section and found a tub of triple chocolate ice cream. And then my path to the checkout took me past the bakery, where the garlic bread was freshly baked. By the time I grabbed my bags, my simple trip for a bottle of wine developed into a buying spree of comfort food and snacks I hadn't had in a long while.

I trudged through the alley to Georgia's backyard and quietly snuck into the basement. Movement from upstairs told me she was in the kitchen and probably finishing up dinner. Immediately feeling bad for being late, I barreled toward the door leading upstairs.

"Honey, I'm home!" I sang out, stopping dead in my tracks when I rounded the corner.

Soft light bounced off the walls of the kitchen from at least a dozen candles around the room. The smell of food was intoxicating, but not nearly as much as the man who turned from the stove and grinned. I inhaled sharply, feeling as if I'd been trapped inside and was taking my first deep breath of fresh air in an eternity. Our eyes met, and I drifted closer, petrified I was dreaming but not wanting to awaken if that was the case.

"Hey," John murmured.

"You're here," I choked out, absentmindedly setting the bags on the island in front of me.

"I'm here," he confirmed. He moved closer and gently grazed my cheek with his knuckle. "You're not dreaming."

"Oh my god." My eyes filled with tears as my hand slid to his chest, where I felt the solid wall of muscle and the warmth his body always radiated.

He covered my hand with his and wrapped his other arm around me, pulling me against his body. I hugged him tightly and listened to the sound of his heart in my ears like it was a chorus of angels. The same heart that was in danger of stopping forever almost two months ago now beat with a steady rhythm that brought peace to my own.

We stood pressed together for several minutes before he stepped back. Confused, I gazed up at him and he cradled my head in his hand. The moment our lips met, I felt the same sparks as the first time. The kiss started slowly, but as soon as his tongue teased mine, I moaned softly and clutched him tighter to me. After a minute, he stepped away and inhaled deeply.

"Dinner first, and then dessert," he scolded playfully. "Why don't you go change into something more comfortable? You look like you've been in front of a grand jury all day."

"Close."

I raced downstairs and changed into my black pajama shorts and his gray sweater. The hardwood floors were cold, so I slid a pair of socks over my feet. "Remember, you said comfortable," I called out once I returned. "So no complaining."

His eyes widened and traveled the length of my body. As soon as I was near, he kissed my forehead and hoisted me onto the counter next to the stove. "Is that my sweater, Miss Donovan?"

"I might have grabbed a thing or two from your closet."

"Something wrong with your clothes?"

I smiled and brought his forehead to mine. "They didn't smell like you."

He gave me a tender kiss and we stayed wrapped in each other's arms before he turned back to the stove. His hand grazed my bare leg as he tended to the sauce. I hopped down and helped him slice the last of the ingredients he needed.

"So, how did you convince Georgia to let you in? What did it cost you? Fingerprints? Hair sample?" I joked as he stood behind me.

"I had to promise we would limit our evening...activities to the basement," he whispered in my ear, trailing slow kisses across my neck.

"If you keep that up, we're gonna have a hard time keeping to that agreement. And I was promised dinner first."

"As my lady wishes."

Fifteen minutes later dinner was served, which meant he mixed everything in a bowl and grabbed two forks. He lifted me up on the island and placed the bowl in my lap, and we scooped out forkfuls of noodles and sauce. When the garlic bread was ready, we simply tore off pieces and dipped them in the bowl. It wasn't the most graceful way to eat a meal, but as we continued to eat, talk and laugh, it was the furthest thing from our minds. We talked about my adventures on the road and life with Connor during his recovery. We agreed not to talk about our troublesome family members. There would be plenty of time for worries and plans, but not that night.

"So I think there's still the small matter of you stealing my clothes that needs to be discussed," he said once we finished eating.

"Hey, if it bothers you so much, you can borrow one of my sweaters."

"Not quite what I had in mind."

He gently pulled me to the counter's edge, and wrapped his arms around my waist. I buried my face in his neck, inhaling his scent. After six months of pure hell, we survived it all. I felt his hand travel under my sweater and his fingers lightly caress my lower back.

"All I care about is that you're finally here," I whispered.

"And here to stay."

Our lips crashed together. I wrapped my legs around his waist and moaned softly when his lips traveled to my neck. My hands tugged at his shirt until he shook his head and scooped me up in his arms, laughing at my sounds of protest.

"Baby, I love you, but Georgia scares me," he said. "And I'm pretty sure she'd know if we did anything on this counter."

As soon as we got downstairs, he kicked the door closed with his foot and sat me near the end of the bed. I pulled him to me and yanked the shirt from his waistband. He chuckled softly as I quickly unbuttoned it and tossed it on the floor. I scooted to the middle and motioned for him to come closer. His eyes darkened as he crawled across the bed.

He gripped my hips. "Mine. And I don't mean the sweater."

I pulled it over my head and tossed it aside, leaving me in just my black lace bra and black pajama shorts. I fell onto the bed and he smiled as he hovered above me. Lowering his head down to my stomach, he trailed kisses and soft bites around my belly button. My skin ignited when he tugged at my shorts before sliding them down my thighs. I protested softly when I realized my panties were still on.

"I know, baby." He gave me another tender kiss. "But it's been six months since I've seen your body and three years since the last time we made love. I'm going to savor every second of this." I caressed his cheek and his hand moved to my panty line. "Every moan." His fingers traveled past the damp fabric and caressed my overheated skin, causing me to shudder. "Every shiver."

"John," I whispered, moving my hips to tease his hand lower.

"Every soul shaking kiss." He unclasped my bra and trailed kisses between my breasts once it fell away. His thumb teased my nipple, causing it to pebble. My skin tingled, needing to feel his touch everywhere.

"Please," I moaned out as he teased the other nipple.

"Let's see if you're as sweet as I remember," he breathed and slid my panties down my legs.

He tossed my legs over his shoulders, and I couldn't hold back the loud moan when his tongue flicked across my clit. My back arched as he licked and sucked the length of my core, and when he slid one finger inside, my breathing grew heavier.

"Baby, please," I panted.

"Just as sweet as I remember," he breathed and kissed both inner thighs. "I think I've tortured you long enough."

"Then why are your pants still on?" I whined, sitting up and tugging on the button of his jeans.

"Because the minute I take them off, I won't be able to control myself." He kissed between my breasts. "And I need to keep my wits about me long enough to make sure I grab condoms before we go any further."

"We don't need them," I panted as his tongue tortured my nipple. "I'm on birth control."

"Someone's going to get their ass spanked for not telling me sooner."

My hand slipped inside his boxer briefs. He closed his eyes and moaned once my fingers closed around him and gently stroked. I unbuttoned his jeans and pulled them down. His cock looked painfully swollen once it emerged. I licked my lips and dropped to my knees.

"Not yet," he grunted, touching the back of my head.

He laid on the bed and gestured for me to straddle him. His hands grabbed my hips and held me in place when I leaned forward and kissed him deeply. I rubbed my drenched pussy on his erection, earning a hungry growl from him before moving me to sit upright. Cupping my breasts in his giant hands, he massaged them, tweaking each nipple with his thumbs, and alternating licks and small bites. I threw my head back and moaned, grinding my hips against his.

We both moved in a frenzy. He held me while I lowered myself onto his cock, gasping at the deep intrusion. His hands roamed my sides as I slowly moved up and down his thickness. Once we found our rhythm, I closed my eyes and let my body take over.

"You feel like heaven," he moaned. "And you look like a goddess. My goddess."

"John," I whimpered.

I leaned forward and rode him harder, crying out when the new angle hit a place deep inside that hadn't been touched in forever. He gripped my ass with both hands and thrust upward. Placing my hands on his chest to steady myself, I felt my climax building. White flashes danced in my eyes seconds later when my body exploded. He slowed our pace as I rode out the waves of pleasure and held my body to his when he let out a loud groan and buried his face in my neck as he came deep inside me.

We stayed locked in our embrace until our breathing slowed. After a few motions, we were lying under the covers. His hands caressed my side, stopping at my ribcage. I mirrored his action, tracing my fingers over the same spot.

"We have matching scars," I murmured. "Kind of a messed up thing to have."

"It is, but we're not exactly a conventional couple. I don't think I've ever actually taken you out on a proper date."

"Not unless you count crashing what you thought was a date between Jake and me."

"Hey, I took you home that night, so I'm not complaining," he laughed. His face turned serious. "I always wanted to take you out somewhere. It was always just too risky."

"Yeah, something about gunfire breaking out during the appetizers doesn't sound very romantic. And these are much better than a matching tattoo."

"Agreed. Matching surgery scars are much cooler."

I giggled. "Neither a spleen between?"

We laughed and settled into a comfortable silence. He swept the hair out of my face and I glanced down and saw the cuts and scars smattered all over his chest. Shaking my head sadly, I bent down and lightly kissed each one until I arrived at the tattoo over his heart. Tears filled my eyes at the thin white line slashed across the hummingbird and the round scar from what looked like a cigar burn over the flower.

"Look at me." He cupped my face with both hands and wiped the tears from my eyes. "We're damaged and we both have our scars, but we're here. Together."

"I'm so sorry."

"You and I are all that matters tonight. No worrying about anything else."

Closing my eyes, I laid my head down on his chest and listened to his heartbeat. "I'm not dreaming this, right? You're really here? Part of me is scared that any moment now I'm going to wake up alone again."

"If you were dreaming, you wouldn't feel this," he said, pinching my ass.

"Ow! Fucker!" I yelped, smacking his shoulder.

He wrapped his arms around my waist. "If you were dreaming, would I be laying here with you in my arms talking about marrying you?"

"Maybe," I whispered, trying to keep my heart from racing.

"And if this was a dream, I'd simply be asking." He kissed my forehead. "Marry me, Larissa Donovan."

"If you're not asking, then what makes you think I'll agree?" I challenged, raising an eyebrow.

"Because I've talked about marrying you since I brought you to Verona and you've never said no. Because you literally chased every lead from one end of the earth to the other looking for me, the same as I did for you. And because there's nobody else on this goddamned planet either of us could ever think about spending the rest of our lives with."

"John," I whispered, trying not to cry. "Yes."

I brought my lips to his and kissed him, softly at first until his hands grabbed my hips and ground them hard against him. My skin ignited at his touch and my lips moved harder and faster against his. I trailed kisses down his neck and across his chest, savoring the taste of his warm skin.

"You said yes, right?" he panted when we both came up for air. "That was a 'yes' you whispered just now?"

"Yes. A thousand times yes. I don't know when or where, but we're getting married."

"The timing is less than ideal thanks to Felton and Massimo. But after they're gone, it's just you and me and the rest of our lives."

"You make it sound so simple."

"It's simple enough to worry about it later," he said, rolling me onto my back and smirking. "Tonight I have a fiancée I promised to ravish a long time ago, and it's time I made good on that promise."

· · · · ● · ● · ● · · ·

John

Her face was pressed to my chest when I woke up the next morning. I kissed her temple, inhaling the smell of coconut in her hair. She haunted my dreams and nightmares almost every minute in that hellhole. Feeling her close to me, finally, was pure heaven. I mentally made a new rule that we'd sleep naked from now on.

For so long, it seemed like an impossible dream that we'd find our way back to each other, and an even bigger fantasy that she'd ever agree to be my *wife*. I brushed a stray lock of hair from her shoulder, smiling when she shivered and burrowed closer against me.

She stirred and I stroked her back as her eyes slowly opened. Her gaze met mine and she smiled. "I didn't dream it," she breathed. "You're here."

"In the flesh, and plenty of it."

She giggled and caressed my face with her hand. "Was that a complaint about last night's activities?"

"Never. In fact, I think we could use several more nights like that."

"That's something I could probably be talked into easily."

"Good to know."

I'd noticed the markings on her inner forearms the night before, but, well, there wasn't a lot of coherent conversation during that time. Now that I was able, I studied them closely. An intricate lace pattern was now tattooed on both arms, just below each wrist and covering her scars from that horrible New Year's Eve. The pattern on her left arm started off blue and darkened to indigo while her right arm started with the same shade of indigo and changed to dark red. I traced the design on her left arm.

"Eddie's daughter, Brooklyn, has a shop and I got them from her," she explained. "They probably look kind of weird by themselves, but together they make a butterfly."

"They're beautiful. Fire and ice?"

"Yeah. I've been called both fiery and ice cold so much it just made sense. They're also a huge middle finger to Felton since I'd never been allowed to get one."

I took her hand in mine and kissed it. "And this is where I change the subject, because that's the last person I want to talk about right now."

"So, who do you want to talk about?"

"My smoking hot fiancée," I answered with a smile before taking a deep breath. "And that I feel bad I don't have her engagement ring with me. It's sitting in a safe in Verona."

"As if that really matters to me. All that matters is that I didn't lose you."

My heart stuttered at her words and then sped up when she brought her lips to mine. The kiss was slow and gentle, made even sweeter by the warmth of her body as she wrapped her arms around me. I gently grasped the back of her head and deepened the kiss, savoring her soft moans. We were both breathless when we broke apart several minutes later.

"I'm sorry. I bet my morning breath is just horrid," she murmured, placing a hand over her mouth.

"Considering everything we did last night, I can say that's the furthest thing from my mind," I laughed. "But I am starving, so we should probably get up so we can eat and take a shower."

Groaning, she crawled out of bed. She grabbed my shirt off the floor and pulled it over her head just before she left, shooting me a mischievous look over her shoulder as she headed to the bathroom.

"Some things never change," I chuckled.

I grabbed my disposable cell phone off the floor and read a new text message. Exhaling slowly, I typed a quick reply and then locked the screen. The knot in my stomach sank like a block of concrete. The phone vibrated with a reply. My fingers shook as I read the message. The conversation she and I were going to have would not be a pleasant one.

"Babe, you coming?" she yelled from the other room.

I shoved the phone under my pillow and stood up. We would talk...after breakfast. And away from any small items since she was bound to throw shit once I told her what needed to be said. She'd be beyond pissed, and she had every right to be. I hated it had come to this, but it couldn't be helped.

After a very long and dirty shower, we made breakfast. Not long after, we sat together at the island eating our food and talking about nothing in particular. As our plates emptied, I felt the knot in my stomach return. She insisted I sit and relax while she cleaned up and while she rinsed the plates, I mentally rehearsed what I was going to say to her once she was done.

"John, are you okay? You look nervous about something."

I exhaled slowly. "There's something we need to talk about."

"What is it?"

I spun her around so her back was to the island and put my hands on either side, caging her in. She grasped my forearms as she looked up at me with a note of unease. "You weren't the only one who called in a favor," I finally admitted out loud, swallowing the lump in my throat.

Desperation can make a person do things they'd never consider doing; things that might sound completely insane at first, but made perfect sense when that one thing offered even the slightest glimmer of hope. For me, that moment of insanity happened during my conversation with Connor shortly after we arrived at Lejeune, and I found out my uncle had doubled the bounty on her. Blinded by the panic, I got a hold of the disposable phone in her purse while she was in the bathroom and grabbed what I needed. The stricken look on her face when she left to meet with her uncle only made my decision easier. Less than ten minutes after she left my room, I used that information and set my plan in motion.

Her brows came together. "I don't understand. Who did you call?"

Knowing my answer would send her into a tailspin, I pressed my forehead to hers and braced myself. "Felton."

Her wrath was immediate. I tightened my arms as she struggled against me, yelling as she tried to break free. She kicked and tried to stomp on my feet, trying to loosen my grip on the counter so she could get away. After several minutes, she stopped moving and her body shook as a loud sob emitted from her.

"You almost died because of him!" she cried. "Why would you do that?"

"We need him, baby."

"No, we don't! Titus is sending me fifteen men, and they'll be here soon. Tavi got word to Rocco, and your guys are preparing to head here as we speak. We don't need him."

"Felton's connected. He knows people who can help us."

"I found the last person who helped him with a gun to your head," she argued as she tried to struggle out of my arms again. "We can't trust him."

"We have no choice," I growled, tightening my arms around her. "Lucas isn't here to help us strategize, and I don't know who Massimo is bringing with him. I'll be damned if I'm going to go head to head with him and hope for the best. No way in hell."

She slumped against my chest and cried. When her body finally relaxed, I loosened my grip and rubbed her back. A few moments later, she sat up and the mixture of emotions in her eyes was a punch to the gut. Anger and sadness, heavily mixed with fear and exhaustion. I kissed her forehead, wishing I could take away all the shit that had saturated our lives for far too long. She leaned her head into my chest and exhaled slowly.

"How do we know we can trust him?" Her voice was tense.

"When you were in the hospital in Tampa and I told him about the bounty, he and I agreed there was only one thing we would ever agree on. Keeping you safe. Considering he kidnapped me and tried to use me as leverage to get Massimo to leave you alone, I have no reason to doubt his sincerity. This is probably the one time I'll ever trust him, but if it means we survive all this, then I'll gladly take that chance."

She nodded glumly. "If you can trust him, I can try."

"That's great to hear since we're meeting him in an hour."

Chapter 14

Judas's Lament

John

SHE PACED THE SMALL elevator as it took its sweet time traveling to the eight floor, throwing me a murderous glare every time she brushed past. I'd agreed that she'd be unarmed at the meeting, which was no simple task since she'd tried to sneak in a small pistol and a switchblade. After the extended and extremely profane rant, she was even more pissed off when she learned I planned to drive us to the meeting on a motorcycle. After muttering under her breath, she wrapped her arms around me. However, by the time I parked, I was sure there was a full set of her fingernails dug into my skin.

I stayed in the corner and let her burn through her rage until I saw it. As we passed the fourth floor, she dragged her thumb back and forth over her collarbone. My eyes met hers for a fraction of a second before she turned away, and I felt like the world's biggest idiot for not realizing sooner that buried under her anger was bound to be fear and a slew of other emotions she'd never admit to. She froze when I moved closer.

Wrapping my arms around her waist, I brought my lips to her ear. "When was the last time you saw him?

"Fourth of July. Two hours later, Lucas called to tell me you were missing," she whispered, swiping the skin under her eye.

"I'm so sorry. I promise you, he won't hurt either of us. He just wants to help keep you safe."

"And he had no intention of hurting you, but yet Franz didn't seem to get that memo," she retorted.

The doors finally opened, and she stalked down the narrow hallway. Law enforcement used the building decades earlier, but it was mostly abandoned except for a few offices on the first floor. I raced to catch up to her so Felton wouldn't answer the door and find her alone and pissed off on the other side. She pounded on the door, and it was a wonder she didn't injure her hand. I wrapped my arm around her waist, fully prepared for her to lunge any second. Her black jeans, t-shirt, and leather jacket fit her mood, proven by the look she gave me when I tightened my grip.

With a low creak, the door opened and we came face to face with Felton Lynch, our nemesis, and potential ally. His face brightened at the sight of his daughter, but fell when she surged through the door right past him. I slowed my feet, causing her to stop in front of an old rickety desk that held several takeout bags and a mug of coffee.

His hand shook as he locked the door. Exhaling slowly, he turned to face us. "Um, it's nice to see you, sweetheart."

In the eleven years I'd known, worked with, and loathed Felton Lynch, he was always well-dressed, well-spoken, and well-heeled. His dark gray hair never dared fall out of place, his suits were never a color other than the blackest of blacks, and his face was always cold and calculating. I couldn't hide my shock that his perfectly coiffed hair was now shaved and only light gray stubble remained. He wore an old black polo shirt and pale khakis. However, the most shocking change was the face that never dared to betray the slightest bit of emotion. His cheeks were sunken and his skin was so pale it looked sickly. The dark circles under his eyes almost glowed as he watched her with a mixture of fear and concern.

"Not your sweetheart," she bit out. My fingers caressed her side, hoping to soothe the tension pulsing through her.

He held his hands up. "I'm sorry. I fully understand why you're upset. You have every right to feel angry and betrayed."

"Upset," she repeated. "Wow. Yeah, let's go with 'upset', Felton. Two hours after I came home from visiting you, I find out he'd been kidnapped. Imagine my surprise when Marianna told me she kidnapped him on your orders."

Her body shook as she spoke and Felton backed away. We both knew all too well about her wrath once it reached a certain point, and while I promised him I wouldn't allow her to kill him, that didn't mean I wouldn't let her get some shots in before stepping in.

He sighed and shook his head. "Anything I say will only anger you further." He stepped forward. "Would it make you feel better if I let you punch me?"

"Have you lost your fucking mind?" I yelled, trying to hold her back.

She bolted low and to the right, a streak of black that didn't stop until she had his throat in her hand. His eyes widened, but he did nothing to defend himself. The murderous look in her eye didn't waver as she shoved him into an old wooden chair next to the desk. He gasped loudly when she released his windpipe. She leaned over him in the chair and he froze.

"You have no idea what would make me feel better, Officer Lynch." Her voice was low and dangerous. "Should I turn a fire hose on you? Chain you to a metal bed frame and put a heat lamp on you so the chains burn into your skin? Or should I use a car battery? Maybe I should load you up on drugs and leave you in a room full of broken mirrors. What do you think, Felton? Which would make me feel better?"

"Liss." I put my hands on her shoulder. She tensed, but then relaxed. "Come on. Let him go."

Her eyes narrowed. "All I can think of is how I sat on your fucking patio and drank beers with your sorry ass on the Fourth of July. As we sat there, what was he going through? What depraved shit was that fucking psychopath doing to him on your command, while you dished out potato salad and told me about your new neighbors?"

"I'm sorry." Sweat dripped down his forehead.

"Sorry?" she scoffed. "You *chose* to call Franz, knowing what kind of predator he was. Of all the other slimy bastards you know, you had that sadist watch over him. The same man who taught me a lot of the same things until you fired him."

His fearful eyes shifted to mine, pleading. I watched her hands grip the arms of the chair. There were at least four ways she could have killed him with her bare hands, but he remained safe so long as her hands stayed put. In all fairness, however, we needed to get down to why we were there.

"All right, you've made your point. Let's hear what he has to say," I said.

Shrugging, she stepped away and stood next to me. Felton closed his eyes and threw his head back as he took a deep breath. I rubbed her lower back and led her toward the kitchen when she stopped. Her hand moved to my waist, and by the time I tried to grab her it was too late.

He had just enough time for a strangled cry of shock before she was on him. His head flew against the backrest of the chair as she crouched over him and jammed the barrel of my gun against his forehead. His knuckles were white as he gripped the arms of the chair and his eyes were the size of dinner plates.

She smiled, enjoying his panic. "This is how I found him. If I'd gotten into that room even half a second later, he would've been dead and we'd be meeting under much different circumstances."

"Larissa," I barked. "That's enough. Give me the gun. Now."

She looked at me before turning her attention back to the chair. "Consider yourself lucky that he wants you alive for now."

Glaring at my outstretched hand, she dropped the gun in the middle of my palm. Feeling the pistol was lighter than it should have been, I raised my eyebrows at her. Rolling her eyes, she dropped the mag next to the gun. Our eyes met, and she nodded, suddenly calm. Blowing out a breath as if the past few minutes hadn't happened, she lowered herself onto the couch.

Felton stood and strolled into the kitchen. "Would either of you like something to drink?"

I shook my head, and we both looked at the couch, where she stayed silent. Nodding, he went to the kitchen and busied himself at the coffeemaker. His movements were slow and shaky, as if waiting for her to strike again. The tension in the room remained high, feeling as if either of them might explode any second.

"Why?" a voice softly asked from the couch.

He shut his eyes and bowed his head. I turned to her and watched as the wall of anger she built to protect her feelings crumbled and fell away. Her eyes were paler that normal, as they often were before she cried. One arm was wrapped around her stomach while the other was across her chest, allowing her to tap her thumb against her collarbone. Her eyes pleaded for an answer.

"Lissa," he began.

"I want to know why," she growled, standing. "Why did you lie to me for all these years? Why were you so overprotective, only to sell me out to Gio twenty years later?" She pointed to me. "And why in the name of god did you pull him into it?"

By the time Felton turned around, her eyes were red. The tears threatened to fall, but her face held a look that demanded answers. He muttered something under his breath I couldn't understand. Her eyes widened, and she lunged, yelling at him in what was most likely Irish. I gripped her around the waist and hugged her to me, tucking her head under my chin.

"All right, ground rules," I bellowed above their voices. "Felton, you sit in the chair by the desk. Liss, you sit on the couch. Both of you will stay in your seats and you'll only use Italian if either of you feel compelled to swear at the other in another language. Agreed?"

"Yes," they grumbled in unison, casting the other one a glare as they did so.

"Felton, you said you'd explain yourself and answer her questions so I think it's time you finally did that," I said, taking one of the old wooden dining chairs and moving it to the middle of the room between the two of them.

Nodding, he took a deep breath. "I guess the best way to explain all this, to help you better understand, would be to start at the beginning; when I met Seamus."

"My father," she interjected.

"Yes," he agreed, wincing at her verbal jab. "I was born Soren Luccetti outside of Naples. My father, Otto, was Italian and my mother, Meara, was Irish. We visited my mother's family pretty frequently, but then my parents told me that whenever we went to Ireland, I had to use the name Felton. I later learned it was because my father was wanted in Dublin and several other small towns. After a while, he stopped coming with us, which was how I could finally make friends with some kids in the neighborhood. I met

Seamus Donovan when I was eleven years old." He smiled fondly. After a few seconds, she cleared her throat, and he nodded.

"We became close friends. So much so that he even spent a couple of summers with me at my grandmother's house. But his parents moved them to the States when I was fifteen and we lost touch. I still visited Ireland, but it wasn't the same. My grandmother got sick, and my mother wanted to stay behind to take care of her. My father insisted I come back to Italy to keep up with my schoolwork. He got a job as an accountant in Sicily, and we moved there the summer before my last year of secondary. High school, as it's called here. My first day of school is when I met the woman who would change my life."

"My mother," she murmured.

He nodded, flashing her a small smile. "Seraphina Morello. God, I can remember it as if it was yesterday. I was sitting in the classroom and heard a voice coming down the hall. By the time she reached the door, she was laughing. It was the laugh that caused me to look up, and that's when I saw her. Took my breath away."

She picked at the sleeve of her shirt and tried to look in-different, but when the mask slipped and the pain shone in her eyes, it sliced through my heart. Hearing how your parents met should give someone hope they'd be able to find a love like the one that brought them into the world. Instead, their story was the beginning of a journey that ended in countless betrayals and bloodshed.

"How did...," she began, but shook her head and looked down. "When..."

"It took a few weeks for me to work up the courage to ask her out," he replied, answering the question she couldn't verbalize. "But after that, we were inseparable. We were in love, desperately in love."

"What did you love about her?" Her voice was almost a whisper.

"So many little things. The way her eyes sparkled when she smiled. Her laugh, her soft, melodic laugh. The way she could lift the mood of a room just by walking into it. She was headstrong but also gentle and loving. Pretty much everything about her."

I was shocked. In that moment, Felton Lynch wasn't the heartless bastard who ruined so many lives. Instead, he was a man reminiscing on a simpler life before it was marred by whatever forces he allowed to intrude. As he described everything he loved about Sera, I was struck by how many traits she passed on to her daughter. I understood and appreciated just how enraptured he was, because I felt exactly the same. She had me so entranced I was willing to do anything to protect her, including joining forces with the man to blame.

"So you loved her at some point," she muttered.

"Yes, I loved her very much. If I'd had my way, I would've married her. Unfortunately, fate had different ideas. I approached my father about marrying her, and he immediately forbade it."

She looked up from the coffee table. "Why?"

He chuckled. "You know your mother's family line. My father was a hardened criminal, but his son marrying into a mob family was unacceptable."

"What did he do?"

He looked her in the eye, not hiding his unease. "Your grandfather was a serial killer. He killed at least six people in Ireland and I lost count of how many in Italy. Ultimately, I think the main problem he had with the marriage was he was afraid of bringing unwanted attention to himself and his activities. Not long after, we moved in the middle of the night to Bari and he took a job at a shipping company near the port."

"Sardi Industries," I offered.

"Correct."

"When was this? Massimo and Gio are only a couple of years older than you, so they couldn't have been old enough to be running the port by then."

"Massimo had just taken over as boss, but yes, he had just turned eighteen and was too young. Instead, Vicenzo, their father's younger brother, was installed as a figurehead leader for the organization."

"Organization," she mocked. "Your dad never realized who the Sardis were?"

"He thought they may have had mob ties, but by the time he learned the truth, it was too late."

"And when was that?" I asked.

"When did you start killing people for them?" she suddenly blurted out.

He looked down and then sighed. "You have to understand. I...um, I didn't have a normal childhood, not really. My mother kept things as normal as she could, but once she decided to stay in Ireland, things changed a lot. He kept extremely odd hours, going out just after dinner and not coming back until very early morning. Not long after Seamus moved away, I came home early from school one day and found him down in the basement. With a young woman hanging from a meat hook at the center of the room.

"Jesus," she gasped. "What did he do?"

"We stared at each other for what felt like forever. He then gave me three options: go upstairs and we'd talk about it later, sit in the corner and watch, or join in. I chose option number two."

"I don't know what I'm supposed to say to that." She stared at him, willing him to look her in the eye.

"What's there to say? I'm a monster. I've always had an interest in darker things, and knives have always fascinated me. So when my father said I could watch, I jumped on it. From there, it became an obsession. Later, when most kids my age were working at cafes or in little shops, my after-school job was with the local butcher. I was mesmerized by what a simple blade could do to tissue."

Her eyes caught mine and I mouthed the word "fuck". She closed her eyes. "Did you kill anyone with your dad?"

"No. I watched him plenty of times, but I never wanted to cross that line because I didn't want to risk your mother finding out. After we moved to Bari, I got a job with the local butcher. Gio visited me at work one afternoon and found me stripping a side of beef. He told me my talents were being wasted and asked if I wanted to make more money than I could ever imagine. I was intrigued. My father refused to allow me to marry Sera, so I planned to save up enough so she and I could run away together."

"So, just like that?" she scoffed. "Gio picks you up from work one day and you decide to just go kill people?"

"Was it easy for you to make your first kill, Larissa?" he challenged. She shook her head and looked down. "It wasn't for me, either. At the time, I saw it as a means to an end, a way to get the life I wanted with your mother. My father was too wrapped up in his own depravity to realize what I was up to. He just thought I was making good money at the butcher shop and putting it away for college. When he found out the truth, he put his own plan in motion."

"Elena."

He nodded. "As soon as he realized what I intended to do, he went to Massimo and Lilliana and arranged the marriage. I met Elena two weeks later at the church on our wedding day."

"Jesus Christ," she whispered. "Your dad was that set against you marrying someone connected to the mob?"

"The joke was on him," he replied. "Massimo chose our wedding reception to announce the Sardi family had formed an alliance with the Genovese. The look on my father's face when he realized he was surrounded by made men wasn't pretty. He left almost immediately and quit his job with Sardi that following Monday. Disappeared without a trace."

Her gaze bounced between the two of us several times, as if deciding whether to speak. After a moment, she leaned forward. "When did you find out she's gay?"

I nearly wrenched my neck turning to face her. "She told you?"

"In private, yes."

"Nonna loves her and accepts her," I explained. "Massimo is why she has to keep it quiet. I guess scary mobsters aren't supposed to have gay sisters."

Felton smiled. "It's great to hear her mother has finally accepted it. When we married, Lilliana forbade anyone from talking about anything to do with wedding night activities." He turned to Liss. "To answer your question, Elena told me on our wedding night. I promised I would never force her to do anything she didn't want to do. We agreed to be discreet, and that we'd come up with a plan when the time came for us to produce a child."

"Thank you for respecting her," I said. "That meant a lot to Lucas."

"Elena is a beautiful person who always wants the people she cares about to be happy. I would and could never do that to her."

"She told you to follow Sera," she murmured. "So you got your wish. You and my mom came here and could be together. How long before you started cheating on this woman you've spent all this time swearing was the love of your life?"

Wincing, he sighed. "I didn't plan to cheat on her. We got to New York and Sera was sent to spy on the Irish at a local strip club. I ran into Seamus, found out he worked for a club, and he agreed to put in a good word for her."

"Did Seamus know she was a spy?" she asked. "I would think someone would've been suspicious that their new employee was some Italian girl."

"No. We told everyone she was from a small village outside Bari, so nobody suspected she was connected to the Genovese. She started working at the club and I started working at the CIA a couple of months later."

"You make joining up sound so easy," I muttered. "All the fucking hoops you made me go through when you knew I shouldn't have even been there, and you make it sound like they just welcomed you with open arms."

"They needed people with college degrees and language skills. I had a general studies degree and spoke Irish and Italian. My identity didn't bring up any red flags, so I was hired to translate letters and recordings," he explained. "As for you, I had to make it look like I'd thoroughly vetted you or it would've raised suspicions."

"So you guys were here, together. And for once you didn't have to hide it," she said, narrating the story as she understood it. "You finally had the woman you loved and your shot at happily ever after, and it sounds like everything was great. Until it wasn't."

He pursed his lips but didn't dispute the accusation in her tone. "Yes."

She opened her mouth to speak, but closed it and shook her head. After a long silence, she took a deep breath. "This is hard for me, Felton. It wasn't my relationship. I wasn't there, so it's probably not my place to judge or criticize."

"It was all my fault. I can sit here and try to justify my actions, but the fact remains, I allowed things to happen that never should have. You have to understand this was the early to mid-80s. Between the IRA and the heightened mob activity back then, we had a lot of covert operations going on in both countries. When I wasn't working long hours at the office, I was doing work for the family. There were weeks where I'd work twelve hours and then either meet with Sardi or Genovese associates or go out on contract jobs for another six to eight hours. By the time I got back to our apartment, your mother was either asleep or already at work."

"Yes, I hear the life of the double agent is exhausting," she scoffed.

She propped her feet on the coffee table and wrapped her arms around her stomach. Her shoulders were tense and I noticed her fingers fidgeting against her sides, as if she was trying to keep everything bottled up. Unsure how much longer she'd keep her cool, I sat next to her. I had a feeling the next part of Felton's story would push her to the limit.

"I'm not making excuses or defending Felton when I say this, not by a long shot," I offered, gently prying her hand away from her side and holding it on the couch between us. "But I know my uncles, and I know their love for forcing people to do their dirty work."

"Elena and Lucas," he murmured, lowering his head. "If I didn't do what they wanted, Gio told me he'd kill Lucas and have Elena married off to Marco."

"Fucking assholes," she muttered. "So they forced you to spy, but I'm guessing your choice to fuck around was all your own."

"Larissa, please know I'm not proud of this. I was young and easily manipulated. It was all so easy at first, the money, the jobs. But then suddenly you're married to the mob boss's sister and doing whatever they tell you to keep your son alive and your wife from being married off to a monster. It was a shitty situation that I didn't know how to handle and I did the best I could."

Her eyes narrowed. "And when did 'the best you could' turn into you cheating on my mother?"

Her hand gripped mine so tightly my fingers tingled. Felton tensed in his seat, gripping his knees as he bounced his legs. She glared and watched him expectantly. I squeezed her hand, forcing her attention to me.

"You said you needed to know the whole story. So let him tell it," I whispered. She closed her eyes and nodded.

Sensing it was safe to continue, he blew out a breath. "There was a waitress who worked at the all-night diner around the corner from my office. She was nice, really sweet. It started out as harmless banter and flirting at first, but the less I saw your mother and the more I heard her talk about Seamus," he broke off at the look of fury on her face.

"So it was my mom's fault, too?" Her hand shook in mine.

"Never. I didn't mean it like that. What I meant was that Seamus kept an eye on her for me like he promised, and they became friends. As the problems in our relationship increased, I imagine she confided in him more and more. And that's probably how the rumors about the two of them started. By the time I heard them, I was unwilling to believe she'd do that, but I used it to justify my own actions."

She stared at him, and then her eyes widened. "It was Karina, wasn't it?" At his nod, I threw out my arm to keep her from standing. "How long, Felton? How long were you fucking that Russian whore before she caught you?"

"Six months," he answered, his voice barely a whisper. "The last words Sera said before she left were how much she hated me.

Two months later, she was married to Seamus and pregnant, so I thought the rumors were true."

"And then you just went on with your life with your whore and not a second thought to her. When did you figure out the truth?"

As if steeling himself up, his eyes lowered to the ground and he exhaled slowly. She gripped my hand so tightly, I winced. She mouthed an apology and tried to relax. The silence stretched into several minutes, only making the tension unbearable.

"Felton," I prodded.

"Your sixth birthday party," he finally answered, meeting her eyes. "Seamus and I crossed paths with each other over the years. He even brought you by my house once or twice while running errands. I never paid much attention to you. A mutual friend invited me to tag along, and I figured why not? That was the day my world turned upside down."

She cleared her throat. "How?"

"I know I've never been an overly emotional person, so this is probably going to sound strange. The minute you bounced down the stairs and I saw you, this odd feeling came over me. I couldn't describe it. And then you walked right up to me, introduced yourself, and then told me all about your school, your birthday, the dog your parents said they were going to buy for you," he paused, smiling. "I'll never forget it."

"Did my dad say anything?"

"No. I didn't realize how close he'd been watching me until Sera came in and saw me. She glared at me but didn't want to make a scene, so she asked you to come help her in the kitchen. I thought nothing of it, but a couple weeks later I ran into Seamus in a restaurant and you were with him. You made a joke and when you laughed, I saw the same left dimple that's been in my family for the last four generations. In that moment, I knew you were my daughter."

Her hands clenched into fists, and her eyes narrowed. "You can use that term all you want, but Seamus Donovan is my father. His name is the one on my birth certificate. All five of them, including the one *you* had forged."

"That might be the case, Larissa, but the dimple in your cheek is the same as the one I saw on the face of my grandmother every time she smiled."

"Aednat?"

Felton tensed before he stood and paced. He scrubbed a hand over his face and whispered to himself, begging forgiveness in Italian and muttering other nonsense. After several minutes, he finally stood in front of us and exhaled slowly. "How do you know that name?"

"It's my real middle name, the one I was told to never tell anyone about."

"Seamus," he sighed, shaking his head. "Of course. She meant so much to him."

"And what has ever meant anything to you, Felton?" she challenged. "Or do you prefer Soren? What did you do when you realized the truth? Cal told me you and my dad had some kind of falling out. Was that the reason?"

No longer tense, he returned to his chair. "Yes. I confronted Seamus, and he refused to confirm or deny anything. He simply told me I was to stay away from both you and Sera or there would be extreme consequences. So I stayed away."

"But not for long. Isn't that right?" She struggled against my arm as she tried to stand. "What did you do, Felton?"

"I swear I did nothing. I stayed away for a while to let him cool off, and then all I wanted was a chance to get to know my daughter.

I'd lost all rights to Lucas. Part of my agreement with Elena when I left was that I would never contact either of them. I couldn't lose another one of my children."

"Bullshit!" she shouted. "Less than a year later, they were dead. Killed by the family you married into and worked for!"

Felton looked shocked and hurt by her words, but the outburst didn't surprise me. Connor and I talked about the possibility Felton had something to do with their deaths, and Liss had made comments in recent weeks wondering the same thing. None of us were certain if he was or wasn't involved, so the question lingered. The only thing I knew for sure was if he had anything to do with it, I didn't know if I'd be willing or able to keep her from killing him.

"They already knew," he said over her loud voice. "Gio asked *me* what I knew about Seamus talking to the CIA. I swear. They didn't get any intel from me."

"I find that hard to believe," I scoffed.

"Seamus never met with anyone in D.C. I found out afterward that he only met with his handler in either Boston or Philadelphia. At the time, I was a mid-level officer and didn't have access to other cases."

"You did nothing to stop it," she argued.

He cursed under his breath. "I know you want to cast me as the villain in all of this, both of you. God knows I've done plenty to justify that. But I swear to you, I knew nothing about what they planned to do to Seamus and Sera until I found you hiding in my backyard that night."

She told me her memories of that horrible night, the images from the dream that plagued her for over twenty years. She was on the road on the anniversary of their deaths, when her dreams were the worst, and all I could do was offer feeble words and hope they provided enough comfort until I could hold her in my arms.

Her face remained blank. "You have this habit of manipulating events so they benefit you. When John became a problem because he knew too much, you had no problem kidnapping him and trying to use him as leverage. But I'm the asshole for being suspicious? Jesus Christ, if I didn't know better, it wouldn't surprise me if you'd somehow intervened in Cuba!"

His eyes burned, and the chilling expression on his face made me shield her body with my own when he jumped to his feet. She jumped at his sudden movements, and when she shrank behind me, I considered pulling my gun on him.

"How the fuck do you think you got to Guantanamo so fast?" he said in a low voice that chilled my blood. "That asshole's compound was in the middle of nowhere. You think that little bitch's distress call saved you?"

"Felton, what did you do?" I whispered.

Squaring his shoulders, he lifted his chin. "What I always do. I protected what's mine. That psychotic fucking uncle of yours forced my hand, so I played along. I signed off on the mission and let them think you were being lured into a trap. As soon as you left Homestead, I called in a favor to a couple of former Special Ops guys I knew down there. They were supposed to provide back-up when things went bad, but they had to shoot their way out of one of Ernesto's roadblocks. The only thing that kept me from having them killed was the fact one of them had enough medical training to keep you stable enough until they got you to safety."

"Talbot?" Her eyes widened. "Do you just make it a habit of employing psychopaths now? How many kilos of coke did you have to pay him with? Or was it thirteen-year-old hookers this time?"

"Kenworth Talbot?" I asked, praying they were talking about someone else.

"Yes, John. The same Kenworth Talbot who runs a group of mercenaries out of Colombia. Because it's not bad enough Felton's a fucking psychopath, he has to surround himself with them, too."

"You don't get to pass judgment on me, young lady!" he roared. "It's not like you haven't done business with your own fair share of shady people."

"And who referred me to most of them?" she shrieked, sneaking under my arm and bolting upright before I got a firm grip on her hand.

"Okay, both of you need to calm the hell down," I commanded, leading her back to the couch.

"It must be so nice to sit in judgment when you have no idea about half the shit I've been through to keep your ass alive," he spat. "Was it a mistake to kidnap John and have Franz watch over him? Looking back, I'd say it was. But what the hell was I supposed to do? Let his uncle keep coming after you until he succeeded? As for Talbot, do you know of anyone else in the area who could've come to your aid?"

"God, for so long I ignored all the horror stories and terrible rumors about you, and then I spent almost a week hearing that most of them were true." She shook her head. "Do you know how hard it is to realize the person you put on a pedestal for so long has a filthier soul than your own?"

"But yet Seamus remains on his pedestal when he did things that make all three of us look like angels," he said. "Why don't I get the same courtesy?"

"Because my father eventually sought to redeem himself for his crimes. And he didn't treat me any different because I wasn't his blood."

"So he's a saint because he got to play Daddy with you for a few years, but I'm a piece of shit even though I raised you?"

She regarded him for a moment before leaning forward. "You know, I was always grateful that you took me in and raised me as if I was your own. Now that I know the truth, it explains a lot of things I never understood growing up, starting with why you were always so overprotective and why Karina was so cold. Cal and Eddie told me just how much she hated my mother and me."

"Yes, and that evil bitch paid for her crimes," he muttered.

We both froze and exchanged worried looks. "What crimes, Felton?" she asked in a soft voice.

He blinked and looked away, as if he hadn't meant to make his comment out loud. "About six months before you went to Prague, she came to me with test results that showed you weren't my biological daughter. I'd snuck through a DNA test through the lab when you were eight years old, but Karina told me the technician had faked the results." He refused to make eye contact with either of us.

She looked away and I wrapped my arm around her waist. "Tell me you didn't do what I think you did," I said, desperate to be wrong.

"I wish I could, but it would be a lie. I told Gio and Massimo that I'd found out the Irish rat was really her father. Gio said to leave it all to him."

My body filled with hot, blinding rage. Before either of them could react, I lunged forward and punched him in the jaw. He crumpled to the floor, and after receiving several swift kicks to the ribs, I picked him up by the throat and held him against the wall. His eyes bulged as I squeezed his throat, drowning out his gasp.

"This is how you treat your children?" I roared. "Completely abandon one and try to toss the other one away like an unwanted toy as soon as you think she might not be yours? Do you have any idea of the chain of events you set off when you did that?"

"That's why she's dead," he rasped, clawing at my hand.

"Who?" My grip on his throat eased a fraction. "What the fuck else did you do, you disgusting piece of shit?"

"Karina, that's why she's dead," he wheezed. "Some of Lissa's DNA was found in the warehouse in Portland. I noticed the blood type on that report didn't match the one listed on Karina's results, so I took samples to a lab and watched them run the test myself. When I learned the truth, I confronted the lying bitch. She finally confessed, and I threw her down the stairs."

The room fell quiet, except for his coughing and wheezing. I stared at him, shocked and disgusted. He'd always been a cold, unfeeling bastard when I worked with him, but to see that same apathy toward his own flesh and blood completely floored me. I gripped the edge of his shirt and glared down at him, wanting nothing more than to give him the cruel and violent death he deserved, when a small hand touched my arm.

"Let him go," her soft voice whispered in my ear.

One look into her eyes and my rage roared to life once again. Her eyes were blank, empty of the fury that tore through her earlier but also of their usual fire. In that moment, I knew she was completely broken, the last of her emotional defenses falling away upon hearing how easily the man she thought of as a second father tried to throw her away like she was nothing. Images of her beaten in the warehouse, chained on the pier, and clinging to life in a hospital bed flashed through my mind and I found my hand slowly creeping toward his throat once again.

"Gianni, he's not worth it," she pleaded softly. "Let him go." I dropped my hands and backed away.

He lowered his head when she stood before him with a glare. "Sweetheart, I'm so sorry."

She pressed her arm against his throat and silenced him. "I'm not your goddamned sweetheart. My name is Special Field Agent Larissa *Donovan*. You are simply a resource for an upcoming operation. Your knowledge and skills will be utilized until such time that you are of no further use. We will be in touch."

Her arms fell to her sides and she left the apartment without another word. He gasped and rubbed his throat gingerly and watched me closely. Shaking my head, I said nothing and left. I raced out the door and scanned the hallway, following the sound of someone pounding on the wall. Turning the corner, I found her beating on the button for the elevator and whispering urgently. I wrapped my arm around her and when her eyes met mine, I saw the tears that threatened to fall. She buried her face in my chest.

"I've gotta get out of here," she whispered. "He can't see me cry."

I led her to the stairs. We emerged from the building a few minutes later and grabbed our helmets out of the saddlebag of the motorcycle. I drove away and with each passing second, I felt the tension melt from her body. When we stopped at the small taqueria she directed me to, she was less tense but the empty and pained look in her eyes remained.

"Snow's coming," I murmured, taking her hand.

She nodded and followed me inside. We ate in silence, and my heart shattered as she stared blankly out the window. After several attempts to engage her in conversation, I knew she'd retreated inside her mind. I reached across the table and squeezed her hand, causing her to look up. She stared at me and nodded before wiping her eyes.

The air was bitter cold when we left and it smelled of snow. I put my arms around her and gave her a tender kiss before we climbed back on the bike to head back to Georgia's. Her arms held me tighter as we drove and by the time we stowed the bike in the alley, a small patch of ice appeared on her cheek from an escaped tear.

Once we were in the basement, I pulled my long-sleeved gray shirt over my head and handed it to her before making sure the house was locked up. When I returned, she'd changed into the shirt and stood near the bed with her arms wrapped tightly around her body. I hugged her tightly, and it was only then that she finally released a heavy sigh and I felt a small tremor. Moments later, I scooped her into my arms and climbed into bed. She nestled her head into my chest as she cried softly. I held her trembling body in my arms and kissed the top of her head. Her cries subsided several minutes later and when I looked down, her eyes stared blankly ahead. I slipped my hand under her shirt and caressed the bare skin on her lower back while she traced her finger over my tattoo.

There were things we needed to discuss, plans that needed to be made, but not that night. Enough words had been spoken that day, stories that damaged her from the weight of their betrayal. In one afternoon, the man she saw as a savior proved to be a monster who helped destroy her childhood and showed just how little their bond meant to him. I felt her eyes on me and found a questioning expression on her face. I gave her a small smile and kissed her before she closed her eyes.

Chapter 15

The Calm Before the Storm

Larissa

I PUSHED A FORKFUL of hash browns around my plate while reading a news article on my phone. John's watchful eyes almost burned a hole in the side of my head as he loaded the dishwasher. I looked up and shoved a strip of bacon into my mouth. He nodded and finished cleaning up. When he was done, he wiped his hands off and joined me at the table.

"Rocco will be here soon to go with me to meet with—" his voice broke off.

"Felton," I finished. "It's okay to say his name."

I was a mess after my conversation with the man in question. Hearing how easily he betrayed me to the Sardis cut even deeper than learning the truth about John's family ties in Portland. I barely remembered getting back to the house that night and spent most of the next day crying. My red and puffy eyes no doubt made me look like a wreck the next day when we moved to a new safe house. Neither John nor Aiden said a word, choosing instead to give me some much-needed space.

He took my hand in his. "You sure you're okay with all this? I can tell it's still pretty raw for you."

"I'm trying to move past it. Did you want me to come with you?"

"Honestly, I think you still need some space from him. So how about you stay here, do your daily check ins and maybe just relax a little." When I opened my mouth to protest, he squeezed my hand. "It won't hurt you to take it easy."

"Fine," I sighed.

"Hey. I know we're both exhausted and right now it feels like the end is a million miles away, but we've made it this far. We've already defied the odds countless times. We have to believe we can make it through to the end. Okay?"

"Okay."

His phone chimed with a message from Rocco, and he gave me a tender kiss before heading out. I took my time finishing breakfast and looked out the window at the falling snow before grabbing my phones. The usual morning text from my uncle hadn't arrived, and I tried not to worry while answering a message from John reminding us about our dinner date that night. My call to Titus went to voicemail, so I immediately called Aiden. He reported that the men Titus sent were stateside and settled into their temporary housing, all eighteen of them. I tried to protest, but he immediately shut me down and said to talk to the boss.

When I told him I hadn't received my daily text from Titus, he told me they'd spoken and he'd gone to ground because the police were sniffing around. He assured me there was nothing to worry about, and we agreed to meet up the following day. My hopes for taking my mind off Titus went right out the window when the first question Lucas asked was if he knew why my uncle was trying to contact him. He agreed it was odd, but figured it had to be important. I told him about the troubles in Belfast, and Lucas said he'd try to get a hold of him as soon as possible.

We hung up and I realized it was almost lunchtime and John would be home soon. As the soup simmered, I tried not to worry. If Titus was in trouble, he had an entire network of people back in

Ireland to help him. There was no point in worrying when I didn't even know there was anything to worry about.

A warm hand caressing my lower back forced my eyes open, and it was then that I realized I fell asleep face down on the couch. I rolled over and found John standing over me with a look of panic that he was trying to hide with an uneven smile.

"Hey," he greeted softly as he helped me to my feet.

"Hey. How'd it go?"

"Later," he answered, clutching my hand tightly as he followed me to the kitchen. "First, I want to have lunch with my gorgeous future bride."

"Flattery gets you nowhere, Mr. Martinetti."

"No, but it gets me lunch with you."

I giggled as we ate giant bowls of baked potato soup. We debated what side dish to bring to Barton and Yolanda's house for Thanksgiving and talked about the nasty snowstorm in the forecast. Nothing in our conversation sounded like we were hiding out from a psychotic madman. It was only after we finished eating that I pressed the issue again.

"All right, lunch is over. Time to talk," I declared.

"You're not going to like it."

I rested against the counter next to him and put my arm around his waist. "Talk to me."

"Talbot," he stated, his tone flat. "He pledged Talbot and his full crew to help us."

Kenworth Talbot and his group of mercenaries were among the best in the world. Their skills were unmatched, but with their talents came an insatiable list of vices that left a trail of destruc-tion wherever they went. A couple of his men had simple tastes, ranging from drugs to specialized weapons. However, Talbot and his closest associates craved female companionship when they celebrated their victories; the younger, the better. It sickened me when I learned Felton hired them to rescue me in Cuba.

"He's out of his mind if he thinks that's happening," I muttered. "I can only imagine what that band of sick fucks wants as payment."

"Felton and Titus covered it, and you know Titus would only agree as long as the payment didn't include their, shall we say, more extreme vices. Money and guns, that's it."

"Honestly, knowing those two are working together makes me nervous. Aiden told me that Titus is lying low because the cops are getting a little too interested in his activities, and now you're telling me he's working with Felton. Those two aren't a good combination."

He sighed. "I know. This is a shitty situation all the way around, but it's what we've got."

"What do you think? Did you or Rocco pick up on anything that would make you think it's a trap?"

"I know you don't want to hear this, but I honestly think he's being sincere. If it was a trap, something tells me he wouldn't involve Titus because he knows what would happen."

"I hope you're right."

We needed all the help we could get. Massimo had endless resources and men back in Italy, and would have access to even more support once he got stateside. My stomach churned at the realization of just how badly the odds were stacked against us.

"You look beat," he murmured.

"So do you."

His deep laugh rumbled in his chest. "Remember when we were kids and how we used to do everything we could think of to get out of naps?"

"My mom wouldn't budge," I said as he led me down the hall. "But she'd lay down with me if I begged her to. My dad was the master of bribery. Well, until my mom caught on."

"Both my parents were pretty easygoing about stuff like that," he said, tossing the covers over both of us once we were in bed. "Nonna was the one you couldn't get anything past."

"Sometimes I wonder what your parents would've thought of me, given my chosen profession."

"Like I said, they were both easygoing with me. For everything else, my dad was the calm one. Nothing really bothered him unless it threatened my mom. He would've loved your knowledge of sports trivia. As for my mom, you would've been her partner in crime."

"Really?"

"She was the rebel of the family. Nonna could barely keep her in line, but she defied my uncles every chance she got. If this tells you anything, my parents' marriage wasn't arranged."

"How'd she manage that?"

"Massimo went out of town to talk to a potential husband for her, and she and my dad eloped. By the time he got back, they'd already escaped to Verona. Luckily, he didn't have the muscle that he has now, and well, you've seen that house. So all Massimo could really do was throw a shit fit and threaten them. A few months later, my dad took the job here in the States."

"She sounds a lot like Nonna."

"Sometimes. Nonna was a mob boss's wife, so she knew she had to pick her battles. Elena was the peacemaker. My mom was the youngest and the smallest, so she learned quickly to strike back when her brothers tried to bully her."

"My dad would've liked you. He would've had fun scaring you into thinking he hated you, but you're overprotective of the people who matter to you, and you kept his favorite whiskey in your office. Mom would be the one you'd have to win over, but that would've been easy once she saw how happy I am."

I curled up against his warm body and wrapped my arm around his waist. He rubbed my back and I smiled. Enveloped in him and his scent, it didn't take long for me to fall asleep. It felt like hours later that I woke up sprawled on his chest. His arms tightened around me when I raised my head and I noticed he had the same worried look as earlier.

I slid closer to his face. "Did you sleep at all?"

"Enough."

"Don't lie to me. Please."

"It's nothing."

"Bullshit. It's obvious you have something on your mind. Out with it."

His eyes fluttered shut, and when they opened, I saw his pain. "Rocco and I got stuck in traffic after the meeting. It took us over an hour to get here and all I could think was if my uncle decided today was the day, you would've been here with no back-up."

"I was fine."

"I didn't know that," he argued, shaking his head. "And when I got here, I rushed in, calling your name, not knowing you were asleep. When you didn't answer, I freaked out until I found you on the couch."

"I'm sorry."

He rolled me onto my back. "We've talked and joked about how we have this weird and unconventional relationship, but today it just really brought home how messed up things are. There are some very real and scary monsters in this world who would be delighted to kill you in ways that no human can even comprehend. As your husband, I want to give you the world, and I will. But I have to help make this world safe for you to live in first, and I will do anything, *anything*, to make that happen."

"Even if it means working with the man who's responsible for what happened to you?"

"You tortured a CIA officer and broke into a hacker's house, and you're asking me how far I'm willing to go to protect someone I love?"

I narrowed my eyes. "Yes, but I didn't join forces with Marianna after all was said and done."

"No, but you were willing to do whatever it took. And so am I."

"You want me to accept Felton's proposal."

"I want you to decide based on how you feel. I'll respect your decision no matter what. But I also know we need all the help we can get."

"So do I. But are we so desperate that we're willing to take his offer at face value? What if it's a trap?"

"I don't think it is. I was there when he tried to bargain my life for yours. I saw the desperation and then panic in his eyes when Massimo hung up on him. He had a complete meltdown after that. I almost had him convinced to release me so I could get you into hiding until Franz stepped in and talked him out of it."

I brought my hand to his cheek and traced my fingers across the stubble. He kissed the palm and his eyes held mine before I put my arms around his neck and pulled him closer. His eyes closed as he lowered his head to the crook of my neck and inhaled deeply. I kissed his shoulder before a silence settled between us, each of us lost in our own thoughts.

"I don't think I'll ever forgive him for everything he's done," I whispered after a while.

He sat up. "You don't have to. And taking him up on his offer doesn't mean you've forgiven him. I'm not going to feel any kind of betrayal if we do this. I don't care, as long as it keeps you safe."

There was nothing I wanted more than to rail at Felton, throw his offer back in his face and walk away. However, the odds against us kept me from the knee-jerk reaction. Hearing John's opinion eased most of my anxiety, which made me feel better about the decision I knew I had to make.

"Okay," I whispered.

"Are you sure?"

"As much as I can be. I'll never fully trust him, but we don't have many people clamoring to help us."

He pulled me into his arms and hugged me tightly. Moments later, he leaned back and cupped my face in his hands and gazed at me before bringing his lips to mine. I leaned against him and said a silent prayer we weren't wrong.

John checked the time and realized we needed to get ready for our dinner date. I was thankful to be wearing jeans and a green sweater, since it was going to be casual. When John caught me admiring him in his black leather jacket, he pulled me close and kissed me senseless. After reminding me we didn't have time to get carried away, we finally headed out.

He parked his motorcycle behind the garage of an old fraternity house near the American University campus. He gestured for me to knock on the door and nearly bounced on his heels as we waited for the door to open. The door opened and Max motioned us inside. Upon closing the door, he pulled me into a hug that lifted me a couple of inches off the ground. Once he put me down, I turned and found the rest of John's men making their way to the foyer. Soon they were all clapping me on the shoulder or pulling me into several bone-crushing hugs.

"It's so good to see you guys!" I said, hugging Rocco.

"It's about time you brought her," Joey teased as he clapped John on the shoulder.

"I was waiting for everyone to get here, so I only had to make the announcement once, jackass," John shot back as he moved to the center of the group and pulled me into his arms. "I'm thrilled to announce Liss has agreed to be my wife."

The yells and cheers were almost deafening as we both received more hugs and well wishes. Everyone led us down the hall toward a large dining room, where the table was already set and covered with dishes of food. John led me to my chair before taking his seat next to mine. I turned and gave him a kiss.

"All right, you two, enough of that," Paolo scolded with a chuckle as he stood up. He held up his wineglass and motioned for everyone to do the same. "Before we all eat too much food and you two start making out at the table, I wanted to propose a toast. To John, our friend, our leader, our brother. Fighting next to you has always been an honor, and now we all get the honor of helping finally rid the world of that horrible uncle of yours."

"Thank you," John replied quietly, raising his glass.

"And to Larissa, our sister, and favorite troublemaker. I know we all met you under quite, ah, explosive, circumstances. But watching you take charge to keep this family safe, and then hearing everything you did to bring our brother home only proves you're the perfect match for him and this family. With that said, I offer not only best wishes to you both but also congratulations to John for finally convincing you to agree to marry him. *Salud!*"

John flipped him off as we all laughed and raised our glasses. Soon after, plates and silverware clinked together as dishes heaping with food were passed around the table. The conversation around the table was loud, just as it had been the last time I ate dinner with these men before we left Verona. My heart gave a small pang of regret that Nonna and Lucas weren't there, but I reminded myself they were safe and we'd see them soon enough.

Jay and Max were regaling me with stories about their adventures at Max's uncle's house in Palermo when I noticed John, Paolo and Rocco were having what looked like a very serious conversation in the corner of the dining room. I excused myself from the table and grabbed my wineglass.

I put my arm around John's waist. "What are you three up to?"

"Discussing your security," Rocco answered, earning a glare from both John and Paolo.

"Seriously?" I didn't bother to hide my annoyance.

John pulled me closer and shot me a stern look. "Bari has been on lockdown for the past two weeks and everyone connected to my uncle has gone silent. It's the calm before the storm. Something is coming, and I'm not taking any chances."

My mood plummeted. "Just one night. That was all I wanted. Especially tonight."

"I'm afraid it's not an option, Larissa," Paolo said. "We can't allow ourselves to get distracted for even a minute. Rocco will meet with Aiden tomorrow, and the two of them will oversee your security when John isn't with you."

John pulled me closer until I was leaning against him. He nodded to both men, who headed back to the table. His fingers traced my jawline before one slid under my chin and forced me to look at him. The deep brown in his eyes burned with the same determination I'd seen so many times before, but I also saw a twinge of sadness. "Did I want to spend a night of celebration having to discuss your security? Of course not. But I cannot and will not allow a single detail to go unchecked if it means it could hurt you."

"Okay." There was no point in arguing with him. For protecting those we cared about, we were both equally stubborn and known to go to extremes. I kissed his cheek.

He blinked at me. "Should I worry that you're being so agreeable?"

Over his shoulder, Max caught my eye and gave a small nod. I grabbed John's hand and smiled. "I've behaved now and then."

I led us back to the table, just as Jay and Rocco came into the room carrying a large birthday cake loaded with candles. John tossed his head back and laughed as everyone gathered around and sang. I hugged him after he blew out his candles.

"Happy birthday, Mr. Martinetti," I whispered in his ear.

We sat in the back of a black SUV as Jay drove us to the safe house. After the cake was served, there were many, many toasts and John and I were feeling the effects. Jay and Max rolled their eyes and ignored us after the third fit of giggles broke out. As John leaned his head back on the seat, I snuggled against him and let my hands wander.

"Behave," he whispered when my fingers reached his inner thigh.

"What's the fun in that?" I traced the outline of his cock.

He shifted in his seat and let out a groan. I watched Max's eyes shift in the rearview mirror and his eyebrows shot up before turning to the front. John's eyes closed as I stroked him slowly. My hand sped up and he cursed under his breath. I brought my face to his and he devoured my lips in a bruising kiss. His hand rested on my inner thigh and teased upward until his lips moved to my neck.

"You're playing with fire," he growled in my ear.

We turned down the alley behind the safe house and Jay parked by an old brick garage. He and Max checked their pistols and nodded to each other, and then Jay looked over his shoulder.

"We'll check the perimeter. You guys stay here," Max said.

"Take your time," I whispered, trying not to laugh at their facial expressions.

John blew out a breath as the door closed. "Just you wait until we get inside."

"Who said I wanted to wait?"

I crouched before him on my knees, running my hands down his muscular thighs. There was no hiding the tent in his black dress pants, so I teased my fingers across the tip through the fabric. He gasped and his hips jerked. My hands worked quickly to loosen the button and zipper. Once his cock was free, I dotted the crown with delicate kisses until his hand grasped my shoulder. My tongue licked the tiny dot of precum that leaked out.

"Fuck," he breathed.

"Not yet."

I slid his cock all the way to the back of my throat. He cradled my head in his hand, resting his thumb on my cheek as I moved my head up and down slowly. My eyes held his and I moaned around him, letting him slide in even deeper. His grip tightened in my hair and I moved my mouth faster.

"Liss, I don't want to stop, but...fuck! The guys will be back any second."

With a small groan of protest, I sat up and his cock slipped from my lips. The heat in his eyes told me there would be plenty more to come when we got inside. Once he was fully dressed and didn't look like I'd spent the past few minutes blowing him, he knocked on the back window. Seconds later, we heard two knocks in reply. He opened the door and took my hand to help me slide from the seat. Max's lip twitched when I nodded at him while Joey rolled his eyes. John shook both their hands and then led me toward the back of the house.

Once the door was locked, he was a man on a mission. Kissing me, he pressed me against the kitchen counter and spun me around. I braced my hands against the cold surface and pressed my legs together when his warm hands moved to the waistband of my jeans. In a flash, I quivered when my bare skin met the cold air. One of his hands pushed me harder against the counter while the other caressed my ass and continued lower until they reached my soaking pussy. I let out a gasp when he sank two of his fingers deep inside.

"So wet," he murmured. "I think someone enjoyed sucking my cock."

"Yes," I panted as he kept fucking me with his fingers. "Please."

Ignoring my protests when he took his hands away, he picked me up and dropped me on the counter. I jumped at the contact with the cold surface, but he held me in place and devoured my lips. Wrapping my legs around him, I yanked his sweater over his head and pulled him closer until his skin touched mine. He groaned and removed my sweater and bra while I kicked off my jeans and panties. Now completely naked, he pressed my breasts together and buried his face in between.

"I'm going to fuck these someday," he whispered before sucking a nipple into his mouth. "Along with that delicious ass of yours."

"John," I whined, pulling at the button of his pants. "I need you now."

"As my future wife commands."

With one arm around my shoulders and another under my ass, he lifted me up. We made it a few steps into the hallway before he pressed me up against the wall. I wrapped both arms around his neck and shivered when I felt the tip of his cock nudge my pussy.

"Fuck me," I whispered. "Please."

"Oh, I'm going to do much more than fuck you." He lowered my body and I let out a loud moan when he slammed inside me all the way to the hilt. "I warned you that you were playing with fire."

"It's my favorite kind of game," I panted in between his thrusts.

He pushed me harder against the wall and thrust wildly. I moved my hips to meet his, barely able to keep up. Throwing my head back to moan, he suckled and bit my neck. His hands gripped my thighs tighter and he watched me as his body devoured mine.

"This isn't a game," his voice husked. "You're going to feel me tomorrow." *Thrust.* "And the day after that." *Thrust. Thrust. Thrust.* "And the day after that."

"Oh god," I cried out when the pressure in my lower back couldn't be ignored.

His thrusts grew even more intense, so much so that I thought he'd split me in two. I threw back and screamed his name when my climax exploded. His pace slowed to ride out the tidal wave of sensations, and I cupped his face in my hands and gave him a tender kiss. Once my body stopped shaking, he resumed fucking me like a madman until he swore at the top of his lungs and clutched me to him while his cock twitched inside me.

We were still short of breath when he carried me to the bedroom and we both fell into the middle of the bed. My body was sore, but I still welcomed his embrace when he covered his body with mine.

"I love you," I whispered.

He kissed my temple. "I love you too. So, so much."

We held each other close until I shivered and he helped me under the covers. He then excused himself to check the doors were locked. Once we were properly snuggled together in bed, he held me in his arms as I fell asleep, bringing an end to what turned out to be our last peaceful night for a long time.

Chapter 16

Unleashed

Larissa

My body jolted to the side and arms closed around me. I blinked into the pitch blackness of my surroundings and tried, failing, to get my bearings as I was moved through the void surrounding me. Struggling against the arms constricting my movement only made them tighten their grip. Visions of my attack in a dark office in Portland made my heart pound. I tried one last time to break free and found myself pressed against a wall of muscle. A familiar scent washed over me and I froze. The air flow changed and my feet met a soft floor below. Placing my hand to the side, I felt a smooth wall. A large hand pulled me close.

"Don't make a sound," John's rough voice whispered. "He'll come back and hurt you." His grip relaxed and helped me sit down on the floor.

"Who?" I whispered. "Who's going to come back?"

"Franz."

Fuck. At the time, I didn't think of the darkness when I first woke up. The snowstorm must have knocked out the power, which turned off the radio and the lamp we kept in the corner of the room to help keep his two biggest triggers at bay. When he woke up to a dark, silent room... Oh god.

I took his hand in both of mine. The muscles in his arm were rigid, and I felt small tremors below the skin. He did his best to keep his breathing calm, but I heard his short, rapid breaths. I racked my brain trying to remember the advice John's counselor gave me.

"Gianni. It's Lissa. You're safe. I promise. The power is out."

"Baby, please don't." The pain in his voice made my heart ache. "I can't risk him hurting you."

"Franz can't hurt me. He's dead. I shot him."

He gasped and relaxed for a moment before the tension returned. "No. This is a dream. I watched him hurt you so many times. He won't do it again."

I needed to bring him back into the present, which would be hard since we were still in the worst possible surroundings. "Gianni, can you do something for me? I'd like you to take a deep breath for a few seconds, hold it, and then let it out slowly. Let's both try it."

His chest expanded against my back and the hand holding me in place flexed before easing a fraction. I nudged his hand upward to rest over my heart. His warm breath fanned over my shoulder as he exhaled and I leaned against him before taking my own deep breath.

"Gianni, it's Liss. I promise we aren't in that horrible place. We're in a safe house in Pentagon City." He let out a breath and slowly inhaled. "What do you feel in your right hand?"

His fingers flexed against my skin. "A heartbeat."

"That's right. You're feeling my heart beating because I'm here in the room with you. Can you put your left hand on the floor and tell me what you feel there?"

"Carpet."

"Yes. We're in the closet of our bedroom."

His head leaned against the back of mine and I relaxed in his hold. "Your hair feels real against my face."

"What does it smell like?"

"Strawberries."

"What does it usually smell like?"

"Coconut." He was silent for a moment and then his body sagged against mine. "Agent Connors grabbed the wrong shampoo on the last grocery run."

Both arms enveloped me and my heart broke when I felt him shaking. He whispered words into my hair I couldn't understand. I placed both hands over his arms and gently rocked back and forth. His body felt heavy against me after a while.

I leaned against his arm. "How are you feeling?"

"I don't know yet," he paused. "I'm sorry."

"Hey." I stood and gripped his hands to help him stand. "There is nothing, *nothing* for you to apologize for. But I think we should get back to bed. I can turn on the flashlight and radio on my phone to help?"

Without a word, the closet door opened and he led us back into the bedroom. Our slow progress across the floor made me realize he was counting his steps. We got on the bed, and he kept a hand on my leg as I fumbled around the nightstand for my phone. Once the small beam of light appeared, his shoulder sagged. Internet was spotty because of the outage, but I was able to turn on a nature sounds app for some background noise. I was thankful the gas furnace didn't need electricity to run, but sliding back under the covers felt like heaven.

"Are you sleepy at all?" I tried to hide the fatigue in my voice, but it wasn't very convincing.

"I don't know."

"That's okay. If I fall asleep, promise me you'll wake me up if you need anything?" At his silence, I sat up. "John, promise me."

"Okay, I will."

I got comfortable and closed my eyes. A moment later, he shifted and his head pressed against my chest. Caressing his cheek, I kissed his temple and then massaged the back of his head. As my eyes sagged closed, I hoped feeling my skin against his was as much of a comfort for him as it was for me.

· · · ● · · ● · ● · · · ·

I glared at the top of Felton's head as he hunched over a sheet of paper in front of him. We'd spent the morning going through and arguing over those plans. John was withdrawn and easily agitated thanks to our rude awakening, snapping at both of us and grousing to himself. It was almost a relief when he left the room to take a call from Paolo, but that left me alone in the room with the last person I wanted to see.

After feeling his stare for the third time, I'd had enough. "Is there something you'd like to ask me, Officer Lynch?"

His eyes went to my wrists. "I'm just...disappointed by some of the changes I've seen in you since the last time we spoke. The tattoos, for example. Did you really feel the need to mar your body like that?"

"Shall I list all the ways you've disappointed me? As for my tattoos, yes, I felt the need for them. I don't expect you to understand."

"I'd like to try."

"It's a bit late for that."

I read through the list of recent travel destinations of several people connected to the Sardi family. Aiden heard chatter about several key people moving around, and we sprang into action. To my relief, I found no flights from Athens, not that I had expected to see one. Those two were far too smart to make their movements so obvious.

John's cousins, Alexa and Athena Sardi, were bred for murder almost as soon as they could walk. Marco was probably the only other person whose bloodlust matched theirs. I was surprised Massimo never sent them after me. Even I knew I stood no chance against them since they preferred to attack in tandem. While I was hunting Sardi associates, I traveled to their estate in Athens hoping to catch them off-guard. The trip was an utter disaster. Not only did I find Marco training both girls, both in the sparring ring and the bedroom, but John found me and I narrowly missed his capture by less than an hour.

"Agent Donovan." Felton's voice persisted, snapping my eyes back to his. "I know I messed up. I know you hate me, and that you'll never trust me again. But I'm willing to try. Can we at least do that?"

I bit back my nasty reply. There was no way for him to know John shared stories from his Asset days, stories that differed vastly from the lies I was told by the man before me. His gambling addiction was very real, but the story about his drug addiction and getting a mobster's daughter killed was a lie. The truth was, Felton chose to rely on several low-level drug pushers who ratted out the daughter, an informant, and got her killed. The lies angered me enough, but John's PTSD episode overnight only rubbed salt in the wound.

Exhaling slowly, I mentally counted to ten. "You want answers, Mr. Lynch? Fine. I used my own name to fly home because I knew the Bureau wanted me. I made a deal with Barton, which is none of your business. Would you care to enlighten me how you found out I was in St. Petersburg?"

"One of Anton Volko's operatives was sent to look for one of his men who disappeared. A man by the name of Petyr." When my eyes widened, he nodded. "Otherwise known as Officer Jackson Michaels. Anyway, Volko's man found Officer Michaels. Imagine his surprise when he spotted his boss's most wanted."

"Nice to know I'm still living rent free in Anton's mind. What about Jackson?"

"We got him out. You were two days away from the Bratva nabbing you. Petracova went underground and Michaels has been stateside since."

I cursed under my breath. His cover was most likely blown, which meant he was on desk duty for a while. I hated that for him, and knew how miserable he felt, but it was better than the alternative. "I know you want to ride my ass for supposedly abandoning my job, but I'll never apologize for not going to Caracas. Not when I found out there was a hit squad waiting for me. This is where I remind you that the hit squad was there because of you. Does that cover all your questions, Mr. Lynch?"

"I'm—"

"I will never forgive you for what happened to John. Ever. And don't even get me started on selling me out to Gio. It really makes me wonder how many other times you tried to screw me over."

"I swear I didn't," he replied.

"Too bad your word means nothing. John and I have been comparing war stories from working for you. Quite enlightening, to say the least."

"I know you're upset."

In the blink of an eye, I sank the switchblade hidden in my pocket into the table a hair away from the side of his hand. "Don't you *dare* tell me you know how upset I am or that you have any idea how I feel."

Strong arms came around my waist and led me away. His calm eyes met mine when I whipped around to confront the jackass who interrupted me. "There's no need to fight over the last cup of coffee. One of you could've just made another pot," John said before turning to Felton. "I see you two are getting along well."

"Just clearing the air," I replied.

Felton watched my every move and I felt my eyes tingle. Growing up with him wasn't a miserable existence. It wasn't a house overflowing with love, but I knew he cared about me. He was the one who took me shopping for school clothes at the mall, helped me with my homework, and attended my graduations.

"I know I screwed up," he said quietly. "All I can do now is tell you both how sorry I am and do everything I can to help you with Massimo."

"You make it sound so simple," I replied, bracing my hands against the table. "I feel like I don't even know you. You've kept so many things from me. I still don't think you've told me all you know about my parents' murders, and god knows what else you've lied about."

He shook his head firmly. "I swear to you, on my life, that I had no hand in their deaths."

"I guess I'll have to take you at your word. Just know that if I find out you lied, your life won't mean shit. Because my fiancé and I have no problem stepping over your fucking corpse and leaving you to rot."

He glared at John. "Fiancé?"

"Yep. Wanna hear how we celebrated?"

"That really isn't necessary," John said. "In fact, I think we should probably head back. It's supposed to snow again tonight, and I'd rather we're off the roads when that happens."

As I busied myself with putting on my jacket and gloves, both men glared and mouthed several angry words back and forth. Felton and I awkwardly exchanged waves and I followed John down the hall. I found him tapping on the elevator button and looking at his phone.

"Well, that was one way to announce our engagement," John said as we crossed the lobby.

I rolled my eyes. "Like you were going to ask him for my hand anyway."

"Fair enough."

We stopped at the grocery store like we did most nights and after debating which bread made the best grilled cheese sandwich, we made our purchases and headed back to the safe house. The snow fell as we made our way to the back porch. Mesmerized, I stood at the top step and watched the tiny flakes swirl through the air. After a while, I felt a hand on my shoulder.

"Your hair has little icicles in it," he told me softly. "Let's get inside before the rest of you freezes."

"Fine."

"You were one of those kids who lived for playing in the snow, weren't you?"

"My dad and I used to sit on the window seat in their bedroom and watch the snow fall. Once there was enough on the ground, we'd go outside and play until I was cold and then Mom would make hot chocolate."

"How touching," a woman's thickly accented voice interrupted.

John moved to my front, caging my body between him and the kitchen counter. I looked over his shoulder and watched a tall, slender woman appear from the darkness. Her movements were deliberate and graceful as her light brown eyes locked on mine. His body tensed with each step she took.

"Lexi," he greeted tersely.

Alexa Sardi smiled. "Ah, Gianni. How surprising to find you with the murderess."

"I thought I smelled brimstone when we walked in. Where's the other demon?"

"She's around," she answered. "Why don't you go look for her while I have a word with your little whore?"

Anger radiated from his body as he traded verbal jabs with his cousin, but with it was an unspoken plea for me to stay silent. The counter dug into my back almost to the point of pain. I gently pushed him forward a few steps, allowing me to fully stand. Her eyes narrowed to slits as they met mine.

She tossed her long black hair over her shoulder and smirked. "I see she has to hide in order to face me. Pathetic."

"Hardly," he scoffed. "She's thought of at least three ways to kill you while we've been standing here."

I'd actually only thought of two, but both were simple and effective. I gave her a small smile and bowed my head. As she continued her scrutiny, I felt another presence in the room. My hand was still on John's back, making it easy for me to tap out the suspected location of his other cousin in Morse code against his sweater.

"Why isn't she running that mouth of hers? Father told me she was quite good at that."

"Just letting you two catch up. It's nice to meet you, Alexa. I'm Larissa Donovan."

She crossed her arms over her chest. "It's hard for me to believe this is the whore with the billion-dollar pussy that just might bring down the empire."

"Is it really an empire if your daddy has to worry about angering the Genovese?" I challenged.

Her jaw clenched. "How dare you insult my father?"

"Oh, I plan on doing a hell of a lot more than insulting him. I'm going to put a bullet in his head and send him to meet his brother. I have no problem giving you a one-way ticket to that family reunion."

"You insolent bitch!" Her fists clenched. "I look forward to turning you over to my father so he can put you in your place."

I poked John's lower back and he twisted to the right, allowing me to grab a can of soup from the grocery bag on the counter and hurled it. Expecting the can to be aimed at her face, she spun around, only to be surprised when it hit her in the lung just below her shoulder blade. She gasped and doubled over, giving me the few seconds I needed.

Charging forward, I punched her in the jaw. She grabbed my shirt as she fell, pulling me down to the floor. Her fingernails clawed at my neck and moved upward. I seized her hand and bent it back until she screeched. Her right elbow flew backward, earning several hard punches to her back before I fell forward.

"Liss!" John's panicked voice yelled out.

"I'm okay," I panted, scrambling to my feet.

Alexa's arm flew around my neck and squeezed. Fighting my body's reflex to panic, I tucked my chin under as best as I could and rocked back and forth. She laughed softly and tightened her hold. I slid the switchblade from my jeans, and she screamed when the blade tore through her forearm, stopping less than an inch from her elbow. The knife clattered to the floor as I rolled away and jumped to my feet.

I grabbed her hair and slammed her face against the wall behind me. The light gray paint was spattered with blood as she slid down the wall and landed on the floor in a heap. I moved to grab her again, but her hand slashed upward and a blade sliced the inside of my right arm. I spun away, heading back to my knife lying on the floor next to the counter.

Something crashed, followed by yelling down the hall, but I had to tune it out and focus on the killer directly before me. She lunged forward and slashed wildly, catching my upper arm with the tip of the blade. I spun around and sliced low, and when I heard the small cry, I knew the target was hit. The blood seeping from her side confirmed it.

She clutched her side, twirled the knife in her fingers and circled me again. I stayed still, never breaking eye contact. Her steps slowed, only to change direction and then move faster. I watched her, calmly waiting for her next move. When she suddenly lunged forward and swung wildly, I leaped back and slashed at her arm.

"I'd love nothing more than to drop your head onto my father's desk," she spat. "Unfortunately, you're to be delivered to him alive."

"Fortunately for me, you're doing a really shitty job."

She screamed and flew at me again. I grabbed her injured arm and pulled her hair down, earning a cut to my left forearm. Wincing, I balled up my right fist and punched her in the face. She lost her footing and fell, but not before grabbing my shoulder and bringing me down with her. As soon as I hit the ground, I kicked my legs to untangle my body from hers.

She seized my ankle and pulled. I flipped onto my back and found her trying to steady the knife in her hand. I wrenched my other leg from under her body and kicked her injured side, causing her to gasp. As she struggled to breathe, I lunged and sank my knife into her neck. Blood poured from her mouth before she fell backwards to the floor. I grabbed the knife out of her hand and struggled to stand up.

"Larissa!" John screamed from the other room.

"In here."

He helped me to my feet. "Thank god."

"Please tell me you found the other one. Because there's absolutely no way I have the energy to do that again."

He took my hand and I hobbled behind him into the living room, stopping short when we rounded the corner. My eyes widened as I took in the sight of a bloodied woman bound to the coffee table with zip ties. Her eyes were closed, but opened after I took a couple of steps.

"Darling, I can't help but notice we have an assassin tied to the table," I observed, grabbing a scarf from the floor and wrapping it around my bleeding arm.

"Cocksuckers!" she screeched.

"And an extremely hostile one at that," I added under my breath.

He smiled. "Sorry, babe. I forgot my manners. Athena, this is Larissa, my fiancée. Liss, this is my cousin, Athena. You met her sister earlier."

"What did you do to my sister, bitch?"

I stabbed her sister's knife into the table right next to her head. "What do you think happened to her?"

"Where is he?" John demanded.

She let out a chilling, evil laugh that left me uneasy. "Gianni, you're interrupting us. You were saying, Miss Donovan?"

"I was saying your sister choked on my knife. Apparently, she thought you two were going to deliver me to your father."

"Where is he, Athena?"

"I saw you," she murmured. "That day in Athens. I saw you watching the house."

"I'll admit I didn't do the best job of keeping myself hidden. Then again, your cousin found me and I had to leave. But I saw plenty of you that day as well, along with your sister and Marco."

She closed her eyes as if savoring the memory. "That was a glorious day."

"I always expected your father would dispatch you two to find me, but he never did. I was disappointed."

"We were given another mission."

"Dare I ask what that mission was? The three of you seemed pretty...cozy when I was there."

John looked uneasy. "Liss."

"Producing an heir."

His head whipped around. "What?"

"You betrayed the family the day you stuck your cock into this filthy whore. Father sent Marco to Athens, hoping to produce an heir. A male heir, one who would replace you as head of the family."

"One he could mold into another murderous psychopath," I said. "I guess the plan didn't quite work out since both of you showed up here instead."

Her face darkened. "Alexa had a miscarriage. My two sons were stillborn. I begged Father to send Marco back, but by then, he had a new plan."

I didn't like where this was heading. "And what was that?"

"He witnessed for himself just how far Gianni would go to keep you safe. It intrigued him. He was also looking for a suitable revenge for his treachery at the ball. That was when he decided he would take you as his bride and mother to his next heir. He put that bounty out on you in order to ensure you were brought to him alive."

"But you said so yourself. I'm a filthy whore. Why would he taint himself with me?"

Her eyes lit up. "Because the best way to torture my cousin would be forcing him to watch Father take you repeatedly until you gave him a son."

The temperature in the room felt icy except for the rage coming from John. I put my hand out to stop him, but he thundered past me. Yanking the knife from the table, he slashed across her face. She winced and closed her eyes briefly before opening them and staring at the ceiling as he stood above her.

"Well, I hate to break your father's heart, but it's not going to happen," he bit out. "She's mine and I'm hers. And that sick fuck can't do anything about that."

She rolled her eyes and laughed. "You know he has his ways. He won't stop until he has her in his bed and you chained to the wall so you can watch and hear every scream as he takes what's his."

"Where is he?" he roared, slashing the other side of her face.

"Over and over again," she taunted. "Oh, and did I mention that if the baby is a girl, you'll be the one to kill it?"

"John." I put my hand on his shoulder, hoping to calm him. Athena knew her life was over, so now it seemed she was after her own revenge with words she knew would torture him long after she was dead.

"And when she finally gives him a son, and she's of no more use to him, he'll either give her to Marco and the men, or it will be your job to kill her."

My heart stuttered in my chest and I shut my eyes tight. His whole body shook so hard the knuckles that held the knife turned white. I continued to say his name softly until he took a deep, ragged breath and slowly exhaled.

"Larissa, I want you to step away from me and go into the other room. Right now, please," he commanded in a voice that was way too calm.

I squeezed his shoulder and backed away. His breathing continued to come out in ragged pants and Athena's eyes grew wider the farther away I moved. "Thank you," he whispered. "Please activate the alarm on your phone. Quickly."

My phone fell near the back door and I raced to grab it. The screen had just unlocked when a scream tore through the house. I pressed the button on my app that alerted Barton, Aiden, and Paolo that I was in danger. The next sound from the other room sounded like a battle cry and I ran. As I turned the corner, he emerged from the kitchen. Exhaling, he dropped the bloody knife. He held me close and planted soft kisses all over my face and neck.

He gave me a quick kiss. "We need to pack. Quickly. The guys will be here soon."

"Don't we need to wait for the FBI?"

He shook his head. "Absolutely not. We have to leave now."

"But—"

"You don't understand. If they're here, that means their father is here, too."

Chapter 17

Dominoes

Larissa

I PEERED OUT THE window from the backseat of the SUV, still dazed from the events of the past few hours. After the alarm was activated, four of John's men arrived within minutes. They found the two FBI agents stationed outside the safe house inside their car with their throats slashed. The next thing I knew, we were in an abandoned building that was apparently used as an underground medical clinic.

When Barton frantically burst through the clinic doors some time later, John lunged at him and had to be held back as he demanded answers. Most of the men left the room, leaving the rest of us to listen to their shouting match as Joey stitched up my arms. By the time they finished arguing, the adrenaline had worn off and I was curled up on an old couch trying to stay awake. John caressed my cheek and I found him standing above me.

He stared at the bandages. "I'm such a shit. I never even asked if you were okay."

"Nothing I'm not used to. Just a few more scars to add to the collection."

He sat down beside me and placed his head in his hands. I leaned my head on his shoulder as he sighed. Barton entered, earning a glare from him when his head snapped up.

"Both of you stop right now," I said. "It's late, everyone is tired, and it's far too early in the investigation to know how they found us."

"I wish I could agree with that, Lissa," Barton replied. "But it looks like one of Massimo's men got to one of the day guards. Your identities are still secure, but the safe house obviously isn't."

"Which is why the FBI won't know our location until there's a need to know," John snapped.

"But Massimo is bound to know you're the lead on the case by now. What about you? What about Yolanda and the kids?"

"Four US Marshals picked them up and took them to an undisclosed location. As for me, the DOJ has now classified me as a special witness in the case against Felton. I'm being moved to another location. I'll give you the number to my secured line so I can be reached in an emergency."

"Georgia? What about her?"

"She'll be in California for the next few weeks. Everyone else is being taken care of. The only one left is you," he answered.

"And we'll be heading out as soon as Rocco and Max finish loading up," John added. "The others should be there soon."

I nodded, and my body suddenly felt very heavy. As the two men talked, my eyes drooped. I nodded now and then, the words they spoke barely permeating through the fog that settled in my head. Moments later, John helped me to my feet, and I vaguely remembered Barton giving me a quick hug and begging me to be careful before he left. I glanced down at my shirt and realized I was still wearing the same bloody clothes from the safe house and wrinkled my nose.

"Once we get to the new place, we'll take a shower," John murmured as he carried me outside.

"Where's that?"

"You'll see when you wake up."

We were soon speeding down the highway, headed to our own undisclosed location. I watched the scenery fly past and tried to ignore the pain in my arms. Joey offered me pain meds, but I needed to stay alert in case of another ambush.

"You should get some sleep," John whispered as he pulled me against his chest. "You look exhausted."

"So do you."

The light from the center console illuminated his face enough that I saw the pain in his eyes. When his arm around me tightened a third time, I knew Athena's words were in his head. As his hand moved to cradle the back of my head, he exhaled a slow, ragged breath. I reached up and cupped his cheek, turning him to face me.

"They're just words, baby. Words of a dead woman who wanted to get inside your head. Don't let her linger there."

For all I knew, everything she said was a load of crap. Deep in my heart, however, I knew it was probably true. Massimo's treachery and depravity knew no bounds, which probably made the images in John's head worse.

"I'm trying. I can't..."

"Tell me how you picture our wedding. You said you've seen it in your head a million times. Is it inside or outside?"

"Liss."

"Inside or outside, soldier," I repeated with a smile. "That should be easy enough."

"Inside. A church. An old church."

"Big one or small one?"

"Doesn't matter."

"Don't give me that. Do you want a big ceremony or a small ceremony?"

"It doesn't matter as long as we have the ceremony. It could be the Sistine Chapel, or it could be a tiny chapel in the middle of nowhere. I don't care. All I need is a priest to declare us husband and wife."

I snuggled into his chest. "Tell me more."

"I know what you're doing," he whispered in my ear.

"All I'm doing is listening to your ideas for our wedding. Is my dress white? I've been debating between white or off-white, but I'm kind of worried white might make my ass look big."

He chuckled and lightly kissed the top of my head before describing me in a white dress as we danced at our reception. I shared some of my thoughts, not realizing the length and style of my dress was up for such a spirited debate. I was telling him my ideas for our honeymoon when his head drooped onto my shoulder. His eyes were closed and his breathing slow and even. Tucking my head under his, I let my eyelids fall and tried to let the sounds of the road lull me to sleep.

The clock on the center console showed it was just after three in the morning when John nudged me awake. The SUV was parked behind a medium-sized building surrounded by several white vans. Paolo and John helped me climb from the back seat and ushered me inside. We passed by a large kitchen and a dark room full of chairs and couches. Seeing my confusion, John explained we were in an old retirement home.

"Second floor, turn left. Last door at the end of the hall," Paolo called after us as John guided me up the stairs.

"Thanks. I'll be down as soon as we get settled," he called over his shoulder.

We entered what looked like a hotel suite. The lights were dim, but I saw a loveseat and TV as we passed through the small living area to the bedroom. Our bags were laying on the bed, but instead of stopping, he led me into the bathroom. He turned on the shower and helped me out of my clothes. His clothes followed and then we were both under the warm water, washing the night from our bodies.

"Where are we? Who owns this place?" I looked up as he massaged conditioner into my hair.

"Staten Island. I'm not sure who owns it. Aiden told Paolo about it, so I'm guessing it belongs to Titus or one of his associates. My guess is the rest of Titus's crew will be here soon."

I nodded and looked at the bruises on his chest and arms. There were several minor cuts across his knuckles and a larger slash on the back of his left hand. He shook his head.

"They aren't nearly as bad as yours. She got distracted by the screams in the other room, and I was able to knock her out. Which reminds me, I need to take a look at your cuts." He pointed to my arm. "One is still bleeding."

After drying off, he removed the bandage and examined the wound. He cursed under his breath when he saw the severity of the cut, and reapplied the dressings. By the time we headed to the bedroom, I could barely keep my eyes open. He tucked me into bed and gave me a soft kiss.

"I need to talk to the men about a few things. I promise I won't be long," he told me softly. "Get some rest."

I nodded and watched him dress quickly. He caught me staring as he finished and smirked. After giving me one last kiss, he left, locking the door behind him. I turned on the small TV in front of the bed and drifted off to sleep. The last thing I remembered was his arms wrapping around me and his warm body against mine.

The air was chilly across my shoulders, but I couldn't move to burrow under the covers. I opened my eyes and found John's head nestled against my chest. His arms wound around me like muscular vines, so I brushed a lock of hair from his forehead and smiled at the peaceful look on his face. Peace was a rare occurrence when he slept. I'd lost count of the number of mornings I watched him push away his worries and put on a brave face once he realized I was awake. Stifling a yawn, I cradled his head in my arms.

My eyes had just closed when my FBI phone rang with a loud pulsating tone that rudely interrupted the quiet. John bolted upright as I grabbed the phone, only to flop on his back after I gave his arm a gentle squeeze.

"Hello?" I answered softly.

"Lissa," Aiden's uneasy voice replied. "We've got a problem."

My heart sank. I was approaching my limit of problems. "What's wrong?"

"Titus is missing."

It was now my turn to bolt upright in bed. I covered my body with the sheet and rubbed the sleep from my eyes. "What makes you think he's missing?"

"He was supposed to meet Fiona last night and never showed. And he hasn't checked in this morning. He always calls both me and her. Always."

I closed my eyes and steadied my thoughts. John was looking at messages on his phone when his brows raised and his face suddenly looked grim. Aiden's urgent voice pulled me back to my call after he repeated my name for the third time.

"Sorry," I muttered, trying to catch John's eye. He was out of bed dialing his phone.

"The last time Fi heard from him was yesterday morning when they made plans to meet. I have a bad feeling about all of this." The anxiety in Aiden's voice made my stomach churn.

I froze just as John caught my eye. "Wait. What the hell was Titus doing in New York? I thought he went back to Belfast."

"He came back a few days ago. As for why, he kept that to himself. I didn't even know until I called Fi one night and she told me he was there."

Alarm bells blared, made louder by the look on John's face. He sat on the bed and shook his head when I raised my eyebrows at him. Something was wrong. Something was very wrong. "Where's Finn?"

"He's driving a bunch of the lads to you guys," Aiden answered. "They're to go where you go. You know that."

"And with Titus missing, you know what that means," I replied quietly.

"No. Lissa, no."

"I have to follow the protocols the same as you. I'm calling Cal. You're to pack up your location and remain on standby for further instructions."

"Okay," he responded after a pause.

"I'm sorry. But this was how he wanted it, and there's too much at stake. We'll keep you in the loop as best we can. I promise."

"Understood," he replied curtly before ending the call.

I buried my face in both hands and took a deep, slow breath to calm my nerves. I felt John's hand on my shoulder and saw deep concern etched on his face when I looked up. Shaking my head, I closed my eyes.

His voice was gentle. "How bad?"

"You tell me. Who called?"

"Barton. There was a shooting in Chinatown last night. Eddie O'Rourke and his daughter were killed."

The news was a punch to the gut, causing me to gasp. "Fuck."

"Why do you need to call Cal?"

"Titus was in New York, but he's missing. If that happens, there's a protocol we all have to follow, safeguards he put in place."

His brows furrowed. "Safeguards? For whom?"

"Key people in his organization. Aiden is second in command and Fiona, well, she's probably the closest thing Titus will ever have to a wife."

I dialed Cal's number. "Lissa, thank god," he answered with a relieved sigh. "I was just about to call you."

"I know about Eddie, but that's not why I'm calling. Titus is missing."

"Fuck!" He yelled before taking several breaths to regain his composure. "Tell me everything that was reported to you."

We made a plan to get Aiden and Fiona out of the city and back to Ireland. Six of Titus's men would join them on the trip, but Finn would stay behind to lead the remainder of the Irish crew. Cal told me to be careful and stay hidden almost a dozen times before we hung up. I tossed my phone on my night table and curled up in bed.

"How bad is it?" John asked.

"Looks like Massimo is trying to take down the Irish from the top in the hopes the rest fall like dominoes. I'll worry less once we get Fiona and Aiden to safety."

"What about Titus?"

"Nobody has heard from him, or knows why he was even here. For now, we stick to our plan and hope he turns up."

"Are you okay?"

I exhaled slowly. "I'm as good as I can be after the last twelve hours. Just have to keep soldiering on. Has anyone heard from Felton?"

He helped me to my feet. "I'll call him while you get dressed and then we'll go eat breakfast.

Talbot and his men arrived in D.C. and Felton picked them up from a private airfield. After hearing about my attack, he told John they were on their way to join us in New York. I insisted he not be told about Titus's disappearance. There was no reason to doubt him, but the last few weeks made me wary.

I had a ton of pent-up anxiety after breakfast, so I spent the latter part of the morning sparring with Rocco and Max in the activity room. After my fight with Alexa, I not only realized I was out of shape, but also out of practice. Max and I focused on knife fighting while Rocco and I worked on hand to hand combat. I finally flipped him over my shoulder when the sound of applause broke my concentration. Glancing up, I saw John standing in the doorway. He nodded at his men, who clapped me on the shoulder and left the room.

"Care to go a couple of rounds?" I joked as he walked closer.

"I believe I learned my lesson the hard way, Miss Donovan." He pulled me into a kiss.

"Yeah, but I could use all the help I can get. Any news?"

"Cal, Aiden, and Fiona are safe. Thomas and Joey are driving them to *the* safe house," he replied. "He said you'd know which one that meant."

I nodded, relieved they were safe. "What about Felton?"

"Talbot has a place in Newark, so they're all holed up there for now."

"And Finn?"

He narrowed his eyes. "How about we have some lunch and check your bandages?"

"I'm guessing there's no way I can say no."

"You're telling me you'd turn down the chance to spend time with me?"

I giggled as we made our way to the kitchen. The last of Titus's men arrived, and we briefed them all on the disappearance. There were very few questions, as his men were well-prepared to handle things in his absence. Soon everyone was settled into their rooms and the place buzzed with voices and activity.

John caught me wincing during lunch, so he gave me a pain pill and dragged me upstairs once I started to doze off. What few protests I grumbled were answered with a kiss, and after that I didn't fight it. When I woke up, his fingers were caressing my spine as he looked out the window.

I sat up. "You're thinking about it again, aren't you?"

He closed his eyes as if my words pained him. "How can I not? Knowing he plans to do that if he gets his hands on you?"

"You know this is how he works. We knew he would never back down from targeting me."

"How are you so calm?"

I pulled his face closer to mine. "Because we're both still standing. Together."

"I can't lose you," he breathed as he buried his face in the crook of my neck.

"I can't lose you, either. I won't. Before I met you, I only existed for the next case or the next lead in the hopes it brought me closer to bringing your uncles down. And then you came along and showed me there was more to life, how to love and how to be loved. There's no way in hell I'm letting some asshole with a god complex take what we have away."

When his lips met mine, my body ignited. He grasped my hair and kissed me hungrily, absorbing the soft moans that came from my throat. I pulled at the hem of his shirt and lightly ran my fingers across the waistband of his jeans, smiling against his lips when he shivered. He let out a low growl and rolled me onto my back.

I motioned him closer and he obliged, covering my body with his. My shirt was tossed on the floor seconds later, and when his mouth latched onto my neck, I squeezed my legs together to quell the need.

A loud knock at the door and Max's loud voice telling us it was time for dinner doused the mood. John glared at the door before turning back to me as I pursed my lips to keep from laughing. He burrowed his head in my chest.

"Son of a bitch," he groaned.

"There's always after dinner."

He rolled his eyes and we both got dressed. Loud, cheerful voices met us in the hall, along with the sounds of a ball bouncing on the floor. The Irish were on cooking duty that night as the mouthwatering aroma of Irish stew hit my nose as soon as we got to the stairs. We shoved the tables together so we could eat as one giant group, and soon the room was filled with the sounds of everyone tucking in for a big family meal.

John stayed close, and as we laughed at Rocco's ridiculous jokes he wrapped his arm around my shoulder. When Rocco complained we were about to kiss, I sprang from my seat and placed a loud kiss on his cheek. The table broke out in laughter and catcalls. Rocco blushed into his beer, earning even more laughter and ribbing from Max and Joey.

My red phone vibrated in my pocket. I grabbed it quickly and every tense muscle in my body relaxed when I saw the display. John's eyes widened and he sat up straighter. I slid my finger across the screen and pressed it to my ear.

"Thank god! Do you know how worried we've all been?" I'd been desperate to hear the voice on the other end all day.

A slow, deep laugh filled my veins with ice. I reached for John, who tensed when he saw my face. He motioned to the table, and the room went silent. With my eyes squeezed tight, I willed my lungs to fill with air so I could speak, but my voice remained stubbornly mute.

"Good evening, Miss Donovan," the smug voice of Massimo Sardi greeted. "I hope you're having an enjoyable evening with my nephew."

My eyes filled with tears that spilled onto the table in front of me. I turned away from the table, unable to meet anyone's eyes as Massimo dealt whatever fatal blow he planned. John grasped my shoulder and spun me around, instructing me to focus on my breathing. He then took the phone from my hand and put it on speaker.

"Massimo," he growled. "Just say what you need to say."

"Ah, Gianni, so good to hear from you. I was annoyed nobody called to tell me you were no longer being held hostage."

"What do you want?"

"So impatient!" he scolded. "Can't a man catch up with his favorite nephew?"

"Not when the man could give two shits about his family, unless he can exploit them for his own personal gain."

He exhaled slowly. "I care deeply for my family. In fact, I tried to pay my mother a visit, but I can't seem to find her. Might you know where she is?"

"She's taking a very well-earned holiday in a private location. She's fine."

"That may be, my boy. However, she's still my mother and I insist on speaking with her."

John rolled his eyes. "Massimo, why don't you quit wasting our time and tell me why you called?"

"I was just getting to that before you so rudely interrupted," he spat. "You see, I was concerned for her safety. I did some digging and had just about given up when a chance meeting put me in possession of this phone number."

My hands shook and I stood to pace the floor, trying to calm my anxiety. My stomach churned, and I focused on my breathing once again. Our eyes met again and John shook his head.

"Well, you really didn't need to steal a phone to tell me you're inviting Nonna to a party. How about you give the phone back to its rightful owner and send him on his way?"

"Oh, but that's where you're wrong. I gave this phone number to an acquaintance, and he was able to glean quite a bit of information. For example, your phone sends and receives a lot of text messages. And most of those text messages go to an area in the Indian Ocean."

"What do you want, Massimo?" I gritted out.

"Ah, there you are, Miss Donovan. I was afraid you'd miss our conversation. You have a debt that must be paid, young lady. And it's long overdue."

"And what guarantees do I have that you'll release my uncle and leave my family alone?"

The line filled with the sounds of multiple people laughing. I pushed back from the table and grabbed the phone from John's hand. Tossing my hair over my shoulder, I resumed my pacing.

"I never said I'd release your uncle, my dear," he scoffed once the laughter stopped. "All I said was I acquired a phone number and gleaned a lot of useful information from it."

"Then what incentive do I have?"

"I'm so glad you asked. My acquaintance was unable to triangulate a specific location of those text messages during their initial search, but assured me they could do so in a few days. Once we find where you've hidden them, it won't take long for me to gather all my men for an old-fashioned welcoming party for my mother," he taunted, pausing. "As well as my sister, your brother and anyone else we come across."

My heart hammered so hard it ached. John kept trying to get my attention, but I turned away, unable to face him at that moment. He spun me around, and I opened my mouth to protest until voices started yelling on the other end of the line. Amongst the shouting, a voice swore loudly and my heart dropped to my stomach. I took a deep breath to calm my nerves, knowing the inevitable had now come.

"When and where?" I stubbornly ignored the angry squeeze of my shoulder.

"Midnight. Gianni will know the place, and I expect him to accompany you."

"Fine."

"And I will advise to all my nephew's flunkies who I know are listening that anyone else accompanying you two will be dealt with."

"Understood," John replied, glancing over his shoulder at Paolo.

Another argument broke out on the other end, followed by more cursing and cries of pain. After a couple of seconds of silence, Massimo's voice returned. "It seems your uncle would like to say goodbye."

My hands shook as I heard quiet voices. John tried to take the phone, but I moved out of his grasp. If this was indeed my last conversation with Titus, I had to be as close to his voice as possible.

"Lissi," his voice rasped.

"Titus, I'm so, so sorry. I wish..."

"Me too."

He coughed. "Can the shithead hear me?"

John pursed his lips to suppress a smile. "Yes, sir."

"Now he kisses up to me," he muttered to himself. "I still don't like you, Martinetti. Your bullshit damn near took away one of the few things on this ball of fucking mud that I treasure. That woman next to you was my brother's world, and she quickly became mine from the moment she shook my hand."

"She's my world, too, sir," he answered, holding my gaze as I swiped away tears.

"You make damn sure she stays that way. It's on you now to keep her safe, keep her happy. If she sheds a single tear because of you, there will be consequences. I won't be there to shoot your nuts off, but someone sure as hell will. You remember that before you do anything stupid. I'm everywhere and I always will be."

"Don't I know it," he muttered. "I would rather die than see her in pain."

"That will happen sooner than you think," Massimo mocked.

"Shut the fuck up!" Titus yelled.

"Titus!" I screamed, almost hysterical.

He sighed. "I love you, little fire. I'm sorry."

"No," I sobbed.

"*Tiocfaidh ár lá*," he whispered, his voice barely audible.

"*Tiocfaidh ár lá*," I repeated.

A single gunshot rang out, followed by loud cheers. The sound of Massimo's voice barely registered when the phone fell from my hand, echoing loudly. As I looked at John's anguished face, my legs buckled under me and I fell to the floor.

Chapter 18

Revelations

John

Time slowed to a crawl. I watched as her heart shattered and she crumpled to the floor like a puppet whose strings were cut. Paolo and Finn were already calling for the men to gather as I scooped her into my arms and carried her out of the room. Halfway up the stairs, she let out a small sound, and by the time we made it back to our room, her arms were wrapped tightly around my neck as heavy sobs racked her body.

I sat on the couch and held her as she cried. Seeing her tear-stained face broke my heart. I reached up and gently wiped the tears away from her cheeks. She whispered her thanks and laid her head on my chest when I hugged her to me. She sat up and faced me, her face set in determination.

"I need a secure line to call Lucas."

"Why?"

"He told me Titus had been trying to get in touch with him. I need to know what they talked about. I also need to make sure Aiden is safe." When I argued, she shook her head. "You don't understand. My ex-IRA uncle wanted to talk to my tactician brother. That's an unholy alliance that, thankfully, is on our side."

I raised my eyebrows. "I knew he ran guns, but we could never confirm or prove it was connected to the IRA."

"He joined up after the rest of the family moved to the States. Pretty active until about five years ago. He still supplies guns for the cause."

"What did he say to you?"

She wiped her eyes when a few tears fell. "'Our day will come'. It's a common phrase used by the IRA. That's why I need to talk to Lucas. Titus was in New York because those two were working on something. I need to know what."

"Where does Aiden fit into all this? Why is everyone so protective of him?"

"He's Titus's son. Fiona is his mother. He's also next in line to take over the...business. There's a lot at stake if he doesn't make it back to Belfast in one piece."

She leaned her head against my chest and stared blankly at the wall ahead of her as I focused on the blank TV screen in front of us. The room was silent as we allowed our separate thoughts to wander. I found myself once again cursing Felton for creating this fucking mess, and hoping we both made it to the other side of all this so he would finally be out of her life.

"What can you tell me about this place Massimo wants us to meet him?"

"It's an old dance hall near JFK. My dad bought it when they first got to the States as an investment. It was supposed to go to me when my parents died, but I signed it over to Gio to help pay off some of my gambling debt."

"How bad?"

"It's not good, and we don't have any time to plan." I kissed the back of her hand. "We've got about four hours. I'm going to get Joey working on the secure line and then try to figure out where everyone is. How about you get your gear ready?"

I grabbed her gear bags from the closet and left her sitting between them on the floor. Joey said it would take at least an hour to set up the line, which left me to find Paolo. He and Rocco were in the dining room looking at a floor plan of the club on a computer screen. Relieved to see they were already working on a plan, I pulled up a chair, only for my heart to sink when I saw the balcony surrounding the dance floor in the center of the room. Rocco pointed out the service hallway leading from the kitchen to the balcony, but we all knew Massimo would have it heavily covered. Finn wandered in a short time later, and when I left them, they were discussing more ideas for getting access to the hallway.

She was putting a small pistol back together when I returned to our room. She looked through the sight for several seconds before shaking her head and tossing it to the side. I sat on the floor behind her, positioning her between my legs. Her hands shook as she picked up another pistol and studied it.

She pulled back the hammer and narrowed her eyes. "How bad is it?"

"The balcony surrounds the dance floor. Two narrow staircases, one at the east corner of the building and another through the kitchen. East corner has an elevator, which we all know will be heavily guarded. The parking lot is fenced in on three sides with limited access to an alley that is very easy to block."

She dropped the gun and stared at the ceiling. "I'm scared." Her voice was barely a whisper.

"I am, too."

"Felton is on his way with Talbot and his men. They had to stop by one of their storage places to grab more ammo."

"Lovely. And the secure line?"

"Joey was working on it. We should have it within the hour."

She leaned her head against my chest and closed her eyes. "What are we going to do?"

"Win."

"Sounds easy enough. What's Plan B?"

"Are you doubting the plan, Miss Donovan?"

She rolled her eyes. "Of course not."

Loud knocking on the door interrupted my reply. Max yelled that the secure line was set up, and we needed to hurry. We both raced to the door and followed him downstairs. She stopped short when she rounded the corner and came face to face with Felton. The temperature in the room dropped several degrees.

"Lissa," he began, sighing. "I wish there was something I could say."

Her eyes blazed and then closed. I knew she was trying to rein in her temper because when they reopened, they were calm but cold. "Thank you for coming," she answered shortly and brushed past him.

We marched down the hall to what looked like a small library or study room. Shelves filled with books lined the walls while all the tables were shoved to the center and were now littered with countless modules and computer parts. Joey pointed to the two headsets next to him and we put them on quickly.

"Lissa?" Lucas's voice was cautious

"I'm here," she answered. "John and I are both here."

"Hey, assface," I added.

"I'm sorry to call you at whatever ungodly hour it is there, but you know I wouldn't if it wasn't important." She took a deep breath. "What did Titus want to talk to you about?"

Dead fucking silence. I knew what that meant, and that once Lucas responded, there would be a fight. Her jaw clenched, and she folded her arms across her chest. Fuck, this wasn't going to be pretty.

"Lucas?"

"I can't tell you. I'm sorry."

She glared at the screen as if Lucas could somehow feel her anger over the line. "He's dead. Massimo fucking shot him when he called me last night. So I'm going to say it again. My uncle was in New York when he could've been safely back in Ireland. Why did he come here, Lucas? Tell me why he came here so I can understand why I had to send his son away so he could be snuck back into Belfast."

"I wish I could, but I made a promise that I wouldn't say anything."

"Cut the bullshit!" she yelled, kicking a chair. "He's dead, Lucas! He's gone and I don't even get to send his body home. I can't even look Aiden in the eye and tell him why he was here. No, instead I get to tell him that his father came here and fucking died because of me."

"Aiden will understand," he replied.

She blinked. "You knew about Aiden?"

"Yes. Titus knew the risks, and he didn't care. We both agreed it was better if you didn't know."

She made a sour face. "So you're telling me it's okay that you two had some sort of plan cooked up that concerned me, but I'm not worth even knowing about it?"

"That's not what I'm saying at all, and you fucking know it, Larissa! I'm saying we both felt—"

"Go fuck yourself," she snarled and tore out of the room.

Joey's wide eyes turned to me immediately after the door slammed. I scrubbed my hand over my face and turned my head skyward. Just fucking perfect. She was going to be an absolute delight once this call was over.

Lucas sighed. "It's bad, isn't it?"

I thought of a response that wouldn't freak him out. "It's not good, man."

"I'm sorry. Go calm her down. She sounded pretty pissed."

"Bit of an understatement, but yeah."

"You guys be careful. I mean it."

A low buzz filled the room when he ended the call, much like the noise in my head after the conversation. Forcing Lucas to a vow of secrecy worried me about Titus's mission. What the hell was he after? Apparently something worth dying for, but I wasn't sure we'd ever know. Whatever it was, I hoped he'd made it happen.

I wandered through the lobby on my way to our room, and it was a flurry of activity. It looked like the Irish had picked up their weapons, judging by the large crates at the bottom of the stairs. I whipped around when I heard heavy footsteps behind me and nodded at Talbot, fighting the urge to wipe the sickening smirk off his face as he sauntered past. God, how I hated that sick fuck.

Our bedroom floor was littered with clothing and gear when I entered. She sat between the two bags, pulling knives from the bottom of one while swearing and muttering under her breath. I crouched down and placed my hand on her arm. She jerked her body out of my grasp and shot me a glare.

I held up my hands. "I'm on your side."

"So are my brother and uncle. Allegedly."

I grasped her upper arms and pulled her up to stand. "Stop. Titus would've had his reasons for keeping it from you. It's a shitty situation all the way around, but now is not the time to let it get in your head."

She blew out a breath. "It's hard to not feel hopeless right now."

"I know. We just have to keep pushing, not allow ourselves to think of the alternative, and do what we can to make sure we're the ones walking out of there tonight."

"That means you too."

"Baby, if it comes down to your life or mine, yours wins. Always."

She held firm. "No! Absolutely not. That's not how this works, goddamn it!"

"If it means you have a life away from all this shit, yes, that is *exactly* how this will work. I love you too damn much to ever—"

My words were lost when she pulled me into a deep, savage kiss. She wrapped her arms around my neck and gasped when I cupped her ass with both hands and lifted her up. Her legs wrapped around my waist before I sat back on the bed. My hands moved under her shirt and lightly caressed her lower back. She leaned back on my lap and held my gaze once we broke apart.

"You are my sin and salvation," I whispered, leaning my forehead against hers.

"Salvation?"

"You saved me long before that warehouse. Before you came along, I'd resigned myself to being my uncles' puppet. It was a dark, shitty existence, but I was okay with it if it kept those I cared about safe. And then a mysterious sniper went and wormed her way into my heart, and everything changed. There's a light in you, one that sometimes glows softly, steadily. And sometimes it explodes and burns hotter than the sun. From the moment I met you, I wanted to be close to that light. And when you finally let me in, I needed that light...and the fearless hellion that came with it."

"Not always fearless," she whispered.

"No, but you gave me hope for something more, too. I want nothing more than a life with you, but if I have to give mine up so you'll survive, I'll gladly do it if it means he can't get his hands on you."

She was silent for a moment before she leaned back and looked into my eyes. "I guess we know what we have to do, then."

I smiled and gave her a slow, tender kiss. She moaned softly and shifted her hips. A soft squeal escaped from her when I rolled her onto the bed, only to be silenced by my tongue as it stroked hers and demanded more. My hand lightly skimmed her breast and moved down to pull her shirt over her head when a loud pounding at the door brought everything to a screeching halt.

"Fuck my life!" I growled into her neck. "Bunch of cockblockers."

"Well, we're supposed to go kill a bunch of people in a couple of hours."

I narrowed my eyes at her. "Laugh all you want. You sure won't be later. Because when this is all over, I'm locking us in a room and fucking you into next week, and if anyone tries to interrupt us, they're getting shot."

She opened her mouth to respond, but then rolled her eyes at the constant pounding at the door. Cursing, she followed me to the living room. I opened the door and glared at the person on the other side, and in that moment, I didn't care that I hadn't bothered to hide the raging boner she gave me.

"Do you think you can stop defiling my daughter long enough to help the rest of us figure out how to save her?" Felton snarled.

"Go fuck yourself, Felton," she spat, shoving past him.

I closed our door and followed him down the hall. "Did you ever consider that if you hadn't gone to Gio when you threw her away, he never would've sent me to Prague. Or Portland."

"What's your point?"

"*You're* the reason I came into her life. If you hadn't shit all over the miracle that was dropped in your lap, I never would've met her. And now you get to watch her walk away with me when this is all over. I'm going to marry her, defile her enough to have a few kids, and never let the best goddamned thing that ever happen to me go. All thanks to you, Felton."

His jaw clenched so tightly I expected to hear bones or teeth cracking. I clapped him on the shoulder before walking ahead, feeling his glare as I turned past the stairs. When he stalked into the room, he looked like he wanted to kill me with his bare hands. Instead, he dropped into the chair next to Finn and listened intently to the discussion.

We decided that Paolo, Rocco and Max would accompany us inside. Finn and the Irish would draw attention to the back entrance while the rest of my men entered through the front after Finn's signal. Talbot and his men would be in the second wave while Felton insisted on staying near her when we went inside.

"Barton is trying to get help from the New York Field Office, but he can't promise anything," she announced. "The FBI has no proof that Massimo was involved in Eddie's death or the attack at the safe house, so they're hesitant to get involved."

"Tell them you've learned I'm meeting with Massimo tonight," Felton said. "That'll move their asses."

I held up a hand. "Be careful in there tonight. Massimo's orders to his men will be to kill as many of us as possible but to take her alive. She's his prize in all this and that cannot happen."

"Understood," all three replied.

Finn asked Paolo a question, but I wasn't paying attention. I glanced at my watch and left them to finish their talk. My heart thundered in my ears, drowning out the sound of my footsteps the closer to our room I got. If this was the last of our time together, I was going to spend it with her.

"Baby?" I called out once the door closed.

"Bedroom."

I stopped short when I found her standing next to the bed. She'd changed into her tactical gear, a pair of black fitted pants and a black tank top. She was focused on adding knives to the holster around her waist when she looked up.

My eyes widened at the quantity. "How many do you plan on taking with you?"

"I have nine here, one hidden on each leg, three on each arm. I still have a couple more."

"Dare I ask how many guns?"

She grinned. "I'd dare you to search me, but that wouldn't end well for you."

My chest tightened when she added another knife to the holster. She grabbed a handful and excused herself to the bathroom. When she returned empty-handed, I took her hand and kissed her temple. She gave me a sad smile and leaned against my chest.

"You should be changing into your wedding dress," I murmured. "I should be in a room across the hall pacing the floor and driving Lucas up the wall. Instead, I'm watching you booby trap your whole goddamned body while everyone downstairs loads up a small arsenal in the hopes it's enough to keep you alive."

Her hands slid to my jaw and guided my face to hers. Her eyes were a beautiful ocean blue, the same color as the tropical paradise I hoped to take her someday. If we lived long enough to make it to that day.

"Kiss me," she whispered.

The kiss was slow and sweet, a simple show of affection under normal circumstances, but packed with so many unspoken promises in that moment. Her mouth opened wider when my tongue demanded entry and it wasn't long before the kiss took on a dizzying intensity that left us both breathless. I grabbed her left hand and placed it against mine.

"When this is over, I'm putting a ring here," I stated, before kissing her finger. "And the only knives we'll have are the ones in the kitchen."

"Sounds good to me," she replied, frowning. "We need to get ready."

I nodded and moved to my bag across the bed. The bathroom door closed, and I knew she'd be the cold-blooded killer the world feared when it reopened. I dressed quickly, no longer able to find any further excuses to delay.

The door opened, and my skin prickled. I'd only seen her dark side once before, but nothing prepared me for the angel of death who faced me. Her hair was tightly braided into several smaller braids coiled at the base of her neck. I saw the hilts of three small daggers hidden in the ornate hair clip above the twists. She never looked more beautiful or lethal.

We stood before the bed and finished gearing up. The only words spoken were when I fastened her body armor too tight. She playfully swatted my shoulder, which lightened the mood if only momentarily. Once we were dressed, we stared at each other for what felt like an eternity. Unable to stand the separation for another second, I pressed her to my chest and kissed the top of her head.

Her body tensed when a knock at the door shattered my last hope that this was nothing but a long, drawn-out nightmare. The sadness in her eyes vanished and her posture straightened. Nodding to each other, we marched to the door.

The car ride was quiet. Her eyes stayed closed with my hand tightly clutched to hers. Paolo drove in silence, occasionally glancing back at us in the mirror while Max texted the rest of the men traveling in the other cars. All too soon, I recognized the buildings in the area and knew we were almost there. Our speed slowed, and her eyes opened. The calm demeanor that enveloped her was unsettling. She slipped out of the back seat behind me and scanned the area with narrowed eyes. The parking lot was surrounded by a chain-link fence on three sides and was littered with large SUVs.

"Joey and Thomas should sweep the area for snipers. Double check the cars and make sure they're empty," she ordered.

Both men nodded and drew their weapons before walking to the far side of the parking lot. I was sure Finn's look of apprehension mirrored mine as we watched them. The remaining men were parked away from the building to keep their presence secret. The air was chilly but calm, as if the night was holding its breath to see who would emerge from the bloodbath we were about to enter.

"Keep things calm when we first get in there," she ordered. "Force him to show his hand before we engage. He'll have the advantage when we walk in, but that doesn't mean we can't spin things in our favor."

She and I exchanged glances, and my hand grasped hers. The silence spoke all the things left unsaid between us. A few moments later, everyone headed toward the building. Felton moved quickly to walk in front of her while the rest of us formed a protective circle. She rolled her eyes, but said nothing until we arrived at the front door.

She smiled brightly at the two guards. "Hi, Donovan. Party of five at midnight."

The taller and bulkier of the two shot her a nasty glare. I recognized him as Tito, the guy who escorted from the dance floor at Massimo's estate. Anger boiled in my veins when I remembered the smirk on his face as he led her away that night with his hand dangerously close to her ass. She told me he'd tried to grope her, which earned him a kick to the balls.

"I'll need to take your weapons," he growled. His partner put his hand on her shoulder.

She grabbed him and twisted his arm behind his back. "Sorry, Tubby, that doesn't work for us. I've got a date with your boss and he said nothing about showing up unarmed. So, if you could just open the door and let us in, we'll be on our way and your friend here won't have his arm ripped off."

He looked like he'd swallowed a glass of vinegar, but opened the door and motioned us through without another word. Felton led us down a dark and narrow hallway, past a sign that asked patrons to please check their coats before proceeding into the main hall. I followed close behind her with one hand ready to grab her and the other close to my gun. The knives sheathed inside the bracers on her arms glinted in the lights in the next room. She scanned every corner of the territory in front of her while her hands hung loosely at her sides.

We entered the ballroom, and all eyes locked onto the darkened balcony in front of us. She stopped midway across the floor and folded her arms across her chest. I stood just behind her left shoulder while the rest of the men surrounded her with Felton directly in front. Her face remained blank as she watched the upper floor.

"Well, if it isn't my blushing bride," Massimo's voice boomed throughout the room.

The balcony came alive when at least a dozen armed men lined the railing and pointed their guns at us. I felt a presence behind us and found two men next to Max with their guns drawn. She almost looked bored as the threat against us increased.

"I'm sorry to tell you this, Signore Sardi, but I'm already engaged to your nephew. It's a pity you missed our engagement party. Your invitation must have gotten lost in the mail," she replied as if they were discussing the weather.

His jaw clenched for a moment before an evil smile spread across his lips. "As the boss of this family, I have the final say in family matters and it's my decision that your engagement to Gianni is over. You will marry me and you will provide me with a male heir. That's final."

"But the invitations have already gone out!"

"Silence," he spat. "As a gesture of goodwill, I'm willing to overlook your refusal to follow my instructions that you and Gianni arrive alone. If you two quietly leave with me right now, there will be no punishments. Otherwise, well, let's just say you'll be in for a very *rough* wedding night."

"The hell she will!" Felton roared, stepping forward. The two men closest to Massimo trained their assault rifles on him. "Your nephew is safe, and so is she. Hasn't enough blood been spilled in the name of this family feud?"

Massimo's eyes narrowed and bounced from Felton to Liss, who still stood stiffly behind him. "You know, Miss Donovan, I find it interesting that you even allowed Mr. Luccetti to accompany you after everything he's done."

"Yeah, well, good help is hard to find. Next thing you're going to tell me is you're going to force him to give me away at this wedding we're not having."

"On the contrary," he replied. "I was going to tell you he's the one who reported to us that Seamus Donovan was working with the CIA. All the blood that's been spilled that he suddenly cares about is because of him."

Chapter 19

Checkmate

Larissa

FELTON'S BODY TENSED. No doubt he felt my eyes boring into the back of his head. He looked over his shoulder at John, but refused to look at me. His actions all but confirmed what I long suspected, which should have angered me. However, all I could muster was a humorless laugh before focusing back on the balcony.

"Lissa?" he whispered.

My attention stayed on the balcony. "Later."

Massimo's laugh was loud and grating, but stopped as quickly as it began. "Marco, go downstairs and fetch me my bride."

I rolled my eyes and pulled out one of my pistols. "Marco, stay there."

The gun stayed at my side while the tension increased. Several of Massimo's men on the balcony looked at him for direction, but he remained mute. After several moments of restless pacing, Marco grabbed the gun from his holster and pointed it in our direction.

"I'm not sure your boss would be too happy with you killing his supposed fiancée, Marco," John said.

"Doesn't matter much to me which one of you I kill. But unless that bitch doesn't move her ass, she's going to have someone's brains all over her," he replied.

It was probably the slightest of movements, the equivalent of a butterfly wing moving just enough to disturb the air, but it launched the room into complete chaos. I knocked Max to the side just as the shot rang out and fired a bullet into the throat of the shooter behind us. The stray bullet tore through Max's lower leg, and he fell. A voice angrily yelled out to hold all fire when several loud booms shook the entire room and filled it with smoke.

Two hands grabbed my arms and pulled me to the side, toward the stairs as the sound of gunfire added to the mayhem. Through the haze, Felton raced toward Max and dragged him to safety. Two figures followed behind me, Paolo and Rocco. Both spun around to return fire before Rocco dove into the corner for cover.

Paolo had almost caught up to us when a bullet suddenly whizzed by me and sailed into the middle of his forehead. I screamed as he dropped to the floor. John yanked my arm, which snapped my brain back into focus. He shot one guard racing down the stairs while I shot another man who appeared to our left.

"Fucking Finn," John yelled as we ran upstairs.

Another guard appeared at the bottom of the stairs behind us, but was felled before he could shoot. Rocco ran into the doorway and gestured for me to run. I grabbed the shotgun strapped to my back and followed John.

The balcony was almost more frenzied. Guards shot at our men down below, but soon turned their attention to the two of us. We moved behind the half wall for cover and Finn and his men soon joined us. They pushed the guards back until they were cornered in what looked like a VIP area in the far part of the room and were killed not long after.

"That was far too easy," I panted after John confirmed the guards were all dead.

"Marco and Massimo are still up here," he grunted as he heaved a body out of his way to check the nearby restrooms with a couple of Finn's crew.

"I meant the low number of men. We all know this was a trap we just played right into," I explained.

I felt a presence just before the shot rang out. The bullet tore through my upper right arm and spun me around before I fell against the back wall. John's furious roar rang out as he ran at the shooter and gripped his head, breaking his neck. The man was dead before he hit the ground.

He crossed the room to me in less than three seconds. "Are you okay?"

Despite the gentle touch of his fingers, I still winced while he looked over the wound. "Clean entry and exit," I replied, hissing when he applied pressure. "Just don't tie it off too tight and I'll be fine. Thank god I'm left handed."

He finished his work and kissed my forehead. The respite was all too brief when we heard a fresh wave of gunfire downstairs. John tried to hold me back, but his efforts were futile when I grabbed my shotgun and ran to the balcony.

Rocco's body was in the middle of the dance floor as the entire room was overrun with another wave of Sardi men. I killed two before they returned fire. John pulled me back and motioned to Finn, who directed to his men downstairs. Two stood at the top of the balcony with us and killed as many as we could before we heard another surge of gunfire and shouting.

I held my breath, prepared for another glut of Sardis, when Gino raced into the room with his gun drawn. The rest of John's men ran in, followed by Talbot and his crew. Finn and one of his men raced back upstairs a few moments later.

He collapsed into a chair and caught his breath. "Talbot has four guarding the door. We need to find that uncle of yours."

"He and Marco are probably hiding in one of the offices around the corner." John turned to me. "How's the arm?"

"Still attached. Let's just find these two and we can worry about it then."

Finn ordered two of his men to remain at the top of the stairs while he and a guy everyone called Tank followed us toward the hallway that led to the offices. The air in the room was still as we continued down the dark corridor. A door opened in the distance and we all slowed our steps.

Something sped past me and hit Tank in the throat, spraying me with blood. I spun around when a vice-like grip closed on my arm pulled me away. John caught my movement over his shoulder and tried to grab my other hand while Finn fired toward the mysterious shooter. Pain wrenched through me a second time when the hand pulled me through the door and slammed it shut.

"Liss!" John screamed.

I slid to the floor, only to be grabbed by the braids at the base of my neck until he yelled and threw me down. Looking up, I found Marco's soulless gray eyes glaring at me as he wiped blood on his pants.

He shoved me against the wall and pinned me with his massive arm. "Alone at last."

"And here you can't use your favorite torture method," I bit out, struggling against his hold.

An evil grin spread across his face, followed by a low chuckle. "That is true. It almost saddens me I won't be able to see if that little pussy of yours is as hot and tight as your mother's. But I still have plenty of ways to keep you subdued until the boss is ready for you. Don't worry, baby. We can still have some fun."

"Seems sad that the only way you can get laid is by either rape or because your boss tells you to fuck his daughters, but to each their own."

I expected the slap, but it still fucking hurt like a bitch. Rolling my eyes, I spat out the blood in my mouth on his boot. His hand wrenched around my throat and squeezed. My head felt fuzzy, but I refused to give him the satisfaction of watching me struggle. He smiled and nuzzled my ear.

His grip eased a fraction. "It's a shame you escaped that night. I could've had a taste then. May have even kept you around as a toy for a while."

"And a dash of pedophilia to complete the psychopath trifecta," I wheezed. "Bravo."

He unleashed an angry growl and hurled me across the room. I crashed against the rotted drywall and fell, but rolled onto my back as quickly as possible. Glancing around the room, I saw several large holes in the walls that exposed the brickwork and pipes underneath. Marco grabbed a pipe from the floor and stalked toward me.

"He never said I couldn't fuck you up a bit before he got here. It's not like a few bumps and bruises would stop him from fucking you."

He swung the pipe, but I scrambled to my feet and ran to the farthest corner. The gunfire in the hallway stopped, but it sounded like people were still shooting at each other downstairs. I felt him behind me and ducked out of the way just in time to avoid another blow. My eyes locked onto a pipe about six feet away from my location. I scurried forward, grabbed for my goal, and swung around as soon as my fingers tightened around it.

A loud clang rang out as the two pipes smashed together. The force nearly knocked me over so I jabbed low, aiming for his knees.

He sidestepped it easily and lunged forward. I dodged several quick swipes before he aimed lower and followed it with a punch, hitting my cheek. Flying backwards, I swung the pipe and tried to get my bearings, connecting briefly with his forearm. Out of nowhere, he gripped my throat and lifted me off the ground.

"Aren't you a quick little mouse," he chuckled, amused by my attempts to break free.

I scratched and clawed at his hand, but all he did was laugh. That is, until I brought up the heel of my hand and slammed it into his nose. I heard a crunch and his grip loosened for half a second, only to clutch me even tighter. Between the blood streaming from his nose and the murderous glare in his eyes, he looked like a monster.

"Go to sleep, little mouse," he whispered, clamping down even tighter on my larynx with one hand and squeezing my injured arm with the other.

I opened my mouth to scream, but no sound came. The strength in my limbs was failing, but I still tried to grab a knife hidden in my hair. My finger tried to close around it, but it slipped from my grasp and fell to the floor. Laughing, he threw me down.

He loomed over me and his eyes scanned my body as it lay on the battered linoleum. Smiling, he kicked my stomach, laughing when I cried out. After two more kicks, I barely had the strength to curl into a ball to dodge the blows. Rough hands pulled at my belt, and I felt several knives slide from their holster and heard them tossed away. My eyes closed, I tried to hear what was going on in the hallway and downstairs, both hoping to hear someone coming to my rescue and also to block out what I feared was about to happen. When he flipped me onto my stomach, I tried clawing at the floor to get away, and kicking at him behind me when that didn't work.

He'd just pulled me back across the floor for a third time when I saw a pair of black boots behind him. Unsure if the person was a friend or foe, I tried to scramble away again. His hand closed around my belt but froze after I heard a loud *thunk*. I looked up and saw John standing behind him with a long pipe in his hand.

"Get. The fuck. Away from her," he panted.

Marco smiled before turning around. "Or what?"

John swung the pipe again, but Marco dodged it and then punched his side. He searched the floor for another pipe, but I shoved the closest one away. Screaming, he tried to kick me, but had to stop to avoid John's blows. Soon, they were more focused on hurting each other. I did my best to avoid them, jumping and running to safe spots on the floor.

A glint caught my eye, and I kicked a few pieces of trash out of the way to find three of my knives that Marco stole. I grabbed them and raced out of the corner as they thundered across the room. Finding an overturned desk in a corner, I hid behind it and waited for the perfect moment. Watching John fight that monster was nerve-wracking. So many times I wanted to dive over the crap piled on the floor and join the battle, but I knew that wouldn't help. No, our best shot was for me to stay where I was and wait for the right time.

John hit Marco in the stomach with the pipe and he doubled over. They moved to the middle of the room, and John's eyes met mine in between punches. He kept his face blank while shifting their bodies until Marco's back was to me. I said a silent prayer and threw all three knives.

The knife in his shoulder blade barely registered. In fact, he tried to reach for it until he realized it was too low and went back to trying to punch John. The next two came in rapid succession, striking his left lung and the back of his neck. John's eyes were like saucers when Marco gasped and wobbled on his feet.

A small pool of blood fell between the men, and John didn't hold back after that. He hit Marco across the face with the pipe, and then rained multiple blows to his face and head once he fell. John let out a loud shout and kept beating the bloodied body on the ground, stopping only when the pipe made a loud bang when it hit the floor. He studied the monster's remains as I approached.

"Liss." He checked the wound on my arm before focusing on my face. "Jesus, baby, you look terrible."

"You should see the other guy," I rasped, wincing when his finger traced my cheek.

His eyes went to my neck, which was no doubt bruised, and cursed. He turned and kicked Marco's already dented head, stopping only when my body swayed. Holding my hand, he led me from the room and back into the hallway we'd been exploring before I was grabbed.

"Did you find Massimo?" I whispered, trying to scan our surroundings in the dark. "Is the floor clear?"

"Floor's clear best as we can tell," Finn answered. "We haven't seen him."

John froze. I looked around until I felt it, too. His eyes shot to Finn, who nodded and continued down the hall. My hand gripped his side as we turned to face the other end. A low, throaty laugh broke the silence.

"Decided to make your last stand, did you?" Massimo's deep voice cut through the sound of gunshots downstairs.

"More like your last stand," I retorted.

"Silly little girl. You think you can beat me? You can barely stand!"

John shook his head. "Marco's dead. He can't help you anymore. And there's no escape down the stairs behind you. You're backed into a corner and out of options. It's time to give it up, Zio."

"That might be the case, boy, but you've hardly won anything. Nothing more than a filthy whore, a byproduct of two spineless, useless people," he spat.

"A filthy whore you planned on raping to produce your future heir, but whatever," I muttered.

The silence chilled my blood. We both stayed frozen in place, desperate to find even the smallest clue. John's hand skimmed my back and slid one of my smaller guns from the holster while I kept my pistol at my side. After a few seconds, he rolled his eyes and let out an impatient scoff.

"The time for games is over. Come out and I'll promise you a quick death."

"My boy, you should be the one asking me for a quick death. You two will not make it out of here alive. I made sure of that."

"Then why hide?" I questioned. "Are you not the boss, the patriarch of this family? If you're so sure your plan will work, then why sit in the shadows and hide like a lost little bird, Massimo?"

"You dare to question me?" he roared. "I have lived through far greater threats than you, little girl. My own father considered me a threat, so I had to kill him when I was sixteen and take his place. I held this family together when his weak brother failed. I built this family from an insignificant speck to what it is today: a global organization feared and respected throughout the world. You're simply a fly in the ointment to be dealt with, a pest who had the audacity to kill my flesh and blood. I fear you no more than I fear—"

We raised our guns and fired into the darkness. A dull thud followed, but we remained stationary for a short time before stepping further into the darkness. When I heard rapid footsteps in the distance, I spun around with my gun drawn. Finn and one other man stopped in their tracks and raised their hands. Shaking my head, I turned and followed John.

Finn's cell phone provided enough light to show Massimo sprawled on the ground with a gaping wound in his stomach and blood pouring from his neck. He looked up at us defiantly as we surrounded his body. John tried to hold me back, but I easily dodged his arm. I crouched down next to Massimo's head and smiled.

"Boo," I whispered, raising my gun to his forehead.

His eyes widened a fraction, but then went slack as the bullet hit its target. Blood sprayed my hand and skipped across the floor before it seeped out into a pool below him. After wiping my hands, I stood and stared at his body for a long moment before walking away. John's hand moved to my lower back as he fell in step with me while the others followed behind. It appeared as if we had won, but I refused to call it a victory. Not yet, anyway.

"One more?" he asked.

"One more."

Chapter 20

Last Rites

Larissa

THE SOUND OF GUNFIRE from downstairs slowed. I limped to the balcony filled with dread at what we'd find below. A sudden roar of unfamiliar voices forced me to move faster, followed closely behind by John and the others. I stood at the railing with my gun drawn, ready for whatever awaited us below.

A large group of men flooded the dancefloor, armed to the teeth with large semiautomatic weapons. They surrounded the room and within seconds, everyone was disarmed, including Massimo's men. The crowd parted and a tall man in a black suit strolled to the center of the room. His eyes wandered to the balcony and locked on mine before reaching for his waist.

"Not a good idea," I bit out, aiming at his head.

He raised both hands and took a step back. "I give my word that no one will harm you. Please come down so we can talk."

The adrenaline was wearing off and my body felt heavier with each step. We followed the narrow path his team formed and stopped a few feet away from him. I lowered my gun as I drew closer, but refused to put it away. John stood close behind me with his hands on my hips.

The lights were brighter downstairs, allowing me to see the stranger better. My best guess was he was in his early to mid-thirties. He was about an inch shorter than John, but with a slimmer build. His expertly styled dark brown hair and clean-shaven face gave him the look of a businessman, but his caramel colored eyes held a certain edge. Those same eyes narrowed as he watched us closely.

He stepped closer, but kept his hands visible. "Are you Larissa?"

"Who's asking?"

"A concerned third party. One who would also ask where Massimo Sardi is."

John's hand moved to the few knives still hidden along my waistband. Finn moved closer to my left side, earning a glare from the mystery man. He holstered his gun and crossed his arms over his chest.

I mirrored his actions. "How concerned would you be if I told you he's dead?"

"Then we would like to thank the people responsible for that, since it would save us from having to do it," he answered, extending his hand to me. "Nico Genovese."

I didn't bother to hide my confusion as I shook his hand. The alliance between the Sardi and Genovese families dated back over thirty years, something Massimo often used to his advantage. I glanced at John, who shook his head.

"It's not public knowledge that the alliance ended," he explained. "We recently got information that shed some light on some, shall we say, less than favorable dealings involving the Sardi family."

My eyes flew up to his. "I don't suppose you'd want to share that information or how you came across it?"

He shrugged. "Normally I wouldn't since it's family business. However, I think you might have an interest. About a week ago, we were contacted by an associate with quite a story to tell. He was at a place out in Hell's Kitchen and an Irish guy approached him."

My stomach dropped. John's hand moved to the middle of my back and I glanced over my shoulder. His eyes met mine and he shook his head. I nodded and turned back to Nico, who watched me closely.

"I'm guessing this story isn't going to end with the usual punchline," I whispered.

"No. It ends with the guy somehow having a ton of intel only someone with close connections to the Sardi family would have. Intel that showed proof that Massimo Sardi had been ripping off my family for the last ten years."

My hand flew to my mouth. The price paid for my vengeance, Titus's sacrifice, cut through my heart like jagged glass. "Oh my god," I whispered.

John wrapped his arm around me. "So, where does that leave things with the Sardi family?"

"And you are?" Nico asked with his eyebrows raised.

"Gianni Martinetti. Larissa's fiancé, and Massimo's nephew."

"Ah, the nephew," he nodded. "Titus spoke briefly of you when I met him. He had...quite the opinion about you, but was adamant that you weren't involved in Massimo's dealings. He said you're a shithead, but an honest shithead who'd been trying to distance yourself from your uncle for a while."

"That sounds like something Titus would say," he said with a low chuckle.

Nico's eyes narrowed. "You telling me the info he had didn't come from you?"

John and I exchanged looks. The Genovese were allies at that moment, but the less they knew about my complicated family, the better. I still had one loose end to tie up with one of those complications, and Nico's presence would make it an even more awkward conversation.

"I wish I could say it was me," John answered. "All I can disclose is the information came from a relative I trust with my life who's in hiding to keep him safe from the family. That's why I'm curious where this leaves the Sardis."

"Fair enough," Nico responded. "The Sardi family is gone. The estate in Bari was seized by the family in Italy and everyone inside was slaughtered. They're hunting down stragglers as we speak. I'll leave it up to you how to handle the ones here that were loyal to your uncle."

I glanced around the room and counted less than ten men who fit that category. John and Nico continued to talk as I took in the number of casualties. Max's leg was propped up on a chair as one of Nico's men tended to the wound. His eyes held an overwhelming amount of pain as they moved between Rocco's and Paolo's bodies. Unable to watch the anguish any further, I wriggled away from John and crouched down next to him.

"I'm sorry," I murmured.

He stared ahead and blinked slowly. "We all knew it could happen when we signed on for this."

"Yeah, but—"

He grabbed my shoulder. "But nothing. You're family, too. I'll miss them, but they died fighting for something they believed in, for someone they loved. It's over now and you lived. That's all that matters. To any of us."

Sighing, I patted his upper arm. He nodded and leaned his head back while his leg was stitched up. John signaled me to join them, but my steps were slow. Mentally, it was finally sinking in that Massimo was no longer a threat. A million possibilities raced around my head before Nico's cell phone rang.

He ended the call and looked around the room. "That was my friend from the Bureau. Apparently, the FBI got a call earlier about a fugitive here?"

"That would be me," Felton announced, moving from the corner where he'd been lurking.

The cigarette case weighed in my pocket as if to remind me how close I was to getting my full vengeance. I touched the trinket in my pocket absentmindedly and took a deep breath. Now that Massimo had all but confirmed what I suspected, it was time for a chat with my darling father.

"Mr. Lynch, I'd like a word." John grabbed my hand and I turned to him. "We'll just be a few minutes."

He nodded, his eyes cautious. I led Felton down the hall and held the kitchen door open for him. The door closed and he watched me closely. I stayed silent and tried not to smile as he squirmed.

"Larissa, I know you have a lot of questions."

He didn't even flinch when I lunged forward, pinned him against the wall, and then sank two knives deep into his upper arms. I then stabbed two more into his forearms. His ragged breaths were music to my ears. He watched me with pain in his eyes, but I couldn't tell if it was physical or emotional. Not that it mattered. After setting my bulletproof vest on the counter, I drew my combat knife from its holster and approached him slowly.

"I'd say we've had enough gun fights for one day, wouldn't you agree?" After listening to his gasps, I held the blade to his abdomen. "Start talking."

"I know how it sounds and looks, but even you know how much of a liar Massimo is," he began, the words coming out in a rush between his pained breaths. "They already knew it was Seamus. I swear it."

"Was that before or after you told them?"

"They came to me and asked if it was true. They knew we'd been friends. Gio asked if I was willing to swear on the life of my son that Seamus was innocent. It was an impossible situation."

"So, you told them he was the rat," I bit out, moving the blade to his chest.

"No! I told them we hadn't been close for a very long time, and I wasn't going to put my son's life on the line for someone I barely knew anymore."

"You expect me to believe that? Given your stellar record of honesty?"

With his eyes closed, he tried to slow his breathing. After a moment, he bowed his head and sighed. "I know I've given you no reason to trust me. All I can do is swear to you once they found out, I did everything I could to save you and your mother. I even told Gio you were my daughter in the hopes he'd spare you two. He just laughed."

"Yeah, since they value family as well as you do."

"I deserve that. But please know, I tried so hard to change once you came into my life. The night I found you in my backyard, I knew I'd been given a second chance."

"Did my parents get the courtesy of a second chance?" I yelled. "Did you, for one second, think about what might happen when a group of fucking mobsters sent a hit squad after a family with a child? Tell me something. After Seamus wouldn't give you what you wanted, how long before you ran to the Sardis?"

I swung wildly, punching him in the jaw. His head flew back and hit the wall, but he said nothing. I shoved his chest hard and slapped him, letting out the anger and hurt that had festered inside me since that horrible night. After all the damage he'd done, I needed him to hurt.

"You left the fate of a six-year-old little girl in the hands of a psychopath! Did they tell you when they were going to go out and do this to my parents? Did you wait around all night and hope for the best? How would you have felt if they'd brought you my fucking corpse that night?"

His face contorted. "How the fuck do you think I would've felt? You're my goddamned daughter! And I sure as hell did a better job keeping you safe than that son of a bitch! What was he thinking by ratting? He was the one who put you in danger, Larissa. His bullshit put a target on all your backs. But that means nothing to you. All you want to do is throw my mistakes back in my face, but Seamus continues to stand on his fucking pedestal!"

"Because his mistake was trusting you!" I screamed.

"Bullshit! If he trusted me, he would've listened. All I wanted was to be a part of your life! To know my child! But that arrogant prick wouldn't hear of it. And no matter how many times I tried to warn him, he just wouldn't listen. I even gave that son of a bitch one last chance to do the right thing, but the smug prick just laughed and stuck a cigarette in his goddamned mouth. Fucker got what was coming to him!"

All the air vanished from my lungs. I lowered my knife and stepped back. Instead of raging at him, I merely stared at the man in front of me. The man who comforted me on that terrible night, took me into his home, and raised me. And then manipulated me into believing his lies and doing his bidding. The same man who was the reason my home and family were ripped apart.

Blowing out a breath, I stood mere inches from his body. "Nico isn't the only one with an interesting story to tell."

I reached into my pocket and produced the case. The antique silver metal was etched with a delicate scroll pattern, and in the center sat an ornate copper octopus. His eyes moved to the case and then flitted to mine as he recognized the item.

"I think it was maybe a month after the murders that Karina found me playing in your guys' bedroom. She screamed at me as usual, but you came in and told her you'd handle it. That was when you showed me this case. We'd been studying sea animals at school, so the octopus fascinated me. You told me it belonged to your grandfather, Michael. I asked if I could have it, and you pressed it into my hand and told me it was mine to keep."

"I remember that day," he responded softly. "You kept to yourself so much in the beginning, hardly ever asked Karina or me for anything. When you asked, there was no way I could say no. The smile on your face made it all worth it."

"Such a pity you never asked me what I used it for."

Taking great care not to damage the latch or hinges, I opened the case and showed him the contents. His confusion lasted only seconds before his eyes widened when he realized what he was looking at. His breath came out as a sob when his eyes met mine.

"I never saw who pulled the trigger that night. I also never mentioned I heard my father laugh before he was shot, or that his cigarette fell to the ground before his body did."

"Larissa, I don't know what to say. I-I'm sorry. All I wanted...all I ever wanted was to be a part of your life," he stammered.

"Mission accomplished."

"That's not how I wanted to go about it. I swear to you."

I grabbed my knife and stabbed him in the stomach. He gasped and his body jolted, but then hung slack. Resisting the urge to stab him again, I grabbed my pistol and held it to his forehead.

"I recommend you choose your last words wisely. I'm sure a great man such as yourself doesn't want it to be a bunch of stammering bullshit."

He looked exhausted, but resigned to his fate. After staring at me for a few long moments, he closed his eyes. "I know you hate me and you always will, but that won't change the fact that I'm still your father, Larissa. And everything I did was because I love you and wanted to keep you safe."

"You loved me when it was convenient for you, Felton. You sold me out the minute you thought I wasn't your blood. Seamus knew from the beginning I wasn't his, but loved me unconditionally. There was never a day that went by that I ever questioned how much he cared for me. He protected me as best he could from the monsters in the world, including you. Hell, Titus even knew the truth, and he still sacrificed himself to save me from this mess. Seamus Donovan is my father."

"*I'm* your father, Larissa! That's my blood that courses through your veins. Those are my eyes that are glaring at me with so much contempt!"

"And it was Seamus's unconditional love that showed me genetics don't matter," I whispered.

His eyes bored into mine. One last attempt to bend me to his will. I took a step back and drew in a deep breath. My hand never felt steadier as I gripped my gun and returned his gaze.

"Goodbye, Felton."

The sound of the gunshot echoed off the walls and hung in the air. I placed the gun on the counter and held the cigarette case in my hands, not once looking at the dead man against the wall. When I heard footsteps, I braced myself against the counter behind me and traced the octopus with my finger. John and Nico burst into the room with guns drawn. As soon as John saw the case, he covered it with his hand and pulled me into a tight hug.

"It's over," I breathed.

Nico gaped at Felton's body before he turned to John with his eyebrows raised. John shook his head and buried his face in my hair. I clutched the case and threw my arms around him and inhaled his scent, allowing the calm that only he provided to wash over me. I stepped back and he cupped my face in his hands and gave me a tender kiss.

"It's over," he confirmed.

Staring at the case in my hands, I opened the lid and showed him the treasure inside. A treasure I was never meant to keep. I closed the case and blew out a shaky breath. It was time to return it to its rightful owner.

John looked over his shoulder. "Nico, you got a light?"

He rifled through his jacket and tossed him a plain silver lighter. "We should clear out of here soon. My guy's only going to be able to delay the FBI for a bit longer. We've got a half hour before they get here."

"I'll just be a few minutes," I answered.

The night air was cool and humid; rain was coming. Two large black cargo vans and a restored dark gray Dodge Charger were parked haphazardly outside the entrance to the building. I couldn't resist the temptation to ogle Nico's car before leaning against it and pulling his lighter out of my pocket.

The cigarette paper had faded to the color of untreated wool with small flecks of blood that had since turned a dull red. My hand trembled slightly and my fingers felt sluggish as I lifted it from the case that kept it safe for over twenty years. I felt strangely calm as soon as it touched my lips. The stale tobacco tasted terrible, but the memories evoked by the smell brought a tear to my eye. I lifted my head skyward and took another drag, unable to stop the small giggle as I remembered one of Seamus's many lectures about smoking.

"Lissi, I better never catch you with one of these disgusting things in your mouth," he said as he crushed the butt into the large metal ashtray he kept in the garage.

I looked up from the picture I was drawing to decorate his desk. "Then why do you do it if it's disgusting?"

He chuckled and pulled another from the pack in his front pocket. "They help me when I'm stressed out."

"What if I get stressed out?"

The flame from the lighter danced briefly before he snapped the lid closed and tossed it on the desk. He tousled my hair and smiled. "First, I don't see how a six-year-old can be stressed out enough to smoke," he paused and took a deep breath. "Second, it's my job as your dad to make sure you're not stressed out. Because if you're ever worried or scared, you tell me or your mum and we'll take care of it. Understand?"

I nodded, confused by his expression. His eyes looked sad and tense, but the kind smile never wavered. Once a couple of minutes had passed, he set the still unlit cigarette down, scooped me into his arms, and hugged me. I pressed both my palms to his cheeks and gave him a kiss, giggling at the funny face he made.

"You mean the world to your mum and me. I hope you know that," he sighed.

"I know, Daddy."

The soft breeze cooled the raindrops on my face. I brushed them aside and slowly exhaled another plume of smoke, ignoring the throb of pain from my cheekbone. The adrenaline in my body was almost gone and my arm hurt like a bitch. Despite the pain, only one word repeated itself over and over again in my head.

Freedom.

My fingers felt the heat as the orange glow neared the filter. One last drag. One last invasion of smoke in my lungs, to be expelled from my body like the last link in a chain that bound me to a life I was about to walk away from. I raised my face skyward and took a deep breath, allowing the night air to cleanse my lungs. The hinges of the case let out a tiny squeak when I slipped the butt inside. My parcel had one last journey, one that wouldn't make sense to most but I knew he'd understand.

A hand touched my lower back and pulled me against a warm body that smelled of blood, sweat, and his own unmistakable scent. His eyes held so much warmth and tenderness as he lowered his lips to mine and gave me a soft kiss.

"Your arm is still bleeding," he grumbled in my ear. "And now you're soaking wet and probably going to catch a cold. If you don't get your ass in this car right now so I can take you to a hospital, I'm going to throw you over my shoulder and toss you in the back seat."

One of Nico's men came out and climbed into the passenger van to the right of the car. A few minutes later, he parked it in front of Massimo's limousine. He nodded to John, slid from the driver's seat, and leaned against the side as he lit a cigarette.

"Fine," I groaned with a roll of my eyes.

"Hey, I'm not the one who's going to get water and blood all over the mobster's car," John said as he led me to the passenger side. "You get to square that with him, though I doubt he'll mind. He seemed quite taken with you."

"Dude, he's like my fourth cousin twice removed or some shit," I argued, spinning around as he beckoned me to get inside. "Any interest he might have is simply because of my skill set."

"Yes, I know," he answered darkly, moving closer. "That's why I'm taking you to the hospital. The sooner I get you out of here—"

We froze. My eyes moved to the man leaning against the van, completely absorbed in his phone and unaware of the presence that made itself known. John's eyes met mine and he gave the tiniest of nods. I stared at the van and heard a click. When my eyes went back to his, they were as wide as saucers.

We were trapped.

· · • • · • • · ·

John

"So, are you both really walking away? That's a shame. We could use a couple of good shots like yourselves."

His words did nothing to calm my nerves while waiting for her to come back inside. I didn't want her to go outside alone, but she needed the time to herself. To close this horrible chapter of her life that had tried so many times to destroy her. I turned away and watched her from the front door so he wouldn't see my glare before I plastered a fake smile on my face and turned to him.

"We are," I answered curtly. "She'd been planning to retire long before all this shit with my uncle started. It's time to do something else. For both of us."

"Well, if either of you ever need help or change your mind," he sighed, clapping me on the shoulder before heading back to the ballroom.

I tore through the door and stalked toward her. Barton could debrief with her at the hospital. It was high time to get the hell out of there. Away from Nico and his prying eyes and agenda, and away from the ghosts of her past. I wanted to get her to a hospital, get her stitched up, and spend the next couple of days with her in my arms.

As expected, she groused and protested, but not for long since she knew I was right. Her eyes were alight with their usual spark, and the weight no longer on my chest made me feel we could do anything. Desire sparked in me as we argued about Nico when my senses suddenly prickled and scented danger in the air. It wasn't until I saw two bodies behind the fence that I realized Thomas and Joey never returned from scanning the parking lot.

In less than a second, all hell broke loose. She grabbed for her holster and the air was shattered by a burst of gunfire. She lurched forward and shuddered as the bullets entered her body. Another shot rang out and the guy next to the van fell to the ground in a heap.

"Oh, Larissa!" a voice sang out, moving closer. "I came to give you and Gianni a proper sendoff."

I pulled her to me and shielded her while I felt my body for injuries. Not as much as a fucking scrape from the concrete. Two more bullets rang out, but ricocheted off the side of Nico's car. Relieved the car was bulletproof, I crouched behind the door and tried to figure out how many shooters I was up against.

"What the fuck? Get more men out here now! We're being fucking ambushed!" Nico yelled from the door.

The door shattered and he took cover inside. I fired between the two Sardi vehicles parked at the center of the lot. The shooter returned fire but bumped the van when he took cover, allowing me to get the smallest of glimpses of his location. I fired two shots and enjoyed a millisecond of victory when his body slumped to the ground.

Cassandra laughed when the gunfire stopped. "Gianni, is that you shooting at my helpers? No matter. I'll just have to do the job myself, as usual."

I shifted her body to the side so I could face the van and limo. She gave a weak gasp and gripped my shirt until a movement out of the corner of my eye made me look up. The barrel of a pistol pointed at my forehead greeted me on the other end of the car. Cassandra gave me an evil grin and gestured for me to stand.

"Hold fire! I've got them!" she yelled. "Grab little Miss Super Spy and come around to the front."

My hand was soaked with blood, but I continued to apply pressure to the wound on her side. Her breaths were labored as I slowly dragged her with me to stand facing the one person I hated more than my uncles. Cassandra's eyes were full of glee as she raised her gun, but they quickly turned to rage at the double click of a shotgun behind me.

"Fucking traitors!" she screeched, firing at the building.

Her next words never came when the bullet I fired hit her in the throat. At the same time, the shotgun fired, sounding like a goddamned cannon and ripping the right side of her skull off the rest of her body. She crumpled to the ground in a bloody pile and silence once again fell across the parking lot for only a few seconds when another bullet whizzed past me.

"Fuck!" I yelled, holding her to me and running to the side of the car closest to the building.

The man with the shotgun took cover behind Nico's car and gestured for me to move behind the van parked closest to the building. Nico and three other men ran outside, and when he saw me clutching her body, he grabbed the man closest to him.

"Tell the Bureau to send an ambulance!" he shouted over the gunfire.

I cradled her body in my arms, tuning out everything and everyone else. Her skin was frighteningly pale and her grip on my arm weakened. I gently ran my hand over the right side of her body to assess the damage. Her back arched and her whole body shuddered when I felt the bullet in her shoulder. She cried out when I found the second wound on her side and pressed her head to my chest.

"Help is on the way. Just hold on a little longer," I pleaded, tucking her head under my chin.

She leaned back and smiled weakly. "Guess I won't be getting blood all over Nico's car now."

"Smartass."

I wasn't sure how much time had passed, but I noticed the absence of gunshots and flashing red and blue lights. A hand nudged my shoulder, but it wasn't until I felt my arm pulled away from her that I realized help had finally arrived. The EMTs hurried her to a gurney and raced to the ambulance. I followed in a daze and barely heard a voice shouting at me to climb into the back. Just before the doors closed, I saw Barton's face. The grim look in his eyes told me everything I didn't want to know.

The screech of the sirens jolted me out of my daze, and everything resumed normal speed. Bright lights burned my eyes, but it was nothing compared to the agonizing beep of the heart monitor and the loud voices working frantically to force life back into her body. Feeling helpless, I forced my eyes closed to block the tears that threatened to fall and prayed like I never had before that some higher power would show mercy and bring her back to me.

Ever After

John

One Month Later

I GLARED AT THE white marble wall adorned with stars in front of me. The last time I'd visited CIA headquarters wasn't pleasant, but this was worse. Her insistence at selecting this meeting spot infuriated and disgusted me. I shouldn't have expected any less, but twisting the knife in such a manner was low, even for her. Still waiting, I counted the stars once more, clenching my jaw that her star was missing.

"John?"

I spun around and glared at the bureaucrat facing me. In seven years, she'd gone from a sniveling suck-up to a fucking unit head. Proof positive that even the most useless people could go far if they were willing to sell their souls and kiss ass.

"Hannah. Quite the interesting meeting place. You fall so out of favor with the higher ups they won't even let you reserve a conference room? Or was making me stand in front of the memorial another way to twist the knife?"

She paled at my words and bowed her head. I could've sworn even her overly bleached platinum hair lightened a couple of shades. Her sudden change of fortune was music to my ears. The last time I saw her was at my disciplinary hearing when she backed up Felton's lies about my supposed drug habit. Afterward, she was praised for her bravery, a rising star who'd go far because of her integrity.

"I'm sorry, John. I wished I'd known."

"You knew. Don't even try that shit with me. You fucking knew. You're only sorry that you got caught. It's kind of hard to cover it up when the right agency gets involved. The smartest thing Larissa ever did was tell the FBI."

She lifted her head defiantly, despite the sour look on her face. I'd struck a nerve. The past few weeks had been hell for Hannah Myers Nelson, unit chief, and supervisor for former officer Felton Lynch. First was the scandal that her employee hired a mob boss's nephew. Then it was revealed that same employee was a mob hitman and spied on the CIA for multiple decades. It had led to some very uncomfortable questions, and the rumors were the DOJ hadn't liked her answers.

Her jaw unclenched and she thrust a manilla envelope into my hand. "Here's the info you requested, Mr. Martinetti."

I thumbed through the papers and confirmed the flash drive was at the bottom. Satisfied that all the information was there, I nodded. "Thank you. I'm sure it wasn't easy to get all this, considering the current environment."

Her body sagged and she nodded. Any relief she felt vanished when she looked up and met my narrowed eyes. She lowered her head, almost as if she expected my next words.

"The wall is missing a star, Hannah."

"She wasn't employed by the CIA at the time," she replied in a rush. "We had to follow protocol."

"Because we all know how important protocol is to you. Were you following protocol when you tried to delay the Marshals from backing up the FBI in New York?"

"I don't know what you're talking about."

"Bullshit," I snapped. "I heard her on the phone with the CIA relay. You're telling me it's a coincidence that the call wasn't logged?"

"I had nothing to do with that, John. I swear."

"The fact is, you have much of the same blood on your hands that Felton did. And I hope that grates on what little conscience you have left."

"I did what I had to do," she snapped.

I stepped closer, and she retreated until her back collided with the wall. "Keep telling yourself that. And when you go home to your boyfriend tonight, enjoy it. Not everyone has that luxury."

I spun on my heels and stalked away. My footsteps echoed through the empty lobby, and without so much as a second glance, I exited the building that gave me nothing but grief while I had the displeasure of calling it my employer. Once I was back in the limo, I let out a slow breath and took comfort in the fact I'd never deal with another intelligence agency after the day was over.

Barton leaned against a tree overlooking the cemetery when the limo parked half an hour later. He'd loosened his tie but was still in the same suit from the service that morning. We exchanged nods as I climbed the small hill and stood next to him.

He kept his eyes fixed straight ahead. "Did she give it to you?"

"Yep. I checked the flash drive on the way here. It's all there."

"Anything else? I'm surprised you didn't tear her a new one because of the report."

I shrugged. "Would it matter? It won't change a fucking thing."

The official report released three days earlier was a whole other level of bullshit. Officially, Officer Felton Lynch was distraught after the death of his wife and became emotionally unstable. His mental state led him to murder Ginnie Matthews, his co-worker and lover, when she confronted him about Liss's paternity test. As his mental status continued to deteriorate, he became obsessed with his daughter's safety. That obsession led him to my family's abandoned building that night, where he interrupted a peaceful meeting between the Sardi and Genovese families.

According to the report, Felton was killed when the men at the meeting were forced to defend themselves as they feared for their lives. That horrible night was written off as a senseless act of violence brought about by a man who had lost everything. The fact he was a hitman and a spy was conveniently omitted. It also failed to explain how a call Liss made to the CIA relay to alert them of Felton's presence disappeared from the logs.

"There was no way the truth was ever going to come out. They couldn't afford for anyone to know they'd been compromised for that long," he reasoned. "I know it's not what you want to hear, but it's the truth."

Nodding, I walked to a set of headstones a few feet away. A wreath of colorful flowers lay against the smaller of the two, the only evidence that remained from that morning's funeral. Several leaves had blown over the ground, which I quickly swept away. My eyes lingered on the simple carving of her name, and for probably the twentieth time that day, my chest ached.

"Yeah."

I stayed crouched down and several minutes later heard his footsteps behind me. The air hung heavy with the words neither of us wanted to say. By the time I stood up, the late afternoon sun was pale. Steam accented our breaths, but the silence persisted.

"Did you get the travel docs?"

I nodded. "Just a couple more stops and this place will be just a memory."

He glanced at his watch and walked away. I stood and watched the sky change from pale white to blush pink. I shivered in the breeze and decided I'd lingered long enough. As I walked back to the limo, I looked around and saw that the cemetery was deserted.

My body felt weary as I retreated into the warmth of the car. I laid my head down and shut my eyes, promising myself it would just be for a few minutes. The presence I felt next to me told me that wouldn't happen. Opening my eyes, I gazed at the face above mine.

I grinned at the annoyed look in her pale blue eyes. "Have I told you that you're the most beautiful dead person I know?"

"The name on my passport is Stella Kowalski," she said in an even tone.

Even angry, she was a vision. Her dark brown hair was long enough for tendrils to tickle my face. Her skin was sun kissed from our recent trip to Florida, making her white lacy dress glow. I wanted to kiss her senseless, but the look in her eyes told me that wouldn't be a good idea.

"You said we could pick each other's names!" I protested, sitting up. "And you didn't hear me complain about my name being 'Jack Burrow'!"

"Jackass," she muttered before stuffing her passport into her purse on the floor.

"That's what you named me, love." I smiled until she winced. "You okay?"

"As okay as I can be for now," she sighed.

The EMTs restarted her heart just before we arrived at the hospital, where she was rushed into surgery. She was shot twice in the lung, and after a very long and delicate surgery, the doctors repaired the damage. The third bullet, however, damaged her shoulder. The surgeon repaired it, but she had a long road ahead of her. My hand caressed her right arm, covered by the black sling that hung over her shoulder.

"You sure you want to do this?"

"I have to," she whispered.

I opened the door and helped her climb out. After making sure her dark gray wool coat was secured over her shoulders, I led her through the grass. Her hand gripped mine as she navigated the snow and wet grass in her high heels. When we arrived at the headstones, she smiled and crouched down in front of the larger of the two.

"Hey, guys. I know it's been a while since I've been here. I'm sorry for that. Things have been...busy to say the least."

She brushed a patch of leaves aside before pulling the metal case from her pocket and holding it in front of her. I still had mixed emotions about the cigarette inside, unsure if the closure she got was worth her injuries. When she set it down on the ground and smiled, it no longer mattered once I saw the expression on her face.

"I got them, Daddy. Every last one of them," she whispered, her voice thick. "I'm sorry that he betrayed both of you, and that it took so long for me to catch him."

Her body swayed in the breeze. I helped her stand and wrapped my arm around her waist. She stared ahead briefly and then leaned her head on my shoulder. I kissed the top of her head and inhaled the coconut scent.

"They're proud of you, baby. I know they are."

She swept the tears from her eyes. "I'm going to go away for a while, but you guys will always be in my heart."

A small sob came from her throat, and she buried her face in my shoulder. Her left arm snaked around my waist and she cried softly. I held her as she released countless years of sorrow and pain, whispering words of love and encouragement. She gathered her courage and faced the headstone.

"Mama, do you remember when you told me someday that you hoped I'd meet someone who I loved with every ounce of my soul? I'd like you both to meet Gianni. He's my...everything. We love each other so much, just like you and Daddy."

I felt ten feet tall. We'd told each other how much we loved and cared for each other at least a thousand times. Hearing her tell those feelings to the people who mattered most to her, living or dead, made me feel like the luckiest man in the world. I led her closer to their graves and tried to ignore the knot in my stomach.

"I really wish things were different and that I was standing in your living room while she introduced me to you both as I fidgeted with my tie and prayed you liked the wine I brought or something like that. Hell, I'm standing here right now hoping I don't sound like an idiot," I explained with a nervous laugh. Her arm tightened around me, and I took a deep breath. "You two know what an amazing woman your daughter is, so I won't bore you with that. Instead, I want to thank you for helping make her who she is today. She's strong and brave. And she has an amazing heart."

I blinked rapidly to stop the tingle in my eyes. "Mr. Donovan, I know we haven't had the smoothest road together. I want you to know that every day I'm thankful that she gave me the second and third chances I know I don't deserve. Now that all this is over, I want you to know that I'm going to spend the rest of my life making her happy. I told your brother the same thing I'm about to tell you. She's my world. Always has been and always will be. I'll love her and keep her safe, sir. I promise you that."

Her eyes were full of tears when she looked up at me. I brought my lips to hers for a tender kiss and caressed her cheeks afterward. We stared at the graves for a few more minutes until she shivered. When I felt her body flinch, I knew the falling temperatures were probably making her shoulder ache.

"Baby, it's time to go," I whispered. "It's getting cold and we have somewhere we need to be. And alive or not, I can't stand to look at that headstone with your name on it anymore."

Sniffling, she nodded, and I led her back to the limo. I hoped to bring her back to the States someday, but for now, it wasn't safe. Even with the Sardi family no longer hunting her, there were still plenty of others from all corners of the world willing to pay millions to see her dead. She was still in surgery when Barton and I decided it would be best if the world believed she died that night. We'd always planned to live hidden on the island until we could travel the world without hiding who she was. I doubted the day would come when the legend of the Asset would fully fade, but that was a worry for another day.

The limo exited the cemetery and turned onto the freeway. She looked out the window and when she saw a sign stating we'd left the Alexandria city limits, she turned to me with a questioning look. When we passed the exit she knew led to the airport, she looked even more confused. I pursed my lips to keep from laughing, happy that my surprise was still unknown.

She looked out my window. "Are we not flying out of Dulles?"

"No. Why? Are you itching to show off your passport, Stella?"

"Asshole."

I laughed and slid her hair off her shoulder to nuzzle her neck. "We have one more stop before we head to the airport."

"Where?" I handed her my phone and motioned for her to look at the screen. Her eyes widened and she shook her head. "John, we can't. Nonna will kill us. The timing is all wrong."

I pulled her into a deep kiss. She tried to push away at first, but brought her hand to my cheek and teased my tongue with hers a few seconds later. When our lips finally parted, her eyes were tender but still worried.

"Nonna told me I couldn't come home until I finally made good on that promise," I explained. "Besides, I met a really smart man recently who told me to never wait for the timing to be right because it never will be."

A week after she was released from the hospital, she begged Barton to allow her to travel to Florida. Ari, the woman who got her the tip she needed to find me, was getting married, and she desperately wanted see it. After assuring us Georgia would be there and making sure every precaution was in place, Barton approved the trip, and soon we were on a plane headed for the Keys.

The sunset ceremony was beautiful, full of laughter and love. Afterward, we met Patrick and Ari in a dressing room, where I shook Ari's hand and thanked her for her help. She hugged me tightly and told me she was glad to see everything had worked out before she and Liss scurried off to the other side of the room to catch up, chatting about Ari's baby bump.

"How long?" a voice asked behind me. He laughed at my confusion before gesturing to the two women with his chin. "I'm Patrick, that little firecracker's husband. How long has she been the reason for that lovestruck look on your face?"

"Three years."

"I can tell she feels the same. Any plans to make it official?"

I nodded, watching her pat the baby bump and laugh. "We had some stuff going on that finally resolved itself. Now we're just waiting for the right time."

Patrick shook his head. "It'll never be the right time. I know that one all too well."

"What do you mean?"

"Almost eight years," he answered, pointing to his wife. "And a lot of shit happened that wouldn't have if I'd just taken the leap sooner. Life's too short to worry about the timing. You love her, she loves you. Make it happen and life will adjust."

As soon as we got back to Virginia, I set my plan in motion. It required several minor miracles, but we were lucky to have friends in the right places who wanted to help make it happen. The limo turned down a rural street, and I knew we were almost there.

"Why do you think I insisted on you wearing a white dress today?" I teased.

"I thought you were going for irony since today was my funeral," she giggled as she ran her hand over my black dress shirt. "Since someone wore all black."

"There's more," I added, handing her a manila envelope. "And this is probably the most important part." She slid the piece of paper out and her hand flew to her mouth. The document fell to her lap as she looked at me with wonder.

"You told me once that our relationship started on lies, that we didn't even use our real names when we met," I explained, trying to keep my voice even. "It's not the perfect wedding we both envisioned, but I'll be goddamned if I'm going to marry you under an alias." I ran my fingers through her hair and kissed the top of her head. "So, if you'll have me," I paused and took her hand in mine. "Me, Gianni Lorenzo Martinetti. I plan on marrying you, Larissa Aednat Donovan, tonight."

"How did I get so lucky?" she breathed, staring at the marriage license in her hand.

"I ask myself that every damn day."

"Jesus Christ, you two!" a voice yelled when the car door opened. "I'm fucking scarred for life already thanks to you two. Can you at least wait until after the wedding to suck each other's faces off?"

Her head whipped around so fast she wrenched her shoulder, causing her to curse under her breath. Lucas offered his hand and helped her climb out of the limo. The minute she was standing he took her in his arms and hugged her.

"Asshat," she sighed with a soft laugh. "You have no idea how much I've missed you."

His facial expression as he hugged her said it all. I watched him whisper in her ear and hug her to him again when she nodded. I stood by the limo to let them have their moment. Several minutes later, his eyes caught mine and he turned to her and motioned toward the building behind him.

Lucas gave me a bone-breaking hug. "You have got to be the luckiest son of a bitch alive."

We stood by the limo and stared at the small chapel in front of us. The exterior was plain white clapboard with two small cathedral style windows on either side of a set of dark wood double doors. The simple steeple held a single cross at the very top.

Lucas checked his watch. "You ready to do this?"

"I've been ready for the last three years."

"Well, then let's get in there and get you guys hitched already."

Nonna had Liss's face cupped in both hands and was kissing her cheeks when we entered the church. The moment she saw Lucas and me, she shuffled across the lobby, threw her arms around me, and buried her face in my chest.

"Gianni," she sobbed. She spent the next several minutes crying, followed by several profanity-filled rants in Italian. Afterward, she looked up at me and smiled through her tears. "My heart. It can't take any more of these scares. From either of you."

"It's over, Nonna. I promise."

"Thank you. Now, let's hurry and get you two married. I'm not getting any younger." With that, she grabbed my hand and led me down the aisle. Once we reached the lectern, she smiled and adjusted my tie. She took my hand in both of hers and gave it a gentle squeeze. "I'm so very proud of you, Gianni. Of the man you've become. I know you two will be very happy together."

The minister, a middle-aged Black woman with long, flowing red braids, stepped to the lectern. Several of Liss's friends filled the pews. Barton and his wife each waved before my aunt leaped up from the front pew to give me a hug that damn near left me lightheaded. Finally, Georgia introduced herself with a stiff handshake before giving me a gentle hug.

"I'm so happy for you both," she whispered before taking her seat.

The music from the pipe organ softly played in the background as I looked around the room. I moved to the right of the lectern and watched Lucas hand Larissa a small white bouquet. As the music grew louder, he led her down the aisle. Her eyes locked on mine, and with each step she grew closer, my nerves vanished. Once they were in front of the lectern, he kissed her cheek, nodded to me and stepped away.

The minister looked at both of us and smiled before she turned to our guests. "We are gathered here today to witness the joining of Gianni and Larissa in marriage. Marriage is perhaps the greatest and most challenging adventure of human relationships. This ceremony will not create your marriage; only the two of you can do that through love and patience, through talking and listening, helping and supporting and believing in each other; through tenderness and laughter; through learning to forgive, learning to appreciate your differences, by learning to make the important things matter and to letting go of the rest. Those of us here today will each bear witness as you both affirm the choice you make to stand together as life mates and partners. Please join hands."

Shaking my head, I hugged her and rested my hands on her lower back. "I'm sorry. But after everything we've been through, I can't just hold one hand for this." Several people laughed. Liss shook her head and rested her hands on my chest.

"Since you've both chosen to write your vows, and it's with those words you express your binding promises to love, honor and cherish one another. Gianni, you may begin."

My hands caressed her sides, and I took a deep breath. "From the moment you came into my world, I knew my life would never be the same. I was drawn to you almost immediately thanks to the warmth of your smile, the joy in your laughter, and the goodness in your heart. I wanted to be a better man, one who deserved the privilege of being your husband. And it's my plan to continue to prove to you I'm worthy of that until my last breath. I promise to let you stick your cold feet on me with minimal complaints, that we'll always snuggle up on the couch for at least one football game every Sunday, and to always share my peanut butter cups with you. As your husband, I promise to love you without reservation, to comfort you when times are difficult, to give my all, to work toward happiness and revel in our good times. I'll respect you, honor you, and cherish you as long as we both shall live."

She smiled through the tears in her eyes, followed by a soft laugh. After a few seconds, she turned to the minister, who returned her smile.

"Larissa?"

If she was nervous at all about a surprise wedding and coming up with vows on the spot, she didn't show it. "This heart here," she paused, leaving one hand in the middle of my chest. "Belongs to the man I love with all my soul. My mother told me she hoped I'd find it someday, and I'm thankful that I was lucky enough to stumble upon him when I least expected it. Today we start the next chapter of our lives, a chapter where I marry my soulmate and best friend. It's my promise to keep my cold feet off you unless it can't be helped, to not eat all your gelato, to love you and stand by you no matter what. My love for you is pure and unconditional. I vow to hold your hand in my hand, to hold your head in my hands, and to hold your heart in mine. I love you and you are my husband for all time."

Her voice cracked and she blinked to keep her tears at bay. I smiled before mouthing the words "almost there". Sniffling, she nodded before we turned to the minister.

"This is the point in the ceremony when people usually talk about wedding bands being a perfect circle, having no beginning and no end," she began. "But we all know that these rings have a beginning. Rock is dug up from the earth. Metals are liquefied in a furnace at a thousand degrees. The hot metal is forged, cooled, and then painstakingly polished. Something beautiful is made from raw elements, the same as love. It comes from humble beginnings, made by imperfect beings. It is the process of making something beautiful where there was once nothing at all. May I have the rings?"

Lucas stepped forward and handed her a black velvet box. The minister opened the box and handed Liss a thick, brushed platinum band. She stared at it for a second and when her eyes shot to mine, I knew she'd found the initials engraved on the inside and realized she was holding my father's wedding band. My parents' initials remained on one side, while I had our initials added to the other. The minister cleared her throat and she turned back to her.

"Larissa, please place the ring on Gianni's finger and repeat after me. 'Gianni, I take you now and for always, for always is always now.'"

Her voice cracked again and was barely a whisper as she repeated the words and gently slid the ring on my finger. Afterward, she held my hand in both of hers and rubbed her thumb over the band. Her gaze met mine before turning back to the lectern.

"Gianni, please place the rings on Larissa's finger and repeat after me. 'Larissa, I take you now and for always, for always is always now.'"

I took my mother's wedding set, a brushed platinum band with a large emerald-cut diamond accented on each side by a smaller diamond paired with a brushed band that matched mine and slid them on her finger as I repeated the words in a clear, calm voice. Her fingers clutched mine tightly and my heart felt like it was going to explode. Our fingers remained entwined as we turned back to the minister, hopefully for the last time.

"No one but you can declare yourselves married. You have begun it here today in speaking your vows before your family and friends, and you will do it again in the days and years to come, standing by each other, sharing the highs and lows of life. I will leave you both with an old Irish blessing that says may your hands be forever clasped in friendship and your hearts joined forever in love. By the power vested in me by the Commonwealth of Virginia, I now pronounce you husband and wife. You may now kiss the bride."

Her hand caressed my cheek, and it felt like a dream. I brought my lips to hers and gave her a slow and tender kiss as our friends and family applauded.

"Husband," she whispered as soon as our lips parted.

"I like the sound of that, wife," I murmured before kissing her again.

I led her down the aisle, to Nonna's outstretched arms. They hugged for several minutes as the rest of our friends and family gathered around to offer their congratulations. We exchanged stories and laughed for a little while before Barton announced it was almost time for their reservation at the restaurant. Nonna wrapped her arm around Yolanda's shoulder as they headed for the exit, not once stopping their endless chatter. It took several rounds of hugs, well wishes, and jokes before Lucas and Barton left. Finally alone, she leaned against me and sighed.

Kissing her temple, I smiled. "Ready?"

"Where to now?"

I took her hand in mine. "Mrs. Martinetti, let's go home."

Epilogue

Larissa

Three Years Later

THE WARM BREEZE BLEW into the living room and carried with it the scent of jasmine. John planted the flowers outside our bedroom window for my birthday and sometimes the scent filled the entire house. Yawning, I laid on the couch and watched the sheer curtains flutter. I was rubbing the sleep from my eyes when two annoyed voices filtered into the room from the kitchen. Slowly, I got up to investigate.

Nonna and Elena were chattering in rapid Italian, arguing over the correct way to cut the two biscotti loaves sitting on the counter. Both made wild motions with their hands as their discussion continued. Their, ahem, debate had just started to include curse words when Nonna looked up and saw me.

She elbowed her daughter in the side. "Ah, Larissa! Are you hungry?"

I shook my head before grabbing a bottled water from the fridge. "Just thirsty, but thank you."

She looked like she wanted to object, but nodded instead. Elena seized on her mother's distraction and cut the loaves. She looked pretty smug until Nonna spun around with a glare that could've stopped traffic. When Nonna announced it was time to cook dinner, I realized how long I slept and wondered when John was due to get home. The clock on the wall showed it was almost six, and I tried to calm my nerves.

"John called about ten minutes ago, while you were sleeping," Elena said as I reached for my phone. "He was running behind, but said he'd be home soon."

I blew out a breath and nodded. "Ah, okay. Thanks, Zia."

"Are you okay? Are you sure you don't want to lie down again?"

"Actually, I think I slept too long. I'm going to go outside and get some fresh air."

"Don't stray too far! Dinner will be ready soon!" Nonna called after me as I headed out the back door.

The covered part of the patio was shielded from the wind, but as soon as I came down the steps, my hair blew in my face. I reached back to pull it into a loose twist at the base of my neck before turning off the stone pathway. After spending the day cooped up in the house, the sand between my toes felt wonderful. Leaning against the small palm tree next to the house, I dialed my phone.

"Hey," Lucas answered on the second ring. "Everything okay?"

"Yeah, I'm just bored. How are you doing?"

It was a loaded question. He'd been restless the past few weeks. More than a few times, he stayed past dinner and talked to John on the patio late into the night. John assured me he was fine and just had a lot on his mind, so I tried not to pry. I knew he'd talk to me about what bothered him if, or when, he wanted to.

"I'm good. I was thinking about hitting the bar in town tonight, but I'm not sure. Maybe I'll just see where the night takes me. What about you?"

Lucas lived his life from one willing bedmate to the next, but his encounters slowed in the past year. I didn't know if it was because of his job, or if he was finally maturing and opening up to the possibility of something more. Whatever was going on in his life, I hoped he was happy or figuring out what made him happy.

"Nonna and Zia were arguing over the biscotti, so I went outside to get some air. Now I'm just waiting for John."

"He was probably ten minutes behind me when my boat left the dock. He said he had a side trip to make first."

"Yeah, that's my fault so I guess I can't complain too much," I replied. "I should probably let you go. Try to stay out of trouble, yeah?"

"Shouldn't I be the one telling you that?"

"Ha ha," I sighed before hanging up.

My sleeveless dark blue maxi dress billowed in the wind as I watched the waves. The water lapping at my feet was cold, so I retreated a few feet and sat down in the dry sand. After laying my phone on my thigh, I leaned back on my arms. The sky was pale as hints of orange and pink snuck in. I closed my eyes and listened to the waves and palm trees fluttering in the wind. When the ache in my shoulder became too much to ignore, I sat up and rubbed it for a few minutes before placing both arms in my lap.

In the three years since my "death", I'd recovered most of the strength and function in my shoulder. The road was long and included two more surgeries and months of physical therapy. However, it was all worth it the day my orthopedic surgeon handed me my sling and told me to throw it away or burn it. I'd probably never have a great bowling game with my right arm, but it wasn't like I did to begin with.

The official report explaining what happened in a random building near JFK airport one night in mid-November three years ago was a waste of paper, which I'd expected. John was outraged that my name was nothing more than another name on the list of casualties. I was happy to have just escaped with our lives.

My mind was still conflicted when it came to Felton. I'd never forgive his many sins, but I couldn't bring myself to fully hate him. He'd always been a complicated man and learning about his upbringing helped me understand to a point. I knew he loved me to the best of his ability, even if he showed it in the most twisted of ways. That said, I never once regretted pulling the trigger that night. Had he lived, I knew he would have meddled in my life and tried to bring me back under his control.

I watched Elena light the candles on the patio table in the distance. We lived on a small island near Tahiti in the South Pacific. The main house was an airy single-story villa with a layout that allowed us to see the sunrise as we ate breakfast. Sunset from either the living room or bedroom patios was always breathtaking. Nonna and Elena had a smaller villa close to the main house while Lucas lived in a house on the other side of the island.

We spent the first year renovating and rebuilding almost every structure on the property. Gone was the stuffy and outdated compound that some rich fool bought decades ago, and in its place was a beautiful home that we'd already filled with memories: Lucas finding a snake under the house and naming it Larry, the dent in the brand new fridge from the cork when we toasted our first New Year's, the first time Elena brought her partner to the island and Nonna hugged her and welcomed her to the family, and so many more. The past three years were a beautiful, loud, hilarious ride that I loved more and more every day.

My phone beeped, and I read the notification from the security station at the island's private dock. A text message arrived almost immediately, and I typed out a quick reply before tossing the phone in my lap. Closing my eyes, I let the sounds of paradise relax me for a few more minutes.

"Stella!" a loud voice shouted.

I tried to ignore him, but when he yelled that horrible name again, I flipped him off. "Jackass," I muttered.

He looked absolutely delicious strolling barefoot across the sand in his suit. The black jacket and pants were a sharp contrast to the white sand, and the deep blue dress shirt almost perfectly matched my dress. As he drew closer, his smile widened and he held up the white paper bag in his hand.

"Good evening, my love," he said in a voice as smooth as silk. "I have your order."

My annoyance dissolved the moment he handed me the bag. I tore it open and moaned at the smell of the onion rings inside. His eyes widened as he watched me shove one in my mouth and I ate it like it was the first thing I'd eaten all day.

He sat behind me and kissed my hair. His hands moved to my swollen belly. "I really wish you'd stay closer to the house in case someone shows up early."

"Sorry," I said after eating a smaller ring. "All I did was sleep today. I had to get out and get some air, feel the sand on my toes. It's not like I went that far, anyway."

"That may be the case, but I'm willing to bet you're stuck in the sand."

"I believe the correct term for when a whale is stuck is 'beached.'"

"And if you were a whale, that's what I would've said, so enough of that," he said. "You're not a whale. You're my hot, pregnant wife."

"Hot because I'm about to freaking melt."

"Don't start."

"I'm just sitting here eating my onion rings."

He rubbed both sides of my stomach. "And how's my other favorite girl?"

"She's the one who made you stop at a hot dog shack two islands away to get these for me."

"Emma," he playfully scolded. "What about the mangoes? After I sliced all those up and everything? I thought we had a deal!"

She kicked against his hand and we laughed. Emmaline Verona Martinetti was due to arrive in less than a month. The same day my surgeon told me to burn my sling was the same day we finally got the green light to start a family. John immediately whisked me away to a surprise honeymoon of sorts in Verona. Aside from a security team led by Max, we had the estate to ourselves. We slept late, lounged by the pool, and made love under the stars and plenty of other places. The morning the plus sign appeared on the pregnancy test was joyous and frightening. John held me close and whispered his promise to ensure me and the baby had nothing to fear, and that our only jobs were to grow and thrive.

Once we got home, he made it his mission to spoil the two of us. He and Lucas transformed the bedroom closest to ours into a beautiful nursery. Whenever my ankles swelled or I had a food craving, he was there with a foot massage or whatever ridiculous snack I desired. It was because of my wild cravings that he had to bring home a large bag of onion rings that I devoured like it was the last bit of food on the planet.

I set the bag on my stomach and leaned into his chest. "How did the meeting go?"

"I think it went pretty well. They're definitely interested. We should know more after they meet with their finance team next week."

"Baby, that's great!"

About a year after we arrived, John and Lucas went into business together and bought a small resort outside the capital city of Suva that closed because of bankruptcy. They spent a year renovating it and turned it into a small, exclusive luxury destination. Business was so good, they'd recently put a bid on a hotel on another island.

"We'll see. Did you work at all today?"

I shook my head. "When Nonna found me asleep at my desk, she made me lie down on the couch. Where I wound up sleeping for most of the afternoon."

Despite my retirement, I kept busy. The first few months of my recovery were difficult, so I distracted my brain and put my doctorate to good use. Under an alias, I wrote and published three research papers. When I wasn't falling asleep in the middle of the day, I spent my time in front of a whiteboard or on a computer modeling equations.

"What are you thinking about?" he murmured before kissing the back of my neck.

I shivered when his lips moved to my left shoulder, where he placed a kiss on my scar before moving to the other side. When I struggled with the limitations of my shoulder and another scar, he sat me on his lap and traced his hand over both marks, kissing them repeatedly. He told me they marked the beginning and end of a long, dark chapter of my life that I survived against all odds. It was slow, but thanks to his love and support, I overcame the emotional pain I sometimes felt when I looked at them.

"Just something Connor told me. I've been thinking about him a lot since he passed."

Barton sent a message three months earlier that Connor had died peacefully in his sleep at the age of seventy-five. It hurt that I couldn't attend his funeral to say goodbye, but I was thankful he'd lived a full life. We honored his memory by setting an extra place at the table and serving grilled steaks while John and Lucas toasted his favorite Jameson.

"What did he say?"

"He asked me if I thought I could have my vengeance and still have a life afterward."

"And?"

I watched the waves for a moment. "Here we are. We're here, in the ordinary world, happy and healthy. *Living.*"

He kissed my cheek. "I can't think of another person I'd rather live with. Even with your onion breath."

He snickered at my glare. As his laughter continued, I grabbed a small onion ring and shoved it into his mouth. He narrowed his eyes as he chewed, which only made me giggle more. Soon we were both laughing, only stopping when his phone rang.

"That would be Nonna or Zia looking for us," he sighed, standing up. "We should head back before they send out a search party."

He held out both hands and helped me stand. Emma kicked to protest the change in position but calmed after he rubbed my stomach and promised her dinner was coming. I paused at a wide portion of the beach and took in the sunset. John hugged me to him, and I stood on my tiptoes to give him a kiss.

"No matter where we are, no matter where we go. As long as I can hold you in my arms, my life is complete. I love you, Mrs. Martinetti."

"I love you too, Mr. Martinetti. Forever."

THE END

Afterword

Whew! From creating a character one afternoon to finishing up the series, this has been quite a ride.

Larissa started out as an idea. A "wouldn't it be cool if..." She was a mental doodle I came up with, and then got on with my schoolwork. Little did I know she was a persistent mental doodle. She'd pop up in my brain over the years, and I'd agree it could be a cool story but it never went further than that.

But she persisted. I was on a bus with my kids the first time she threw random names at me:

Mental Doodle: Two names...Barton Kane and Felton Lynch

Me: Okay. Who are they?

Mental Doodle: Barton is my FBI handler. Felton is CIA.

Me: And...what am I supposed to do with them?

Mental Doodle: Dude, figure it out. And figure out my name while you're at it.

The names sat in my notes app on my phone for a couple years. I'd stare at them every now and then, but no story came. When things in my personal life required an outlet, I started writing a completely unrelated story about an IT exec dealing with a stalker. While writing the (totally unplanned) sequel, I decided to take a chance. I'd try to weave this mental doodle character in and see if there was any way I could spawn some kind of story. During the course of writing that book, "Annaliese" became Larissa and those two chapters were the spark I needed to get her onto a piece of paper.

Finishing up this series feels surreal. Part of me is sad and will miss this character who's been in my head for more than half my life , but I'm also excited to tell new stories and possibly bring new life to old stories.

Patrick and Ari: Ari is the FMC dealing with a stalker in the first book series I ever wrote (The Beloved Duo). She and Patrick's story is a good one, and I've considered publishing it. The only problem is some of what happened to Ari is based on a true story, and part of me reluctant to relive that story. So while I'll never say never on bringing this series back to life, I will say it won't happen anytime soon.

What's Next? I'm going to take some time off and celebrate one of my babies graduating from high school! After that I do have a new series to write, which I plan to start later this summer. This is a whole new group of characters, new locations, new everything. It's also going to be less romantic suspense and more thriller. Please look for updates on either my social media or mailing list!

PS... Instagram peeps! The songs from the last two chapters of
the book are:

Chapter 21: Can't Help Falling in Love – UB40

Epilogue: Ordinary World – Duran Duran

Acknowledgements

Many thanks to everyone who picked up a copy of this book and decided to give it a chance. I cannot express how grateful I am.

A million and a half thanks to my family... My husband who still knows more about being an artist than me and has gotten wise to my procrastination methods when I don't feel like writing. Well played, sir. Well played indeed! My boys who have learned to accept that their mom writes about other people and it helps keep her sane. And I think they may have finally learned to stop looking at my monitors when I'm writing!

To Jess and Andrea, thank you for keeping me in the shallow end and talking me down when I start to freak out. Andrea, I hope some day our paths will cross and we can sit around and gossip while I watch you stab things over and over. Jess, here's to daily mischief and getting Bruce some more friends.

Thank You!

Thank you for reading Mutual Assets! If you liked the story, please consider leaving an honest review here.

Want to read a bonus chapter from Seamus's POV leading up to that terrible night? Click here to join my mailing list. You can unsubscribe at any time.

About the author

Samara Black was born and raised in Oregon. She started writing short stories and weird poems at age nine. She continued writing as a hobby in college, typing out silly stories with her roommate and came up with the idea for her first book series when she should have been studying for an economics test. After several dysfunctional friendships, toxic relationships, and family entanglements she had enough source material to write stories about characters with messy lives and even messier problems that come their way.

Samara currently lives in Seattle with her family, including several pets who think they're in charge. In her free time, her hobbies include reading, photography, chasing pests out of her garden, and annoying her teenaged children.

Instagram: @author.samarablack

www.ingramcontent.com/pod-product-compliance
Lightning Source LLC
Chambersburg PA
CBHW070509310726
48976CB00002BA/393